Praise for the novels of Robyn Carr

"The Virgin River books are so compelling—I connected instantly with the characters and just wanted more and more and more."
—#1 *New York Times* bestselling author Debbie Macomber

"Carr has hit her stride with this captivating series."
—*Library Journal* on the Virgin River series

"A strong, uplifting tale."
—*Library Journal*, starred review, on *The View from Alameda Island*

"A blissful beach read."
—*Kirkus Reviews* on *The Summer That Made Us*

"A satisfying reinvention story that handles painful issues with a light and uplifting touch."
—*Kirkus Reviews* on *The Life She Wants*

"Classic women's fiction, illuminating the power of women's friendships, is still alive and well."
—*Booklist* on *Four Friends*

"A heart-grabber that won't let readers go until the very end."
—*Library Journal*, starred review, on *What We Find*

ROBYN CARR

Return to VIRGIN RIVER

mira

mira™

Recycling programs for this product may not exist in your area.

ISBN-13: 978-0-7783-1167-6

Return to Virgin River

First published in 2020. This edition published in 2021.

This edition published by arrangement with Harlequin Books S.A.

For questions and comments about the quality of this book, please contact us at CustomerService@Harlequin.com.

Mira
22 Adelaide St. West, 40th Floor
Toronto, Ontario M5H 4E3, Canada
BookClubbish.com

Printed in U.S.A.

For Melanie Stark, with love,
and in loving memory of Cindy Stark Stoeckel.

Return to
VIRGIN RIVER

1

KAYLEE SLOAN TOOK THREE DAYS TO DRIVE FROM Newport, California, to Humboldt County. She could have done it in one and change, but she didn't even try. She visited a couple of friends on the way—Michelle, who lived in San Luis Obispo, and Janette, who lived in Bodega Bay. Yes, they were her beloved friends and had been since she was small, except they had really belonged to her late mother. Not only were they each a welcome respite in a long drive, she needed some of their nurturing.

Kaylee was headed into the northern mountains for a six-month escape to write. She had packed as much as possible and leased a house in Humboldt County from old friends of the family. The nearest town was an isolated little burg called Virgin River, a place she knew only vaguely. She'd been to this mountain house before, twice with her mother and twice on her own. It promised no distractions. She was a suspense novelist and was facing a hard deadline on a book. Her writing had been slow and difficult for the past year, during her mother's declining health and since her death.

As she drove north from Bodega Bay, the landscape became more and more impressive. It was as she remembered— soothing. The redwoods were majestic, the mountains lush and green, the sky a rich blue and the ocean vast and endless. Kaylee made her home in Newport Beach so was no stranger to the ocean, but these trees! They were huge and powerful.

The house in Virgin River belonged to old friends of her mom's—Gerald and Bonnie. They'd used it as a summer house for over thirty years. When she mentioned to Bonnie that she thought it would be a good idea to get away, to change the scenery and perhaps escape the constant reminders of her mother's death, Bonnie offered her the use of the house.

"The family will stop going up there after July," Bonnie said. "I doubt anyone will be going in the fall. Maybe a couple of the kids and their families might want to for a long weekend, but that's iffy."

Kaylee could handle that, no problem. She was fairly close to the Templeton kids. She'd known the four of them all her life. And she knew that their cabin was spacious and inviting, warm and comfortable. It was full of leather furniture, soft blankets, lots of decorative accent pillows and deep and cushy area rugs surrounding a big stone fireplace. And the porch was perfect; the views it offered were extraordinary—mountains and valleys and magnificent sunsets to the west. In fall the changing colors would knock her socks off.

She desperately needed to separate herself from Newport Beach, to isolate herself enough to force concentration on the book she was under contract to finish. Living in her mother's house was too overwhelming and seemed to invite her continued mourning; she felt she had to shake things up to get a fresh start.

Kaylee was raised as an only child. Her parents separated when she was five and divorced when she was six. Her father had very little contact with her after the first couple of years and seemed like more of an acquaintance than a parent. He had remarried and had a new group of children; he later divorced again and yet again. She thought it was only a matter of time before wife number four appeared. On those few times Kaylee met her father's subsequent families she was polite, but disinterested. She never did understand how her father could leave her spectacular mother, Meredith, for those poor substitutes. She never became close to him or any of his wives or children. He hadn't really even been in touch, until recently. Her mother's illness seemed to have had a startling impact on him. It was as if he was suddenly interested in the family he left behind so long ago. With Meredith's death came even more intense interest from Howard Sloan.

Meredith had been a wonderful constant in Kaylee's life. It was just the two of them and Kaylee's childhood had been rich with happiness and perfectly normal. Her mother had been everything to her—her best friend, protector, cheerleader and idol. And then Meredith was diagnosed with lung cancer, though she'd never smoked or lived with asbestos nor worked in a high-risk environment. The doctors pronounced her chances of recovery and survival excellent; everyone expected her to triumph over the disease, but they were wrong. She passed away six months after her diagnosis.

Kaylee was pitched into a well of despair. During the six months of Meredith's treatment and the six months of grieving that followed her mother's death, Kaylee hadn't written a word. She was moderately well-known as an author of suspense novels. She wasn't rich and famous, but she was known among writers, librarians and reader groups. She managed to earn a respectable living, and she had worked very hard to get to that point. Her publisher, so understanding and supportive, had granted her several extensions on her deadline and offered to help in any way she needed. She knew, however, that their patience would eventually come to an end and they would not be able to schedule her next book until she actually delivered a manuscript. At this point in her career, to not publish a book for a couple of years could have a very negative impact. Thus the need for a change of scenery and her determination to get back to work. She knew it was what her mother would want. Meredith had been her biggest fan and her most ardent supporter whether she was trying to get a book published or dating a new guy. She had always been there, always on her team.

Kaylee wondered if she'd ever recover from the loss. She hoped six months in the mountains would signal a new beginning, but she hadn't been sure what to do about her mother's house, now her house. Her friend Lucy Roark offered a solution. Lucy worked for a vacation rental management company. Kaylee met her for a drink and Lucy casually asked, "Have you thought about renting your house for a few months? It would make a fantastic short-term rental. I could manage it for you. In fact, we have a network that spans the continents, in case you'd like to go away for a few months."

"And how is that done?" Kaylee had asked. "Do I just lock it up and leave?"

"Our owners usually pack up their personal items. People are always looking for furnished rentals in Newport Beach."

It didn't take her long to accept the Templetons' offer to rent their mountain home, and she had to insist they take the rent money. They were inclined to let her have it because they loved her. Then Lucy hired a crew to pack up and store Kaylee's items. That alone served many purposes. The thought of a hideaway in the mountains was encouraging and it helped her accomplish the overwhelming task of finally going through her mother's things, giving away what she didn't want to keep. The house was beautiful—Meredith had been an interior designer—and with a deep cleaning and some fresh paint and polish, it was show ready. A couple well-known to Lucy's firm was excited to rent the house for six months as they had grandchildren nearby. Kaylee was happy to let them have it through the Christmas holidays. She could barely stand to think about Christmas. Without her mother, the holidays would be unbearable.

Kaylee was about eight the first time she and Meredith spent several weeks at the mountain house with the Templetons. She thought of Bonnie and Gerald as family, and their kids were like cousins to her. Over the next twenty-six years, Kaylee had visited a few more times. The nearby town was small with hardly any services available. The last time she was there, ten years ago, there was a bar and grill fashioned out of a cabin— that had been a welcome discovery. The place would have no distractions for her and she found herself looking forward to the rest of the summer and fall.

Now Kaylee prayed she could set things right, eke a life out of this tragedy, carry on as Meredith would want her to. The idea had seemed impossible. But as she drove up into the mountains past Fortuna and the trees overwhelmed her, she began to feel hopeful for the first time in a long time. The place was filled with lovely memories that were coming back to her. She had been visualizing the cabin filled with old china, colorful quilts and solid hardwood floors covered with plush area rugs and knew it was the perfect escape. She remembered laughter and good food and long walks. She had fished in the river with Gerald and a couple of the Templeton kids.

She followed the directions as her GPS chirped them out. The road was narrow and shrouded by large trees. Every now and then she'd pass a break in the trees and the sunlight would blast her eyes. Off in the distance, she saw a curl of smoke. She hadn't thought about the risk of forest fires and hoped that wasn't anywhere near the Templetons' house.

She remembered the house was perched on a hillside. As she drove upward, her desire to settle in and write grew and grew. Her writing was usually at its best in winter, when it was cloudy and damp and chilly enough for her to light a fire at six in the morning and hunker down for a long day of writing. Winter in Newport was usually mild and sunny, but when those dark, cloudy winter days came on, Kaylee burrowed in and lost herself in her story. It was August now so it wouldn't be too long until the weather would start to change. Soon, with the changing of the leaves, she'd be entering months of cozy fireplace days.

Another twenty minutes and half as many miles brought her to the road on which she'd live. There were only a few widely separated homes, all sitting above the road with fairly long drives leading to them. She could see that one was surrounded by fire trucks, the drive blocked, rivers of water soaking the road. A lot of pickup trucks were blocking the road and there, at the end of the drive, was a house, or what was left of one. The firefighters were reeling in their hoses. The house, a two-story, was charred on one side, and it looked like flames had licked the outside from the dormer windows.

"Those poor people," she said aloud.

The flowers that lined the front walk and what was left of a porch were trampled and drowned; mud flowed in rivers and a gang of men were standing around the front of the house.

"Your destination is on the left," said the GPS voice.

She slowed to a stop and looked around for another house.

But there wasn't another house. And the number on the mail-box confirmed the bad news. Her getaway, her mountain villa. It was one big smoldering pile of ash.

"Oh shit," she said.

She pulled over down the road, out of the way of the fire trucks. One was labeled Virgin River Volunteers and the other, bigger truck said Cal Fire. She walked up the drive and headed for that gang of men. Some were wearing yellow turnouts, those thick flame-retardant overalls. Others were in jeans and denim or plaid shirts and she assumed they were just observing.

"What happened?" she asked the first man she came to.

He was kind of grizzled looking, with a stubble of beard, thin hair up top and watery blue eyes. He scratched his chin. "Fire," he said.

"Obviously! Was anyone hurt?"

"Nah, she's been sitting empty since after Fourth of July. Heard someone's gonna be renting it. But I guess that deal's off…"

"Me," she said. "I'm renting it. Holy God, what in the world caused it to burn up! I mean, if no one was in it…"

"I guess those Cal Fire guys will help figure that out. Wasn't no lightning; we got clear skies. We're just lucky the postman saw smoke and the whole damn hill didn't take light!"

"Dear God…"

"We coulda been out here for days," he said, giving his brow a wipe.

"The Templetons," she said. "Has anyone called the owners?"

"The fire department will call once they get the number. You got the number? You can call 'em. It ain't no secret. It's just gonna be a while before anyone figures out what set it off and how bad the damage is." He turned and looked over his shoulder at the charred mess. He shook his head. "I hope you have somewhere else to stay."

"That's going to be a problem," she said. "I guess I could drive back over to the coast and look for a hotel or something. Unless there's one around here?"

He was shaking his head. "I can give you a spot on the couch if you're hard up," he said.

A man in yellow turnouts walked over to where she stood. He was holding a shovel. "Did I hear you say you know the owners?"

"Yes, I've known them almost my whole life. I was renting the house from them and I just arrived to...to...this."

"It's pretty ugly in there," he said. "It can be fixed, but it can't be fixed fast. No way anyone's staying there tonight. Or this month for that matter."

"Do you have any idea what caused it?" she asked.

"I'm not an investigator, mind you. Just an old fireman. I suspect an electric blanket. It looks to me like the fire started in the bedroom. On the bed."

"They left an electric blanket on?" she asked. "And that could start a fire?"

"It didn't even have to be turned on," he said. "It's best to wait on the investigator to make a judgment, but I've seen it happen. I don't think that house is for rent anymore."

"What am I going to tell Mr. Templeton?" she thought aloud.

"You can start off by telling him there was a fire in his house, a pretty bad one, and the place isn't a total loss but it's uninhabitable. We'll call someone to come out and make sure it's locked and the windows are boarded up. Wouldn't want anyone to go in there and get hurt. Wouldn't want what survived to be damaged or stolen. We don't have a lot of that sort of thing around here but..." He shrugged. "The damage is considerable."

"I'll say," she replied.

"So much for your vacation," the first man offered.

"I wasn't here for a vacation," Kaylee said. "I was here to work. I rented it for six months of quiet so I could finish a project. Hey, can I look around in there? So I can tell Gerald what it looks like?"

"You can't go in there. It's hot, steaming, could be unstable," the firefighter said. "I'll take you around back and shine a light in the window. You might be able to get a glimpse. The kitchen is smoke damaged but most of the fire got the upstairs. There's no way you're going to see that until much later."

"Okay, let's have a look," she said. Then she shuddered. This was a tragedy; the Templetons treasured their mountain house. When their sons were young, they'd spent a lot of time here. Sometimes Bonnie and the boys came for nearly the whole summer with Gerald flying up from LA as often as he could get away. And now, they loved to visit with their grandchildren.

It was such a charming stone house with wide porches on the front and back. The inside was beautiful in an unfussy way, plastered walls and wood accents. The kitchen was large with a long breakfast bar, the fireplace in the living room made things so cozy and there was an open staircase to the second floor. There was also a cellar, partially finished, that Bonnie had talked about turning into a wine room, but as far as Kaylee knew, it still just served as storage.

She followed the fireman up onto the back porch; part of the roof hung down as if damaged, but the man just moved around it and she followed. He pointed the light into the kitchen window and Kaylee peered in. She gasped. Everything was black.

"Smoke and water damage," he said. "It wasn't burned."

After a moment he moved over to the dining room window and pressed his flashlight up against the glass. It looked just fine. Not even the furniture was damaged. "I guess the fire didn't even reach the first floor. But the ceiling is damaged and probably dangerously weak," he said. "The roof is ruined by fire and the places where we opened it up to vent it. It'll need a whole new roof, I'm pretty sure."

"And a lot of other stuff, too," she said, surprised by the lump in her throat. She began to have visions of kids sitting around the coffee table playing Monopoly or Scrabble. She envisioned their makeshift tents constructed out of old blankets and quilts and sleeping bags on the floor of the back porch. Toby, the youngest of them all, never made it through the night.

She suddenly recalled when she was here once with her mom who was depressed, doing a lot of crying, and she tried to remember, was that about the divorce? And then there was a time she and her mom came alone and her mom had been so happy and carefree. That had a lot to do with her mom's new friend, Art. Art was around for at least a couple of years and he had lightened Meredith's mood. She didn't remember her mother being brokenhearted over him when their relationship ended. She had asked her mom what had happened and the answer had been so unsatisfying. It was something like, *I guess it had just run its course, but of course we're still friends.*

"As a renter, I don't think you're obligated to call the owners and explain all this," the fireman said, disrupting her memories.

She wiped away a tear before it could fall. "They're very close friends. The owners. Of course I'll call them." She pulled her phone out of her pocket and began to snap a few pictures. She took a shot of the damaged overhang above the porch from several angles. She asked the fireman to shine the light inside again and she tried to get shots of the kitchen and dining room, though they were dark and murky, taken through a window as they were. "This is going to break their hearts. They love this house."

"The fire department will be in touch with them anyway, but you call if you want. Be sure to tell them they'll be hearing from the chief. And also, tell them there's not much they can do right now. No need to rush here to see. They should contact the insurance company, though."

"I'll call right away," she said. "Listen, I've been driving for several hours and I need to figure out where I'm going to stay tonight. Is there a restaurant or something nearby?"

"Jack's Bar and Grill in town," he said. "Or you can go back down 36 to Fortuna where you have a bunch of spots to eat and several motels. Jack's is about ten minutes; Fortuna about forty minutes. You by yourself?"

The lump in her throat returned. "By myself," she said and felt that familiar deep and painful longing for her mother. Her best friend. Her soul mate.

There seemed to be a lot of noise involved in the packing up and retreat of two fire trucks. Kaylee was almost grateful that she couldn't really call Bonnie and Gerald until things quieted down. She found a thick log from an old tree on the ground across the street from her parked car. It was nearly four o'clock and she was fighting tears, not so much over the charred house but more from the memories it brought. The plan had been to separate herself from all the sweet memories of her mother but in coming here she had only unearthed more.

By the time she clicked on the phone number, she was completely alone. And it was quiet as a church, sitting as she was beneath the huge pines.

"Hello, Gerald? It's Kaylee. I've arrived in Virgin River and I have terrible news."

"I already know, Kaylee. The Cal Fire chief called me just a half hour ago. He said you were there and had seen the house. Honey, I'm so sorry. I can't imagine what happened!"

"They said they suspected an electric blanket," she informed him.

"He told me, but I find that unlikely. We never left the house to come back home without unplugging everything except the refrigerator."

"Then I guess we'll have to wait for their investigation to find out the cause. It's a mess, Gerald. Not completely destroyed, but a mess. What the fire didn't damage the water and equipment did. The fireman I talked to said someone would come back to board up the windows and make sure it was secure. I can text you a few pictures, but I wanted to talk to you first."

"Please, Kaylee. Fire them at me. Oh, poor choice of words."

"I'll send them as we talk, so you can ask me any questions." She put the phone on speaker and texted off a group of pictures from her phone.

"Good God," he finally said in a hoarse whisper.

"The fireman said you should phone your insurance company but there's no reason for you to rush up here."

"Aw, honey," he said. "Just when you think you're moving forward, something like this—"

"Your poor house," she said. "I know how much you love this house."

"We loved the idea of you living in it," he said. "Thank God it was empty when the fire started! It'll take some time to find out the cause and cost of repairs, but I'll be sure to let you know when I do find out. Will you just head back home now?"

"Well...not tonight. I've done enough driving for one day. I'm going to get a bite to eat and maybe a glass of wine, then probably find a motel. There's that place to eat in town, I guess. Jack's?"

"Yes, Jack's," Gerald said. "He's been there about ten or twelve years now. We know him. Tell him we're friends; ask him for any tips on good places to stay tonight. He's a straight shooter. And he knows everyone."

"I'll let you know where I'll be once I figure it out."

Kaylee remembered Jack's, though it looked to be much bigger than the last time she came here. It was a large two-story cabin at the center of town, tucked into a bunch of houses and maybe a park or very large yard. There was no big neon sign announcing Beer or Girls Girls Girls. If it weren't for the five men gathered on the porch holding beer bottles and an Open sign on the door, it would've looked like someone's house. There were quite a few trucks parked down the street, plus a couple of cars and SUVs. It appeared Jack's was hopping.

She parked and walked up to the porch. It was a little intimidating until she recognized a couple of the guys on the porch as firefighters who had doffed their turnouts and now wore jeans and boots. One of them nodded at her and smiled.

"You doing okay, miss?"

"Yes, thank you. But I think I need to have a beer or something."

"You do that. Let us know if you need help with anything. Even if it wasn't exactly your house, it was going to be your house tonight before it caught fire."

"Thank you, that's very nice."

"We have a fire-victims committee. You know—food, clothing, that sort of thing."

"Fortunately, I hadn't moved in yet, so I didn't lose anything."

"It can still be unsettling."

She just smiled at him, thinking that was so sensitive.

One of them held the door for her and she stepped inside. And looked around.

It was almost a town in a room. A couple of elderly women sat at a table by the hearth. An entire family with five small children occupied a long table. A half-dozen men leaned against the bar at one end. Two middle-aged couples occupied a table, laughing and talking over their drinks. A table for four held women who were knitting while they nursed beers and wine. A woman was hustling from the back with a full tray of food and there were a couple of men behind the bar—one very handsome man in his late forties or early fifties with just a smattering of silver threaded into his brown hair and another man with coal-black hair, also sporting just a hint of gray.

She went to the end of the bar and sat on a stool. The handsome brown-haired guy was before her at once, wiping off the bar and slapping down a napkin.

"Evening," he said. "What can I get you?"

"Any chance you have a nice, cold chardonnay and some peanuts?"

"I can do that," he said.

"And is there a guy named Jack around?"

He turned back abruptly. "That would be me."

"Ah. Well, I was headed for the Templetons' house when everything fell apart. The fire department had just put out the fire as I was arriving. So now here I am, homeless for the moment. I spoke to Gerald Templeton and he asked me to tell you hello. And he said you might have some good ideas about where I should spend the night. A good motel or hotel not too far away?"

"The fire!" Jack said. "I heard about that. Damn it, that's a nice house. The Templetons are great people."

"They're very old friends," she said. "I've known them since I was about six."

"Let me get your wine, then we can talk." He busied himself behind the bar for just a moment and before returning to her with the wine, he spoke over his shoulder. "Mike, back me up, will you?"

"Absolutely," Mike said.

He put down the wine and a bowl of nuts appeared. He reached under the counter and pulled out a second bowl holding pretzels. They shook hands, introducing themselves. "So, were the Templetons coming up for a while?" Jack asked.

"They weren't planning to. I don't know if their plans will change, given the damage to their house. I was renting it from them. I needed somewhere quiet with a change of scenery so it was to be mine for six months, though it was possible someone from the family might come for a weekend visit."

"And now you're stuck here with no house?"

"That about sums it up. I rented out my house in Newport, so just going back home is not an option; my renters couldn't wait to get in there. Fortunately, I have friends in the LA area, but they don't exactly have quiet lives..."

"Couldn't you explain to your renters...?"

"I suppose, but really, I made a commitment and they seem to be nice people who were counting on living near their grandchildren for a few months. And I'm just one person. I could be tucked away in a guest room somewhere. I'll have to think about where. Meanwhile..."

"Meanwhile, you should let me treat you to dinner. Salmon, rice, asparagus, corn on the cob. It's delicious."

"Sounds great."

"I can give you a place to stay, too. It would be temporary, I'm afraid. We have a guesthouse out back, but my sister is coming for a visit at the end of next week, so the place is booked."

"That's very nice of you. You don't even know me. I'm capable of staying the night in Fortuna or any place you recommend."

"I understand if you'd rather not stay with strangers," he said. "But there's no need for you to drive over to the coast, especially since your plans are up in the air. I'll give my wife a call. Her name is Mel and she's very flexible."

"Is it typical for you to offer housing to someone who wanders into your bar?" she asked.

He had a surprised look on his face. "I was going to say no, but the truth is that anytime there's a situation that leaves someone without a bed and bath, I've been known to offer. We also have a cabin not far from here. That stays pretty busy, too. Especially in good weather."

"I hate to impose."

"Think about it while I check on the customers. After you've had a little of that wine, I'll get you some dinner. By the time you're done, you'll know what you want to do. The welcome mat is out. You're a friend of friends. I've known Gerald and Bonnie since I got to town over ten years ago. I like them. I think Gerald helped me with the roof on this place, back when it was just a small cabin. It's doubled in size since—we added on."

"Thanks, Jack."

Before and during her meal, a few bar patrons stopped by to ask her if she was all right, if there was anything she needed, because by now half the town had heard about her and the fire. When she was done with her meal, feeling full and relaxed, Jack brought her a cup of coffee, though she hadn't asked for it.

"You might want to go out to my place and check out that casita. Give yourself a couple of days and look around. There might be other rentals around here and maybe all your plans won't be ruined after all. Sometimes things just work out. Here's the directions. It's not far and Mel is waiting for you."

"You are unbelievably nice," she said.

"Doesn't cost anything to be nice, right, Kaylee?"

2

IT DIDN'T TAKE MUCH CONVINCING TO HAVE Kaylee driving up the road toward the Sheridan house. It was at a beautiful location. The drive plateaued near the top where two beautiful ranch-style houses sat on big lots with twin porches that both faced west, looking over the valley for miles and miles. Kaylee spotted pastoral fields of crops, a large vineyard, scattered houses and grazing livestock.

The drive made a Y, veering off to the left to wind around the house to the back or to the right, ending in the front of the house. She could see a portion of the guesthouse in the back, just beyond a play area for kids with swings, a slide, a basketball hoop and a putting green. On the porch at the front of the house, a woman sat braiding a little girl's hair. That would be Jack's wife. And daughter?

Kaylee didn't even have to think about it. She didn't drive around to the casita but up to the front, parking and getting out.

"Mrs. Sheridan?" she asked.

"I'm Mel," she said. "And you must be Kaylee."

"Yes, ma'am."

"Come up here and sit with me. All right, Emma. Go take your bath and I'll be in shortly. Come, Kaylee. The sky is wonderful tonight—a million stars. That moon is like a lamp, lighting up the whole valley. It's almost my favorite time of day. Jack tells me you've had a stressful day."

There was just something about Mel from the second Kaylee met her. She was like a warm blanket. Welcoming and nurturing and completely accessible.

"It was a shocker, that's for sure," Kaylee said.

"He said you were going to be renting the Templeton house, but he didn't tell me why you came to Virgin River," Mel said. "Have you been here before?"

"Yes, a few times. The first time I was just a child and came with my mother. But the most recent was about ten years ago. I think the bar was a new addition then and I remember being glad to see it. Up till then I can't remember there being any place to eat. The Templetons are very old friends and they offered me the house for a getaway."

"Ah," Mel said. "A very polite person would just let that go, but I'm cursed with rabid curiosity. Tell me it's none of my business if it's too personal, but what are you getting away from?"

"It's kind of a long story," she said.

"I'm not at all tired," Mel said, smiling. "I certainly understand if you are—"

"Well, I think it boils down to running away from grief. I'm a writer. Fiction. Suspense, to be more specific. I've had some modest success and I have a contract. In fact, I have one book left on my contract, but I've had the worst time writing. I just can't focus. It was almost exactly a year ago that my mother was diagnosed with lung cancer. Everyone was so optimistic, including the doctors. And yet, my mom got sicker and sicker and she passed away in December last year. I was living in her house. Of course, I stayed with her when she got sick and later when Hospice came. And then after she died and I was alone in her house, I was lucky if I managed a sentence a day. I really couldn't think of anything but my mom. I needed to change my scenery, so I decided to look around for some place to go for six months, if only to finish this last book on the contract. Then," she said with a shrug, "then I don't know what happens. Maybe I look around for a teaching job. I taught for a while after college, writing at night and on weekends and vacations. But I might be done writing."

"I'm so sorry, Kaylee. You must miss your mother so much."

"Unbearably," she said. "We were so close. I'm an only child. We were best friends. Her friends were my friends and my friends were also her friends. She read every book I wrote before I even sent it to an editor. I'm lost without her. I knew I would be for a while, but sometimes I feel like I'm getting worse, not better."

"Do you have to finish that book? I mean, do you have other options?"

"I could give the advance back. I'm just not ready to give up yet. My storytelling always swept me away. Saved me. Till now."

"Well, it's not surprising. You suffered an enormous loss. But I think you were smart to come here. A change like this can be good. You know what I learned about grief? It's always there and it's always at the center of your life and then one day you realize with some surprise that you had a fairly good day and you wonder if grief left. Or if it got smaller. It didn't," she said, shaking her head. "It's the same size. Your mother will always be that important. But your world will get a little bigger. And when your world gets bigger it feels like your grief gets smaller. You took a very brave step in coming here—the change alone will make your world a little bigger."

"I will always miss my mom," Kaylee said, and the damn tears gathered in her eyes.

"Of course you will," Mel said. "But your world will inevitably expand. Jack said he fed you dinner. How would you like a cup of tea? With honey?"

"That sounds perfect."

"Let's go inside and make it together. There's a small refrigerator and microwave in the guesthouse. We can poke around in the kitchen for a few things you can take with you for the night."

Kaylee followed Mel. "As a matter of fact, I brought a cooler and picnic basket with some groceries. I knew that once I got to the Templetons' house, the nearest grocery store would be at least a town away and it might be a day or two before I could shop."

"That was smart. There's a small store in town but you're probably going to have to drive to Clear River or even to Fortuna to stock up. Sit down while I put on the water and make our tea."

Kaylee looked around the spacious kitchen adjacent to the great room and dining room. "Your home is beautiful."

"Thank you," she said. "Jack and some of his friends built it. Then his sister and her husband built the house next door. Brie is an attorney with an office in her home and she loves to hike. If you decide to hang around a while, she can give you some great tips on hiking trails. Sometimes a little bit of nature is just the thing. The views are spectacular."

"I'll probably go back to the LA area, since the house isn't going to be available."

"LA? I went to school in LA and worked there for a long time."

"What kind of work?" Kaylee asked.

Mel put the tea in the pot to steep, bringing it to the table. "I'm a nurse practitioner and midwife. I work with Dr. Michaels in town, right across from Jack's. Here's an idea. Jack knows everyone. That's kind of a by-product of having the only watering hole in town. Why don't you ask him to make a couple of phone calls and check with a Realtor or two, see if there are any vacation properties for rent around here. Maybe you won't have to hurry back to LA."

"I don't want to impose..."

"He wouldn't mind," Mel said. "I'm sorry you can't just use the casita for the whole time you want to be here, but Jack's got family coming the end of next week. Besides, that little guesthouse wouldn't do. You need a real house with a real kitchen."

"And a porch," Kaylee said.

"It wouldn't hurt to ask. I'll call him right now. What are some of the specific things you want?"

"A cozy place. A view would be nice, like the Templetons have from their front porch. The weather is going to cool off; a fireplace would be good. I don't think I could be happy in some fishing cabin buried in the woods. Do you know the Templetons' house?"

"I've met Bonnie and Gerald and a couple of their sons, but I've never been to their house."

"It's bigger than I need—four bedrooms. But it has a nice living room and kitchen and a porch in front and back. And their view isn't as great as yours, but you can see down the hill and the mountains to the east and west. I remember shiny hardwood floors, old quilts and wood paneling. It's not fancy but it's homey. Comfy. As I remember it, it feels like it kind of hugs you."

"Wonderful description. You should be a writer." Then Mel grinned and said, "Stand by." She pulled her phone out of her back pocket. "When I first got here about ten years ago, we had no cell service anywhere. I used to carry a pager—that's how antiquated this place was. The internet was dial-up. Jack," she said into the phone, "Kaylee is here, we're having a cup of tea and got to talking." Then she repeated everything Kaylee had said about a rental. She said she'd see him in a while and signed off. "See. He's happy to make a couple of calls on your behalf. Let me get your number. I'll put it in my phone. And I'll give you mine and Jack's."

They chatted while they finished their tea, and then Mel walked with her to the guesthouse and opened the door for her. It was perfectly charming and certainly adequate but she wouldn't choose something that small for a six-month stay. It was hardly more than a motel room and she wanted to spread out and work, if possible.

Kaylee went back to her car and moved it to the side of the guesthouse. She brought in her suitcases, cooler, picnic basket and a couple of boxes of stuff that she wouldn't bother to unpack until she found something long-term, if that even happened. She had a special suitcase with some mementos of her mother, things she couldn't bear to be away from for too long. She was fairly sure she'd be putting everything back in her car and heading south in the morning. She'd start making a list of people she could call who would put her up for a while, until she found something semipermanent. In fact, she could call Lucy and talk with her about finding a rental somewhere.

By the time she'd gotten into her pajamas, she'd begun to long for her mother's house and, of course, her mother.

They used to talk three times a day. Nothing in either of their lives passed without some mention, and major life crises or events could take hours to discuss and sort out. They were each other's go-to counselor. Kaylee didn't have anyone to fill that void.

She thought about what Mel had said to her before leaving her to settle in.

"It might be time to give yourself a pause. A break. You can't rush healing. And healing is more important than anything else, including finishing a book."

Early the next morning, Kaylee decided to take a walk. There was a small coffeepot in her casita. She brewed a cup and then stepped outside. There were a couple of chairs just outside her front door, so she sat in one. Everything was bright and clean, the air much clearer and sharper than at home. She saw Mel walk to the house next door with her children and within moments she was walking back home. She gave Kaylee a wave before disappearing into the house. A few minutes later she saw Jack's truck driving down the road away from the house, both Jack and Mel inside.

So the day begins for the people of Virgin River, Kaylee thought. Jack was probably going to the bar, though it was quite early. She left her coffee on the ground by her chair and took a leisurely walk down the road, enjoying the sight of fog nestled in the valley as the chill ran up her back and arms.

I can do this, she thought. *I can breathe in the cool morning air, wake up to the mountainous beauty, wave to the neighbors, and then I will get to work.*

She showered, sat in the only chair in the room, feet propped up on the end of the bed, laptop balanced on her thighs, and she opened up the document. She had left off on page seventeen. She reread from page one as she had a billion times before and hadn't even gotten to page seventeen when her mind began to wander. She thought of going to lunch with her mom and maybe a girlfriend or two, hers or her mom's, it didn't matter. She thought of shopping trips, always quick ones since neither of them liked to diddle over the racks. She thought about those nights neither had plans and they'd binge-watch some new series. And they often read the same book at the same time, cautiously discussing without spoilers until both had finished. Kaylee loved doing that.

There was a time a few years ago when Kaylee had to attend a conference cocktail party and had nothing to wear. She wanted to look good. Not only would other writers be there but also publishers, agents, editors and booksellers. Meredith had said, "You need just the right little black dress." And Meredith needed one, too, for an entirely different event. They wore the same size but their age differences and therefore style preferences precluded sharing a dress. Off they went to one of the better stores in LA. *Better* meant middle range, because they were hardly Rodeo Drive shoppers, but this called for something more upscale than the mall. Neiman Marcus, they thought. Or Nordstrom.

They loaded the appropriate dresses on their arms, chose neighboring dressing rooms that opened into a large viewing area with several mirrors. Kaylee's first choice hugged her butt like it was three sizes too small while Meredith's emphasized her belly. The next two were almost the opposite—Kaylee suddenly had a belly and Meredith looked all hips and butt. The next one for Kaylee looked more suited for a ninety-year-old attending a wake while Meredith had one fit for a seventeen-year-old.

"You need Spanx," Kaylee told Meredith. "I'll have the saleslady get one."

And it went downhill from there with them dying of laughter at the sight of Meredith trying to pull on the body shaper and then Kaylee trying to help her tug the girdle up. Neither got a dress that day but they did have wine with lunch, continued the laughter and vowed to try again in a week.

Kaylee was laughing out loud at the memory, but tears were running down her cheeks as well. When she thought of Meredith, that sort of thing happened. So many good times, lost.

"Oh, Jesus," she muttered, wiping her cheeks.

She remembered that Mel said something about grief never getting smaller but how her world could get bigger. She wasn't sure how that was done, but it was time to try. After she considered it for a few minutes she slid her laptop into her shoulder bag and headed for her car. She'd drive into Virgin River, which you could miss if you blinked, maybe have another coffee and whatever breakfast sandwich Jack offered. She'd try to write at the bar for an hour. Before her mom got sick Kaylee used to go to a coffee shop or a neighborhood restaurant called Carlisle's where she could have a glass of wine and a New York–style pizza slice. She felt less like she was in detention if she wrote for a while in a coffee shop or bar.

As she walked to her car she heard the smallest peep and slowed her steps. She looked up first. Then down. Right there by her front tire was the tiniest black-and-white kitten. What was a person to do? She scooped it up in her hands and instinctively held it close to her cheek. "Aww. You are lost, little one." She wasted a good ten minutes looking around for more kittens or at least a mother, but this guy was alone.

And then she did the one thing everyone cautioned against. She took him into her casita and gave him a bowl of milk and told him she'd be back in an hour or so.

"Well, well, Kaylee Sloan, just the person I wanted to see. I was going to give you a call a little later," Jack said as she walked in the door.

"Do you need the casita sooner?" she asked.

"Nah, you're fine. But I talked to an agent who leases rentals. Her name is Gloria, very nice lady, and she's going to see what they have. I gave her your number. She'll probably be calling soon."

"Oh, thank you! Um, did you lose a kitten?"

"A kitten? No. A kitten?" he repeated.

"Cutest thing, all by himself. Or herself. I don't know much about cats."

"How big is this kitten?" Jack asked suspiciously.

"He could fit in a cup," she said. "Black and white."

"There are feral cats around, but we have a dog. And with the wildlife in the mountains, kittens without a mother don't survive long and if they do, they're fighting cats. Where is it?"

"In the casita," she said. "I couldn't leave it alone. You have a dog?"

Jack nodded. "Ralph. He's a border collie. My son found him under the Christmas tree we put up in town every year so we had to keep him. He's kind of lazy but he'd probably try to herd a kitten. He's still herding us into the kitchen whenever he can."

"I never saw a dog," she said nervously. "I'm a little wary around dogs. I was bitten when I was a child. Pretty badly. Badly enough to set up a good-size phobia."

"Ralph won't bite you. He stays close to David, my son. Besides, Ralph's partying days are over. Did you, um, feed that stray kitten?"

"No. I just gave him some milk and left him in the casita so he wouldn't get hurt or lost."

"You fed him. And what are you going to do with him now?"

"There must be a no-kill shelter around here somewhere," she said.

"Nah, you should keep him. You two need each other."

"I've never had a cat..."

"I hear cats are easy. Sometimes they're independent and couldn't give a shit about you, but some people claim to have very affectionate cats. And he or she's a baby. That should give you an edge. Plus, you fed him—that's commitment in his eyes. There's a pet store in Clear River where you can get some supplies. I'll give you directions."

"I won't even know what to buy!"

"It's a pet store," Jack repeated. "Tell them you don't know what to buy and they'll load you up. How was the casita? You sleep okay?"

"It was very nice, thank you," she said in a somewhat frustrated tone. Had he just sold her a kitten? "Do you have some kind of breakfast sandwich? And coffee?"

"You bet. Preacher's in the kitchen. What do you want on it?"

"Sausage, egg and cheese, please."

"Sounds easy. Stay tuned." He turned and went to the kitchen. A moment, and only a moment later, he placed before her a perfect sandwich, cut on the diagonal, with some home fries and a tomato slice on the side. "Anything else? Ranch? Mayo? Ketchup?"

"Cholula hot sauce?"

"A girl after my own heart," he said, producing the desired hot sauce. Next came a mug of coffee and an ice water. "Be careful, now," he said. "After a couple of Preacher's meals, you'll never cook for yourself again."

She added her sauce, took a bite and let her eyelids drop in heavenly wonder. It was fabulous. "There are onions and peppers in here," she said. "Brilliant!"

Before she finished the first half, the magic that was Jack's Bar began to happen. People wandered in, recognized her as the girl from the fire, introduced themselves and tried to think of a house she could rent. She met Connie from the store across the street, Tom Cavanaugh from a local orchard, Jillian, who ran a small farm of specialty fruits and vegetables, Luke Riordan, who owned some cabins on the river, and Dr. Michaels, who worked with Mel. They all mentioned other neighbors and in no time at all she felt she'd met or heard about everyone in the town. When she finished her breakfast, she dabbed her lips and pushed her plate away. "I was going to see if I could write for a little while, but I think I have to go to the pet store."

"Congratulations," Jack said with a grin. "You're a kitty mother."

"I haven't decided I'm going to keep him," she said.

"But why not? Everyone needs a companion. Especially a writer. So, what kind of stuff do you write?"

"Well, mysteries. Scary mysteries."

"Are you famous?"

She paused before giving her standard answer. *Only to my mother.* "Hardly anyone knows me. Thanks, Jack. That was absolutely great."

"I'm hoping you'll be a regular," he said.

She gave him some money and he gave her directions written on a napkin. "Try not to find any more kittens. My daughter is almost six. Very vulnerable to small, cute animals."

"I'll keep my eyes closed," she said with a laugh.

And she thought, *In eight months nothing has changed and suddenly, in one day, I feel like life could be interesting again.*

Kaylee had never had a pet. When she was quite small it was because her parents worked and there was no time to take care of a pet. When she was six, not long after her father left them, she got that nasty dog bite. He was just some wayward dog loose in the park and of all the children there, he bit Kaylee. That eliminated the puppy notion, plus there was even one fewer person to take care of a pet. Her mother liked cats but when she was around Grandma's cats, her sinuses plugged up and she sneezed a lot. Grandma had to put the cats in a room when they visited, but that didn't help too much because the dander was everywhere.

Kaylee had a girlfriend who had two cats—one was sweet and cuddly and the other one seemed to think she was leasing her space to the humans. Her friend's cats didn't bother her sinuses at all, so that was one issue she wasn't worried about. But because of her closeness with her mother, a cat as a companion had never occurred to her.

"So, I found a kitten," she said at the pet store.

"How old?"

"I have no idea," she said. And she made her hands into a small cup.

"Boy or girl?"

"I also have no idea," she said.

"It's a little hard to tell when they're babies, but... Well, you better see the vet right away—it might need formula. You'll want to have it neutered because if you don't, you'll have a batch of new kittens before you can say 'here-kitty-kitty.' Now, what do you need?"

"I was hoping you'd tell me."

An hour later she was on her way back to Virgin River with the back of her SUV full of supplies from kitty litter and food to a scratching post. She had a cat carrier so she could take the kitten to the vet. And once she got back, she spent the better part of an hour on her hands and knees looking everywhere for that kitten. She called for it over and over, but there wasn't a sound. She was just about to give up when she pulled her head out from under the bed and something landed splat on her head, claws bared. And she screamed as if someone had come after her with a bloody knife.

She held on to the kitten with one hand and ran her fingers through her hair with the other, fully expecting to find blood. "You're an evil little thing, aren't you?" she said to the kitten.

Ah, but she had a sweet face. Or he did. She turned the cat over and gave it a close look-see. She thought it must be a girl, but she wasn't completely sure. She decided she hoped it was a girl and she pressed her face into her soft black-and-white fur. And the kitten bit her nose. "Jesus!" she swore. "Maybe that means you're hungry. Or maybe you're just plain mean! My luck. I hear there's a no-kill shelter nearby so watch it!"

Then she put out the pan and kitty litter, having no confidence at all that would work. She opened a can of food and put out a bowl of water. To her surprise, the kitten went right to it. Kaylee crouched down to get a better look at the kitten's delicate bites and heard a little purr. "Aww," she said, giving the kitty a stroke.

When the kitten was done eating, Kaylee placed her carefully in the litter pan, hoping for the best. The saleswoman at the pet store said, "It's going to take quite a few tries but eventually she'll do her business in the litter box because cats prefer that—they like to bury the evidence."

Every twenty minutes or so, Kaylee put her in the box and waited. Nothing happened. They spent the rest of the day like that and Kaylee was too distracted to get any writing done. Eventually when Kaylee got tired, she held the kitten in her lap and began a mental conversation with her mother.

I found a kitten. If you were here we'd have to take her to a shelter but I could use some company. She's not great company yet but all my writer friends have either dogs or cats. I'd rather have you. Of course I'd rather have you, but that choice was taken from us. So now I've gambled on a cat that clawed my head and bit my nose. Stop laughing! I'm doing my best, you know. Here I am in Virgin River where I know no one and am relying on the kindness of strangers...

And then, predictably, she began to tear up.

I miss you so much. I dream dreams of us sometimes and I'm not sure if that helps or hurts. Oh, Mom, I know you expect me to be tough and smart and capable and I don't think I am. I don't think I ever was... I'm just lost without you.

Eventually she fell asleep, the kitten in her precious little kitten bed beside her.

The next morning Kaylee woke to the sound of scratching. The little heathen was scratching the sheet and she had pooped on the bed.

"Great," Kaylee said.

There was some serious tidying up to do and after Kitty had some breakfast and a brief visit to the sandbox, Kitty went in the cat carrier Kaylee had bought. That would keep her from hiding or having an accident. Then Kaylee took a walk. Though the scenery was lovely and the August morning was cool and fresh, those were not the reasons she faithfully walked each day. It was a holdover from those first weeks after her mom had passed, back when she couldn't seem to find a reason to get out of bed. At the time she told herself she was simply exhausted from putting together a celebration-of-life event, entertaining friends and family, and not sleeping well at night because the darkness brought increased longing. Then she realized she was grieving and depressed and began to fear she might melt into a puddle and disappear. That seemed briefly desirable, but the image of her mother's beautiful face twisted into a disapproving frown provided some stimulus to get up and move, to shower when really, who cared? She forced herself to eat though she wasn't hungry and forced herself to move when what she wanted to do was curl up and just fade away.

Thinking her mother might be watching and that she would approve of Kaylee's efforts kept her going. And taking at least one long walk every day became routine for her.

After her walk, she showered and went through the motions of getting comfortable, brewing a fresh cup of coffee and propping the laptop on her thighs. She began reading the work in progress from page one. Again.

But she realized she was reading page seven for about the twentieth time and she had just had it. "This can't go on," she said aloud. "I have got to get my mojo back. If I can't write, what can I do? After the money I have runs out, take to the streets?"

"Mew," came the answer.

It was nearly lunchtime when Kaylee walked into Jack's Bar. There were quite a few people gathering. She saw Mel sitting up at the bar while Jack stood behind it so she went to the stool beside Mel.

"Well, hey there, I was just getting ready to give you a call. That Realtor I told you about, Gloria Patterson, has a few rentals in the area she'd be happy to show you, if you'd like," Jack said.

"Did she happen to describe them at all?" Kaylee asked.

"Not really," he said. "Except to say they were pretty nice, a couple had porches, one in town here and the others scattered around the hills. You want some lunch?"

"I don't suppose you have salad?"

"They've gotten pretty good with salads once the population of women grew a little and we were all getting fat on Preacher's food," Mel said.

"How about a half a sandwich and a salad," Jack offered.

"I could do that. And I'll call the Realtor. Maybe this situation will get resolved soon, but I have to say, that little casita is awfully nice. Mel, I wonder if I could impose on you to borrow your washer? I have a small load of laundry." She didn't want to mention it was a load of sheets with the comforter. She was afraid they'd throw her out. That kitten was small enough so the spot barely showed, but still...

"Of course," Mel said. "The back door is unlocked and the laundry room is between the garage and kitchen."

"And the dog?"

"Ralph won't bother you, except maybe to ask for a pet or treat. He's very quiet and good-natured. Now, hurry and call Gloria," Mel urged. "I'm dying to know what she's got."

"Me, too," Kaylee said. She looked at the number Jack had written on a small slip of paper and keyed it into her phone.

"Gloria Patterson, please. This is Kaylee Sloan." Then she began a series of questions. Are the houses furnished? Is there a view or at least pretty surroundings? How many bedrooms? Is the kitchen modern? Fireplace? Central heat? Available for six months? How are the utility bills handled? What's the rent? And finally, "I'd be happy to meet you at three. That's perfect."

Then she relayed what she'd learned to Mel and they began to chat about everything related to living in the area—what some of the neighboring towns had to offer, where to go antiquing if Kaylee was into that sort of thing, what the fruit and vegetable stands along the road and the farmers market in Fortuna had to offer.

"Soon it will be cool enough for soups," Mel said. "I'm a lousy cook but Jack is amazing and Preacher better still. But I still love the farmers market and if I bring home a big box of beautiful fruits and vegetables, Jack can turn it into something delicious."

"I think that after I settle on a house I should look around to rent a Jack!"

"I have no advice on where to find one," Mel said. "He took me by surprise."

Somewhere in a conversation punctuated by laughter, Jack brought lunch for both of them.

"I'd love to hear about your work," Mel said.

While they ate, Kaylee explained that she wrote suspense novels, the kind that made you wonder what that sound was in the dark of night, the kind that made you check the locks.

"I'll go to the bookstore," Mel said. "I love to read, it's my primary relaxation, but I warn you—I only read the kind of books you write when I'm feeling very brave and secure."

"What do you usually read?" Kaylee asked.

"I love romance and love stories. In my work, I require happy endings. And hopefulness. I like to read about people working things out."

"You do know they're fictional people working things out..."

"Not when I'm reading them," Mel said. "After you get yourself settled in, if you find you need supplies or clothes or just want to look around, I'd be happy to tag along. I have to plan, though. I have patients to see and the kids, but Jack is great at backing me up in the kid department. My sister-in-law next door helps. She works at home and has a daughter and the cousins keep each other busy. We could shop and lunch, either in one of the bigger towns or check out the stuff in the villages that are a little more remote."

"Assuming I'll get settled in..."

"Excuse me," a deep male voice said.

Kaylee looked up into the gorgeous blue eyes of a handsome man. Her mouth formed an O.

"Hey, Landry," Mel said.

"Hey, Mel," he returned. "Forgive me for eavesdropping, but I take it you're looking for a rental."

"I'm looking at some this afternoon, as a matter of fact," Kaylee said, a little distracted by the blueness of his eyes.

He pulled his phone out of his pocket. "If you don't find what you're looking for, I have a house I rent out from time to time. My dad and I lived on adjoining properties and after he passed away, I moved into his house because it's bigger. The house I'm renting is really nice. It's only seven years old and small but comfortable. If you want to see it, I can give you directions."

"You'll be home later?"

"The rest of the day. Here's my number. Text me if you want to see it and I'll send you the address. I'm only ten minutes from here just on the other side of 36. I heard you talking about what you want. It has a porch and a view."

"I'm Kaylee Sloan. And you are?"

"Sorry," he said with a laugh. His grin exposed one slightly crooked tooth in a sexy smile. "I'm Landry Moore. No wants or warrants. Mel might vouch for me—she cured my bronchitis two winters ago."

"I think he's pretty safe," Mel said with a laugh.

"If I don't see you later, I guess we'll run into each other around town. Probably in here."

"Thank you," she said. "It's very nice of you."

"My pleasure," he said. "Good hunting. Mel, see you around."

Once he left, Kaylee looked at Mel and lifted one brow. "I should stay away from his house. He's pretty handsome. I suppose he has a wife and seven kids."

"I think he has an ex-wife. No kids. He's kind of a loner, but friendly when he turns up. I like him," she said with a grin.

3

AFTER THE LUNCH CROWD THINNED OUT AND
Mel went back to her clinic, Kaylee ordered a Diet Coke,
settled at a table in the corner and got out her laptop. She reread those seventeen pages again. Then she wrote a page in
the third-person narrative about a woman looking for a new
start in a small mountain town. It wasn't exactly a journal but
it also wasn't exactly not. She needed to get words, any words,
on a page. Anything to get those writing juices flowing.

At three she was sitting in her car in front of Gloria Patterson's property management office in Clear River. After in-
troductions and little conversation, they took Gloria's car to
look at rentals. The first one had a nice porch and view but
was a wreck inside, wallpaper peeling off and old-fashioned
linoleum floors that were all cut up from wear. The kitchen
appliances looked old and unreliable. The next was all knotty

pine inside and reminded Kaylee of smallpox. The third was very nice but it was a converted fishing cabin and therefore extremely small, just barely larger than Jack and Mel's casita. There was no fireplace but there was a wood-burning stove and a small but decent galley kitchen.

"I'm going to have to sleep on it," Kaylee told Gloria.

"No problem," Gloria said. "If you have the time, I'm expecting a couple more rentals to come available in a few weeks."

Of course she didn't have a few weeks. She really didn't have a few days. It would probably be home to Newport or the surrounding area and this whole notion of a change of scenery would be out the door. Maybe she could make the nice little converted fishing cabin work, buried in the woods though it was.

From her car, sitting in front of the property manager's office in Clear River, she texted Landry.

If the offer is still open, I'd love to see your house.

It took only a minute before she could see the moving dots indicating he was writing. He texted back the address and she told him she put it in her GPS and would see him within the hour.

It only took her about a half hour to drive from Clear River, on a winding road that climbed up the side of a hill. She saw the houses, a big one and a small one not terribly far away. There was a path between them and the distance was about that of a city block. She knew it would be the smaller, plus Landry was standing in front of it, raking a flower bed that bordered the front of the house. Not only was there a porch but also a porch swing and a couple of chairs. She couldn't help it—she took a deep and hopeful breath.

She parked in front and got out of her car. Now that they were both standing, she realized how tall he was. He was about six feet to her five-foot-four. He had light brown hair to go with his blue eyes, paint splatters on his boots and jeans, tanned forearms and, she couldn't help but notice, broad shoulders and big hands.

"Does the house come with a gardener?" she asked, giving him a smile.

"If you want," he said. "I was just trying to clean it up a little to make a good impression. I take it the Realtor didn't have any winners?"

"Well, there's one I liked."

"Good, then look at this one and see how it compares."

"So, tell me about this house?"

"I had been living in the city—San Francisco—but it was crowded and expensive and my dad was here, so I came up to stay with him for a while. It wasn't long before I decided this was a better place for me, but I wanted my own house and shop. We built this little house together. We did it in one summer and I finished the inside in the winter. It's not very big. It was meant to be a small one-bedroom house with a kitchen and a large shop in back. I make things. Sculptures and pots and artsy-fartsy things. I meant for it to be more of a shop than a house, but you know how plans are. I'd been here a few years when my dad passed away. I moved into his house, knocked out a bedroom wall and recreated the shop in the back of his house."

"My mom passed away," she blurted out and immediately regretted it. It was a reflex, that's all. It was her life now, after all. She felt defined by it.

"I'm so sorry," he said.

"Thank you. And I'm so sorry about your father."

"Thanks. I fixed up this house so it could be used if anyone came to visit, like family or friends, and moved into my dad's house. I moved everything from my shop into my dad's house and restored the guest room in the smaller house, but I never furnished it. So, it's still small, but…"

"You're an artist?" she asked.

"I try," he said. "I dabble in clay, ceramics, metal, glass. I think I'm more of a craftsman than artist, but sometimes I surprise myself with something I think could be considered art. And I build. When my work slows down or doesn't sell, I work construction. I'm basically unemployed," he added with an engaging grin.

"It sounds like a wonderful life," she said.

"It's not nearly as expensive to live here as in the city. In the city I had to live in a small flat and rent space to work—it was inconvenient. I have to be flexible. I also do cabinets, trim, just about anything. I've even worked as a framer. And I train dogs."

Her eyes got very big. "Dogs?" she said.

He frowned and peered at her. "Dogs," he said. "I'm only working with a couple right now but I've had as many as eight at once. It's not a big business, not full-time. I'm just kind of hooked."

She gulped. "Do you train them to be attack dogs? Guard dogs?"

"No," he said. "Hunting dogs or support dogs or just plain nice family dogs. I trained a PTSD support dog once—he was amazing. I'd love to do more of that…"

"So, you have dogs?"

"Hey, you have a problem with dogs?"

"I'm afraid of them," she said. "I was bitten when I was six. Badly. I don't think I got over it."

"If I have dogs in training, they don't run free. I have a fenced area where they train or play and I have my own dog, an English setter named Otis. He's an amazing partner and helps with the training. I usually bring an extra dog who's in training into the house at night to be sure they cohabit, and Otis is less okay with that every year. He's ten. I guess he's entitled. He's been with me a long time." He frowned again. "I manage the dogs very carefully. You're in absolutely no danger. Ever. I can't have a trainee get loose—can you imagine the terrible mess if I lost one?"

"Hunting, huh?" she asked. "Support dogs?"

"All kinds of support—for owners with anxiety or diabetes or phobias or, like I said, PTSD. If you decide to stick around, I can help with that fear thing, though can I stress to you right now—you should never trust a dog you don't know. They're animals, after all."

So, he could help her, she thought wryly. It was universal, that desire to fix things, especially with men. She didn't want to be fixed. She wanted dogs to stay away from her. She had a spontaneous urge to flee before he went any further with his offer.

"Let's just have a peek at the inside," he said, walking onto the porch. "It may not be what you're looking for, but you came all this way."

Before she had even gotten to the porch, he was holding the door open.

"Would you prefer to look around by yourself?"

"It's okay. You can come in. It's your house. There might be things you want to point out."

"Sure," he said, standing aside so she could enter. "This is the living room."

She stepped through the door. Damn. It was lovely. Modern, decorated in earth tones of beige, rust, brown and a small bit of yellow. It was one large room. There was a sectional sofa and easy chair with an ottoman on one end, a dining table on the other. It had an open kitchen with a small breakfast bar and two bar stools. The living room furniture looked soft and comfortable, accented with pillows in a variety of colors and a large square coffee table, all sitting on a large, white-and-beige, deep shag area rug. The floor and furniture were polished to a high sheen; the countertops and cupboards looked as though they'd been recently wiped down. The appliances were immaculate.

"This is beautiful," she said before she could check her words. *The rent probably just went up*, she thought.

"No fireplace, I'm afraid. I have one in the bigger house. The bedrooms are that way. A master and guest room, but like I said, I never furnished the guest room. If you need to use it for guests, just give me some notice. I can get it furnished. Go ahead. There's a big closet and good-size bath."

She passed a small powder room and stepped into a lovely bedroom, if a little masculine. There was a king-size bed and again, the colors were beige and brown. The bed frame was large, the headboard tall and tufted with a wheat-colored fabric. There were two bedside tables and a bench at the foot of the bed. That was it for furniture. She glanced over her shoulder at him and he indicated a couple of pocket doors. She slid them apart and they opened into a master closet that was very large. And of course empty, since he wasn't living here.

"Wow," she said.

"Yes. When I built it, I robbed the bedroom of some space to make the closet larger—I always had a lot to store. Everything from camping gear and art supplies to linens. There's a small stackable washer and dryer right there, too. If you have to wash something large like a rug or comforter, my washer is larger and available. The spare room is just down the hall two steps. It was my shop or studio, whatever your preference. It's only a room. There's no closet, no bath, nothing but a space.

"There's a back door off the kitchen but not much of a back porch. There's a path into the woods and a stream back there. Oh, and there's bear repellent under the kitchen sink..."

"*Bear repellent?*" she nearly shrieked.

He laughed. "And you were worried about the dogs. By the way, I rarely get a dog who doesn't play well with others. I mean, it has happened, but... Enough said, the dogs won't be a problem for you."

"What's the rent on this house?" she asked, a little afraid of the answer.

"Oh, I don't know," he said. "I've gotten five hundred before, but I'm willing to consider an offer. It's been sitting empty for a while."

Five hundred? she thought in shock. That wouldn't get a one-bedroom and closet in Newport. In fact, she couldn't rent a room in a house for that! "That sounds more than fair," she said. Even without a fireplace it was so much bigger and nicer than the places the Realtor had shown her. Here, she could put her laptop on the dining table or sit in the living room with it on her knees. She might even get an outdoor chair with ottoman and do some work on the front porch. "You're sure about the dogs? Because I don't know anything about dogs except that they make me uncomfortable. I have friends who put their dogs outside or send them to bed when I visit..."

"It's guaranteed. I could put it in the lease if you like. By the way, I didn't hear how long you need a rental."

"Through the rest of the year. I'm renting out my house in Southern California and they plan to stay through Christmas because they have grandchildren nearby. But we're both flexible on when in January we return to our original places."

"But through Christmas. That's nice. This little town really lights up at Christmastime. For myself, I kind of hate it."

"You do?" she asked, wondering if she might have found a kindred spirit.

"Well, yeah," he said. He pulled off his hat and ran a big hand through his hair. "The people I'd most like to be with on a holiday are gone and seems like the ones I'd least like to be with are around. I find holidays really awkward. Except the food. I end up eating a lot of really good food because of Christmas. There isn't much more to recommend it."

She almost said, *I hate it, too.* But she used to love it. Then her mother was dying as Christmas approached and she thought she'd never again have a survivable holiday. "Well, I think I'd like to rent your house. If you're sure about the—"

"I'll be extra cautious," he said. "I don't want you to be scared."

"Thank you, because I don't want to be. I guess that's it, then. When would you like me to move in? I mean, when is it available?"

"Whenever you like." He dug around in his pocket, pulled out a key ring and wrestled a key off. "This is for the front and back door, but don't panic if you forget to lock. We don't have burglars around here." Then he grinned and added, "Too much barking, for one thing."

"Great," she said. Then she startled and said, "Oh, I guess pets are allowed?"

He just lifted both eyebrows.

"I found a kitten hiding under my car." She formed that little cup with her hands to indicate her tininess. "I couldn't leave it. So I bought food, kitty litter and toys. If it doesn't work out, I hear there's a no-kill shelter nearby."

"Don't give up on him," Landry said. "Pets bring a lot of comfort. As long as they're fluffy and not slimy."

"I'll be back tomorrow morning, then," she said.

★ ★ ★

Meredith used to say that Kaylee was stronger than she realized. "I think it's a combination of being very clever and also lucky, but you always land on your feet." It was true she always seemed to come through in the end. She didn't get into a couple of writing programs she really wanted to try, but she actually wrote anyway and sold her first book at a very young age. She fell in love, had a great wedding, had her heart broken within a year, and though it was one of the most painful things she'd ever been through, she came out of it stronger, more independent, and had learned some valuable lessons about trust. And about men. Lesson number one, when you know someone is lying, trust yourself, not him!

She'd been only twenty-four when she married and divorced, yes, in the same year. She had her share of wonderful experiences and successes and no shortage of disappointments to survive. Now, at thirty-five, there was but one thing she hadn't bounced back from. She could hear her mother's voice telling her to be patient. "Give yourself some time to heal but don't be self-indulgent. You don't need forever. We'll still be together anyway. We'll always be together."

Hah, Kaylee had thought. A little over eight months and she still missed her mother so, felt so lonely at times. And though she could see her mother's bright, laughing face and sometimes hear her voice, she was never coming back. She dreamed of her sometimes, just a little scene here or there, wanting it to be more, to feel real, to hear some of her sage advice or laugh together till they almost lost control... And she would wake up, sometimes feeling warm and sentimental, sometimes feeling the loss all over again.

What would Meredith think of this new twist, her daughter moving into a rather handsome man's guesthouse? If she were a little bit more stable and restored, she might even see the potential for a relationship. But a man was about the last thing Kaylee needed. She needed her best friend. There was just no substitute for Meredith.

When she drove up to the Sheridan house, Mel was sitting on the porch. She had a bottle of wine and two glasses and was once again braiding Emma's hair.

Kaylee stopped and got out of the car, shouting to Mel over the open car door. "Are you waiting for me?"

"I am," Mel said. "I'm not on call tonight. You can celebrate that with me if you like. I'm dying to hear about the places you saw today."

"Let me park, check on the kitty and I'll be right back."

Emma's head jerked up as if she'd gotten an electric jolt; she was all attention. "Kitty?" she said.

"Can you bring your kitty?" Mel asked.

"Sorry, I forgot Jack wanted me to keep that kitty kind of secret." She nodded toward Emma.

"Jack's a coward. Bring the kitty. Emma would love to just hold it for a little while. If that's okay."

"It'll just be a few minutes."

Kaylee did what she had to do, placing the kitty in the litter box, getting some results, then putting her back in the little carrier. She opened a can of food and carried everything back around the house to the front. Emma sat down on the porch floor, crossed her legs and reached out her little hands, just waiting. The expectation on the little girl's face made her shine.

"After you hold her a little bit, then we have to feed her. She's so little that I have to offer her food three times a day." She put the kitten in Emma's anxious hands. "Be very gentle, sweetie."

"I'll be gentle," Emma said. "I know how. I held babies. Real babies."

"Then I guess you're an expert."

"The apple doesn't fall far from the tree," Mel said. "Emma wants to be a baby doctor." She lifted the wine. "Is white okay?"

"Just perfect."

"So, what did you find?"

Kaylee quickly explained the first three houses and then Landry's. "It's really pretty beautiful. Very nicely decorated, plenty of room, a nice porch with a swing and it's immaculate. Like it's been cleaned with a toothbrush. One thing, though. It might be a problem. He has dogs. I told you, I'm not very good with dogs."

"A bad bite, you said," Mel remembered. "But Landry sometimes trains dogs. It's not his main business but he's developed something of a reputation. Mostly hunting dogs, I think. But if he's a trainer, there shouldn't be out-of-control dogs tearing up the countryside. Right?"

"I hope so, because that could spoil the whole thing. He said he's also some kind of artist."

Mel nodded. "I've seen some of his pottery and glass— very beautiful. He ships a lot of stuff to San Francisco and other places and he usually has a booth at some of the town fairs. There are lots of artists tucked away in these hills. We have a good friend who paints wildlife portraits. Colin Riordan. He and Landry are friends." Then Mel's eyes twinkled. "He's cute."

"Colin? Or Landry?"

"I guess they both are, but I was commenting that your new landlord is cute. Are you in the market?"

"Nah," Kaylee said. "I'm in recovery. I struggle every single day with my mom's death. I'm not ready to open up to anyone new."

"But your life is getting bigger," Mel said. She lifted her glass in Kaylee's direction. "May it get bigger and bigger."

It took Kaylee a little more than an hour to wash her linens, clean the bathroom in the casita, load up her belongings and kitten and head across town to Landry's house. As she drew close, she passed a vegetable stand. It was mostly late summer vegetables like squash, melons, berries, cauliflower and broccoli. There were still tomatoes but the lettuces and kale were looking a bit tired. The artichokes were amazing, and she loved artichokes. She had seen a nice grocery in Clear River the day before; she planned to make a run later for butter, bread, bacon, tuna, sliced turkey, cheese. Also chips, salsa, garlic, eggs and a few other things.

This was a sign she was going to settle in.

Once she got everything into the cabin, her next task was settling her kitten. She showed her where they'd keep the litterbox, then got some toys out of the bag and shook out the soft, fluffy bed, which the kitty immediately began to claw.

Next, Kaylee set up her music—she chose her Beatles playlist. She ate a couple of tomatoes with avocado. She did a quick inventory of the kitchen to see if there was anything she had to buy in order to feed herself dinner.

She made tea. Then she sat down and read those seventeen pages again. Blah, blah, blah.

She opened the document she had titled *A New Start* and began to write.

She wanted to feel safe, cozy and completely confident. After all, being alone was hardly a new thing for her. And this temporary space had everything she needed from a porch swing to a flower bed bordering the house. In days gone by, all she had to do was burrow into a comfortable chair, open her laptop, place her mind in a story and write. Not that it was easy—even the easiest writing was filled with constant revision, change and improvement. But it had always felt good before. Now, with her best friend gone, it was like her talent was gone as well. She didn't know where to look to find her magic again.

She should give herself and her best friend names.

Sometimes she felt like her mother was still alive. Sometimes she thought of her alive and well, robust and funny and cynical and pouring a cup of coffee or glass of wine in her house in Newport. Countless times she felt her hand reaching for the phone to give her a quick call. "I'll go get us Mediterranean and we'll eat on the patio," Kaylee would say. "Do you have good wine?" And before she finished the thought she would remember Meredith wasn't there.

Her thoughts were interrupted by the sound of barking dogs and she went to the porch cautiously. Landry was in the fenced yard behind his house with a couple of dogs. She didn't know what kind they were. Two were blond and hairy, one was sleek and black. Landry was throwing ball after ball for them to chase. He stopped, put three balls in his pocket and called the dogs with a shrill whistle, and all three trotted over to him, wagging their tails fiercely. They sat. Then he lowered a hand to one, then another, then threw a ball to the third. Only that dog ran to fetch. Then that dog sat and was told to stay while the second dog was invited to fetch. Then the third. Remarkable. They took turns and politely waited.

"Cool," she muttered to herself. But she had no desire to be anywhere near them. She sat on the porch swing and listened to the barking, the whistling, the quiet, rinse and repeat.

She put her kitten in the carrier to keep her out of mischief while she was gone, packed up her computer and drove to town.

Given it was midafternoon, there were only a few people in Jack's Bar. He called out her name, greeting her, and even though it had only been a couple of days it had much the feel of Cheers—friendly and familiar. She went to the bar for a Diet Coke, found a table in the corner away from the door and bar, and opened up her computer.

She forced herself to write one page of her novel. She was desperate to make some progress and the best way she could think of was to toss a dead body in there. To make it interesting, the body had several bullet wounds and was discovered by one of her favorite recurring characters—a seventy-eight-year-old woman, a busybody with a fierce interest in forensics.

Then she flipped over to the other document.

The last thing she had any interest in was a man or a romantic encounter. She noticed that Landon spent a lot of time outdoors with his horses and his garden. She couldn't help but see him. A lot of him. The way his jeans fit seemed to be particularly appealing, not that she was checking him out. She told herself she wouldn't have noticed the jeans if it hadn't been for his lovely personality. He was so comfortable around her, so accommodating and affable. His eyes were so shockingly blue and his smile both frequent and engaging. When he smiled at her she felt her pulse pick up a little. She couldn't help but watch him when he was in sight.

She wondered if they might become friends while she lived in his guesthouse. And she hoped to become better friends with the bartender and his wife—they were so kind and generous, not to mention fun.

"Hey, it's the fire girl," someone said. She looked up to see Mike, the guy who had been behind the bar the first night she was in town. She had since learned that he was Jack's brother-in-law and lived next door to Mel and Jack. Today he was wearing a badge on his belt. "The writer."

"We're going to have to go with names and not reputation," she said, sticking out her hand. "Kaylee Sloan."

"Mike Valenzuela, how you doing?"

"Great," she said. "I didn't know you were the police."

"Constable for this town. How's the new place?"

"It's very nice," she said. "Just what I was looking for since the Templeton house is off the market. I'm lucky—it was just a lucky break."

"Have you heard from the Templetons?"

"Not since I talked to him right after the fire. Gerald said he'd give me a call once he learned more about the cause. He thinks he'll have to come up here and plan some repairs. He or one of his sons."

The door opened and a tall man came in and walked toward Mike and Kaylee. "Hey there," he said. "I think I saw you at the fire. I'm Paul Haggerty."

She recognized him as one of the many men gathered around the dregs of the fire. "Kaylee Sloan."

"Did I hear you say the Templetons were friends of yours?"

"That's right. I was going to use their house for a few months."

Paul pulled a card out of his pocket. "Next time you talk to Gerald, tell him I'm hoping for a chance to bid on the remodel. I have a construction company in town. He knows me, but I don't know if he'll remember I'm a builder. I do a lot of remodels and upgrades around here."

"I'll be sure to pass that on."

"Thank you. Are you doing okay?"

"She's renting that extra house out at Landry's," Mike said.

"It's nice out there. I helped Landry tear out a wall in the big house and he works with me from time to time."

"Oh, this is the girl from the fire," someone else said.

Over the next hour she chatted with Connie, the owner of the Corner Store; Noah, the minister; Colin and Luke Riordan, names she'd heard before, and then of all people to drop by, Landry came in, greeting her as if they were old friends. There was a lot of hand shaking and howdies, a couple of beers, a couple of sodas, a black coffee. Mel came in to take her afternoon break with her husband. Kaylee met the cook, Preacher, and his wife. Before she realized what had happened, she'd been in the bar for two hours and the place was beginning to fill up with construction workers or farmers or people from businesses around town.

At five Jack asked her if she was staying for dinner. "Not tonight," she said. "I have a kitty to feed."

"Something to go?"

She'd been to the store; she did a mental inventory of what she had on hand, but somehow it didn't create a picture of a meal in her mind. "A salad to go?" she asked.

"Sure. Can I give you a chicken breast with that?"

"Absolutely," she said. "And a hunk of bread?"

"You got it."

A few minutes later she made her way out of the bar with her sack of takeout. She had noticed that Landry left just before she did and when she got home she saw that he was in the fenced yard with the dogs. He waved to her.

"You need anything, Kaylee?" he shouted.

She lifted her bag. "I'm all set, thanks."

"Have a great night," he yelled.

"You, too," she called out, waving.

Now, that wasn't such a big deal. Just neighbors being

friendly, that's all. But there was much about him to enjoy, not the least of which was his kindness. He didn't have to ask if she needed anything. He was also handsome. And sexy. And right next door.

She fed her kitty, ate her salad, put on her pajamas and sat on the big bed with her laptop. The sun was setting but she had not achieved much by way of writing, so she opened the laptop while the kitty played beside her on the bed, frequently jumping onto the laptop keys. She forced herself to deal with the dead body in the story, though nothing could have interested her less.

Then she flipped over to that other document, to the fantasy world of her new fictional characters Caroline and Landon. She decided that her own life story lacked pizazz so she made a few adjustments for Caroline. Instead of grieving the loss of her best friend, she decided it would be more interesting if Caroline was a young widow and no one in her new town knew the details.

The only job she could find was a temporary position as an assistant to a producer who happened to be shooting a docudrama in the small town she chose for her escape, for her second chance. It was nothing but busywork, handing out scripts, setting up chairs for a reading, making sure everyone had what they needed, whether that was a coffee or a masseuse. Once, just a few days into her new job, the director stopped her and said, "Do us a favor and read this scene."

"But I don't act," Caroline said.

"No problem, we're not looking for acting from you. Just read so my leading man can do his thing. It's only a rehearsal. And he needs it."

"Okay," Caroline said. "But don't hold it against me."

"Of course not."

There were about ten people total around the set. She could fake it. She took the script, gave it a quick read, understood the emotion and pauses, silences and outbursts. It was all of two pages. She stood before the outrageously attractive leading man. He gave her a reassuring smile, coincidentally just like Landon's.

They began. It was an argument that would end with her in tears and him putting his arms around her to reassure her. She accused him of being interested in a woman named Carla, snapped back when he tried to make excuses, stood speechless before him while he fought back, and then (because it said so in the script), she began to cry and fuss about the pain his indifference caused.

The small set was on location in the woods, and when the rehearsal of the short scene was at an end, there was a deafening silence all around. Stillness. Everyone was frozen.

Caroline wiped away the tears she had forced. She had wanted to cooperate as well as possible, after all. She looked around. Silence and open mouths faced her.

"Well, holy shit," the director said. "I've never seen anything like that."

"I'm sorry," she said. "Was it terrible?"

"Terrible? Darling, you're an actress," the leading man said.

She came back to reality and stopped typing.

Crap, Kaylee thought. *Why can't I fantasize like normal people? The next-door neighbor waves at you and you write a scene that reeks of romance and yearning. That's not normal.*

I think it's adorable, her mother's voice said. *What can it hurt?*

"A man is the last thing I'm looking for," she said aloud.

Whatever. He seems like a pleasant distraction.

"Hush, now. You know that's not what I want."

But she played around with that scene, went back to the beginning of this totally outrageous story and reset it, giving it a proper beginning, and typed for three hours. Kitty fell asleep next to her and when she couldn't keep her eyes open any longer she closed the laptop. She slept like that, a laptop and a kitten sharing her space on the bed.

She slept well and with a smile.

4

THE UPSIDE TO BEING KNOWN AS THE GIRL FROM the fire was, she was not considered a stranger. She might be learning the names of the folks around town and their connections to each other slowly, but they all had her down. No matter where she went—on her daily walk, shopping, stopping at the vegetable stand, hanging out at Jack's—she was greeted as if she were a friend. And because of the fire, she had a history here. There was something comforting about that.

She was still feeling a little lonely, especially in the evenings. This was naturally time she would either phone her mother to share events of the day or maybe she'd drive the few miles from her apartment to her mom's house. They often ate dinner together. There was no changing that history so she often reached out to some of her friends who were not yet sick to death of her grieving and would talk to her, Face-Time with her.

"I'm sorry that the only thing I seem to be able to talk about is how much I miss my mom," she said to Janette.

"That's okay, cookie. It won't always be like that but while it is, I'm here to listen. I listen for a living, you know. Now tell me a story. Tell me about the book."

"Which one?"

"Are you working on more than one?" Janette asked, surprised. She knew Kaylee hadn't been writing much since her mom was diagnosed.

"Well, the one that's due, that *was* due before Christmas, is a suspense novel, and right now the suspense is whether or not I am ever going to finish it. It is two and a half chapters in length. It's boring and disjointed and I have very little interest in it. But I had a wild idea about a woman starting fresh in a small town. She's working for a local movie producer. She rents a small house from a man who trains dogs and of course, she's afraid of dogs."

"Kaylee, what's that story for?"

"For me. It's alternative journaling. Fictionalizing my experience while I make sure to add a few legitimate feelings and thoughts. I won't do anything with it."

"That's brilliant," Janette said. Janette, as it happened, was a counselor. A marriage and family therapist. "I sometimes recommend that to my clients. But why don't you just keep a diary? I bet in ten years it would be really interesting."

"You have no idea how not interesting that would be," Kaylee said. "I went to counseling after my divorce and at the insistence of the counselor, I kept a journal. I read through it about six or seven years later and found it so embarrassing, I destroyed it. It's a terrible experience—expose all your deepest, darkest feelings and emotions and take a clear look at them later. Oh God, that is humiliating. It's much better to make up a story without naming names."

When she was dead and gone and someone unearthed these stories, they might see some similarities between her and her fictional heroines, but they'd never be entirely sure. And she was writing down her real experiences and feelings, which the counselor said never hurt. She didn't advocate mailing the vitriolic letters Kaylee wrote to people like her ex, her estranged father, women friends who ultimately turned out to be crappy friends. But giving all of them new names and faces and exposing them secretly inside a novel... There was a real satisfaction in that.

One of Kaylee's writer friends kept killing her ex-husband in book after book. He never went easily. He suffered. It was delicious. Kaylee had a little fun with the demise of her ex as well. It was kind of irresistible.

The next day, Gerald Templeton called Kaylee. Bonnie had been sick. That was why Kaylee hadn't heard from them. Bonnie was feeling better, but not good enough to take a big road trip. In another week, if she was up to it, they were going to come up and have a look at the fire damage. Their oldest son, Rick, lived in Oregon, and he was hoping to meet his parents there.

"That reminds me, Gerald. I met a man named Paul Haggerty. He said he knew you and to please remind you that he's a builder. He's hoping you'll consider him when you get around to repairs and renovation."

"I remember Paul," Gerald said. "Did you get his number?"

"I have his card," she said, happy to be assisting in some small way.

Kaylee had been there a couple of weeks, wandering around by day, calling friends and writing in the evenings. She was a frequent visitor at Jack's Bar and often had dinner there. Sometimes Mel would drop by and they stole a little girl time. She walked the roads up, down and around the mountain near her rental house. Given the elevation of this little mountain town, the weather was not as hot and steamy as those towns in the valleys. Right now Sacramento would be simmering. But in the mountains, it was so pleasant. She discovered that on the side of Landry's house there was a large garden and if it weren't for the frequent barking around his property, she might have taken a closer look. She did see Landry from afar now and then. He could usually be found having his morning coffee on the porch or maybe watching the sunset or, most often, working with a dog or two in the yard.

She bought her own bear repellent, a can so large she had to wear a backpack to carry it. And the upside of that—it was too heavy and bulky for her to run. It would bang her in the back. Thank God, she thought. No running or even jogging.

It was early evening, the sun just starting its downward path, when she was returning from her second walk of the day. As she passed in front of his house, raising a hand in hello, the rug beside him appeared to jump up. *The dog.*

"Hey, Kaylee, how's it going?"

She froze. She'd seen this dog from a distance. This was the closest she'd been to it and it was a very big dog. He was there on the porch with Landry. There was no fence and, of course, no leash. She couldn't move. She imagined the dog would leap off the porch and fly like a torpedo toward her and take her down.

"How about a beer?" Landry said. "Or maybe a glass of wine?"

She was speechless. Didn't he realize there was a monstrously large dog standing beside him, glaring at her?

"Kaylee?"

She was paralyzed. She held her hands clasped in front of her and took a cautious step backward.

"You okay?"

"I... Ah... I have some stuff to do."

"Okay. But are you okay? You look a little...freaked out. Hey, are you afraid of Otis?"

She shook her head. "Sorry. I have to—" She took slow and very cautious steps backward, then turned and forced herself to move unhurriedly down the road toward her house. Her heart hammered in her chest and her breath came in short gasps. She tried telling herself that Landry wouldn't let anything bad happen, but fear was in charge.

She looked back at Landry's house. The dog wasn't actually all that big. Too big for her, that was for sure, but a moment ago it seemed as big as a horse, teeth bared. Now he stood relaxed beside Landry, casually wagging his tail. He almost looked like he was smiling. The place on her calf where she'd been bitten so many years ago ached. She knew that was in her mind because that was not a chronic pain she had.

She lifted her hand and gave him a wave and went inside. She leaned against the door and waited until her breathing evened out. "Sheesh," she said, unnerved. She was shaking. She sat on the couch and concentrated on just calming down. Once she was under control, she drank a large glass of water. Then she poured herself a glass of wine. She turned on the TV.

In ten minutes, her scalp stopped sweating and dried out. Her hands stopped trembling. The voice of the news anchor became familiar and calming, even if the news was not. She wasn't sure how long she sat there, cradling her glass of wine. All she was acutely aware of was that her door was closed and she was alone. Safe.

There was a sharp rapping at her front door and she jumped in surprise, sloshing her wine. She brushed at the spill with her hand, annoyed by her jumpiness. "Who is it?" she asked, but she knew.

"It's me. Landry. Can I have a minute?"

"Do you... Is there... Is the dog with you?"

"No, he's in my house. He's staying right there."

She let out a breath. Whew. She opened the door and he stood there holding two beer bottles by their necks.

"Let's have a beer and talk," he said.

"Talk? About?"

"Come out and sit on the porch," he said. "I think you just had a panic attack. About the dog."

"I'm not comfortable around..."

"We can talk about that."

"I don't think talking about it is likely to change anything," she said. "I've talked about it before. It's a very old trauma."

He lifted the beers toward her.

She sighed. "I have a glass of wine. I just poured it. Let me get it." When she got back to the porch, he was seated on the porch swing.

He took a deep drink of his beer. "Here's the thing. I think I told you, I've dealt with this before. You should always be careful around dogs you don't know. They can be unpredictable and sometimes unfriendly. You did the right thing—you stayed still and didn't bolt. That's good. But Otis gave no sign of being mean or vicious. I think if you're going to work through this, Otis might be a good place to start. He's very gentle and he'll take commands from anyone. Like *anyone*. He follows the commands of a two-year-old if necessary. He's been a good companion to several children who are trying to get over their fear."

"What's the point? I'm not likely to want a dog. Not after being badly bitten. I was only six. I had to have a couple of surgeries."

"It's not so you can be a dog owner," he said. "You don't even have to be a dog lover. It's so your heart doesn't pound so hard you faint or throw a clot. The point is not to get you to love dogs. It's so you don't have to feel that terror every time you see one. If you feel better when you avoid dogs, there's nothing wrong with that. It's a question of taste, isn't it? Probably you're a kitty person. It's just about getting over the fear. Not the healthy, reasonable fear. The irrational fear."

"How do you suppose I do that?"

"With the right dog, for starters. A dog you can absolutely trust."

"Hmm," she said, thinking she really didn't like the idea of being around any dog. "How did you get into this?" she asked, taking a sip of wine.

"Kind of the reverse of your situation. I found a dog who had been abandoned and abused. I was just a kid of fifteen and I carried the dog home. I called her Izzy. I wanted to keep her and get her strong and my dad thought it was a bad idea. He thought the dog's temperament might be permanently damaged, that she might get scared and attack or run off or just hide in a corner and shake for the rest of her life. But I talked him into it and then I looked everywhere for someone who could show me how to help her gain trust again. There was a trainer over in Fortuna and I went to talk to him. Then I took Izzy with me. He thought she might be about two years old and based on her physical condition, might have been used for fighting from the time she was a pup. Even the trainer said I'd probably be fighting a losing battle. I had to hand-feed her for months. I slept with her and took her everywhere but school. In six months she was the best dog that ever lived. And she was happy. I think she forgot about the abuse." He looked at her and flashed his grin. It was an engaging, infectious grin that demanded a smile in return.

"And I got hooked on training. To have a dog, especially a difficult dog, follow your commands because she wants to—it's exhilarating. It gives you a friend for life."

"And now it's your job?"

"Just part-time. Because I enjoy it. Dogs deserve to be well trained. I think it makes them happy. I know it makes them social. And it makes a good family. Frustrated dog parents are unhappy and unhappy parents are sometimes angry. That's no good for anyone."

"Why don't you teach people how to train their dogs?"

"I do that, too. But not everyone has the right temperament. It takes a certain kind of confidence. For me, it's satisfying to turn over a well-behaved pet or partner..."

"Partner?"

"I train hunters and support animals, too. They're working dogs."

"And guard dogs? And police dogs?" she asked.

"No. Canine officers should train their own dogs; it's part of the bonding experience. I don't like the idea of guard dogs. Get an alarm. Or just an ordinary dog will bark at just about anything that stirs. Most people want guard dogs that will scare people, even attack. That's not what I do. I want to work with people who want happy dogs. That's a tall enough order."

"And you have many other things to do," she said. "I'm very curious about all your art. But I'm more curious about your experience with this town. How long have you been here?"

"I grew up here. It was just me and my dad. This was his property. I was little when he and my mother got divorced. She went back to the city and we stayed here. He was a lineman with the county—back then it was power lines."

"So, you spent almost your whole life right here?"

"Not all, no. I went to college in San Francisco, lived there a few more years, before I decided I didn't have to pay those high city prices. What about you? Where did you grow up?"

"Southern California. Newport."

"One of those California beach girls…"

Before long, he began the second beer while she sipped her wine. They talked about areas of the state they liked, the differences between the northern mountains and the southern beaches. She told him she'd been married, though briefly, and had been divorced for nine years. He mentioned that he had been married eleven years ago, that his hadn't worked out, either. It was one of those pleasant, superficial, just-getting-to-know-you chats. She heard her phone ringing in the house and decided whoever was calling could leave a message because she was enjoying this time with her landlord.

They parted ways as the sun was getting low over the pines and a small chill was settling over the land. "We'll have to do this again," he said.

"By all means," she said.

When she was back inside, she checked her phone. It was Howard, her father. His voice was a little hysterical.

"Kaylee, where the hell are you? I've left messages, you haven't returned my calls, so I stopped by the house and there's a strange couple living there! They said you'd moved to Northern California for the rest of the year! Call me or so help me God, I'll come looking for you."

She sighed deeply. It was tempting to just ignore the message, but clearly he was going to keep calling. She didn't understand the urgency. He seemed to have spent much of his life avoiding her until Meredith got sick. Then suddenly he was calling frequently, wanting to see her, wanting to form a family with her.

There just didn't seem to be a polite way to tell him he was much too late.

Kaylee had grown to hate the words, "Well, he *is* your father." From the time Howard had left them, he had not been an attentive or doting father. In fact, he rarely visited her. He would come to the house occasionally, and even at the age of seven or eight she knew he was coming more to see Meredith than her. It became more evident as the years passed that he regretted leaving Meredith, and on his visits he would spend a great deal of the time visiting with her, not Kaylee. Kaylee would say hello and then go watch TV, and Howard and Meredith would sit at the kitchen table and talk like old friends. By the time Kaylee was a teen she had come to understand Howard wanted to talk to his ex-wife about his unsuccessful relationships.

"Doesn't that make you mad, that he complains to you about his wives or girlfriends?" she once asked her mother. And Meredith said, "No, sweetheart. It makes me very grateful that he left me."

Meredith was fine with his visits, given they weren't too frequent. Because Meredith was classy. Her heart no longer ached for the marriage that fell apart and she'd had plenty of gentlemen friends in the years since the divorce. She had a good social life.

But then Meredith got sick and Howard amped up his visits, causing Kaylee to be jealous of the time he spent with her mother. Whenever Kaylee complained, Meredith would say, "Go easy on Howard. He is your father."

And to be fair, Howard had paid child support and helped with her college expenses. He'd done well for himself in the real estate business, which was lucky since he had to pay a lot of support. He'd had a total of four children.

She decided to get it over with and called him back. "Hi, Howie," she said in greeting because she knew he hated it. He always instructed her to call him Dad. But for some reason she kept forgetting… "No need to panic. I wanted a change of scenery for a few months so I could finish a book."

"Where exactly are you?" he demanded. "And why didn't you tell me you'd be out of town?"

"I'm in Humboldt County, and I didn't mention it to you because I'm thirty-five years old, we're not close, you don't tell me where you're going all the time. In fact, I don't expect you to."

He sighed. "Okay, I deserved that," he said. "I wasn't there for you when I should have been and there seems to be no way to make up for it now. But with your mom gone, I wish we could spend a little time together. I was going to invite you out to dinner. I think we're both missing her."

The last thing she needed was an evening of reminiscing with Howie. "Sorry, but I came here to work and that's what I'm doing. Maybe when I get back to Newport."

"Are you getting a lot of work done?"

"I'm trying," she said. "I…I still find it hard to focus, hard to concentrate. But I'm giving it everything I've got."

"Maybe I'll come up in a few weeks," he said. "You can show me around and we'll have dinner."

"I don't have a guest room, Howie."

"I can make arrangements," he said. "Think about it and we'll talk about it later. I'll give you a call next week."

"All right. Take care."

"You, too. Love you."

"Goodbye."

She never said she loved him. She wasn't sure she did. She wasn't sure she wanted to.

Kaylee took Kitty to the vet that Jack recommended— Dr. Lynne Murphy. "Well, Kitty turns out to be a boy," the vet said. "And I'd guess about eight weeks old. He'd have to be that old to eat solid food and use the litter box. Let's give him a couple of weeks of growth and then start his shots. Meanwhile, would you like me to chip him?"

"Chip him?"

"A microchip that ID's his name, owner, vital information so if he's ever lost he can be returned to you."

"Oh yes, please."

"Is he going to get another name besides Kitty?"

"Oh man. This is actually my first pet. My mother was allergic and I know nothing. I guess that's obvious."

"Not to worry. This cat will probably raise you. So, he should be neutered because if he's not he will not only make more cats, and he'll make a mess, spraying his scent around your house. We'll give him shots, make sure he's in good health and check his weight. After about four months of inoculations and after he's been neutered, if you keep him as an indoor cat you'll be on your own unless you need us. He's a pretty little guy."

She had them put Tux on his chart as his name because of his black-and-white markings. She pretended not to hear when the doctor said, "Original."

The next afternoon when Kaylee was at Jack's having lunch, Jillian Matlock came in carrying a large cardboard box filled with vegetables. "It's your lucky day, Jack. Is Preacher around?"

"Yep. Stand by." He turned and banged on the wall that separated the bar from the kitchen. "Brought him some goodies, did you?"

"The harvest is winding down and these are good but not pretty enough to send out." Preacher came through the swinging door, drying his hands on a dish towel.

"Hey," he said. When he saw Jillian, he smiled. "Goodies?"

"For my special friend. The last of the Russian Rose and purple calabash, some artichokes, onions, turnips... Late stuff."

Kaylee got off her stool and slowly gravitated toward Jillian and the box of veggies. There were peppers, cucumbers, a bunch of green and purple leaf lettuce and a few other things she couldn't name.

"Have you two met?" Jack asked.

"The fire girl," Jillian said. "We met last week. How are you?"

"I'm Kaylee," she said with a laugh. "I'm great, thanks. Is this stuff from your garden?"

"I'm a farmer," Jillian said. "I have a few acres dedicated to heirloom vegetables and other organic stuff. They're some little known varieties mostly used by restaurants as garnish. Also my sister is a chef and she makes a variety of sauces, relishes, and a few dressings and pastes. She's a cooking miracle. She's working on some soup starters as her new line—absolutely amazing stuff."

"You oughta see Jillian's place," Jack said. "It's incredible. And she farms year-round."

"Look at those artichokes," Kaylee said. "They're huge!"

"I'd love it if you came by," Jillian said. "I'll give you a tour. Whenever you're available. I'm just about done for the day if you're free now."

She glanced at her laptop, which hadn't seen a lot of action today, and said, "I'm free."

"Great! You can follow me home! I'll take you around in the garden mobile."

Kaylee did just that, driving down Highway 36 behind Jillian and then down a long road, through the trees and up to a beautiful Victorian mansion. After she parked she admired the house.

"Completely restored, mostly by Paul Haggerty," Jillian

said. "I found it and rented it and started a small garden, then I bought it and the ten acres it's on and planned a farm. The house is wonderful; I'll take you through it after we tour the gardens. Colin and I live here, but my sister, Kelly, uses the kitchen to cook. She has a commercial kitchen in Eureka where she produces her sauces. But she's always trying new things, usually on a large scale, and this kitchen is perfect. Come in and meet her."

Kaylee followed Jillian inside and met Kelly, who appeared to be up to her elbows in dough.

"Bread," Jillian said. "I love it when she bakes bread. You can smell the aroma all the way to the coast. If you're interested, we can see the gardens first, then the house."

"Oh, I'm interested. I want to see anything you have time to show me."

"Good, I love showing it off."

Sitting in the garden mobile next to Jillian, Kaylee bounced around the huge gardens behind the house. They were like a quilt of many colors and textures, lush and looking tasty. Most of the outdoor gardens were picked clean except for the melons, pumpkins and some late squash. But there were several greenhouses in the back, filled with raised beds that held fruits, vegetables and flowers. "Mostly edible flowers that chefs like to garnish their plates with. I just started doing that a couple of years ago."

"How do you get your stuff to the restaurants? Because unless I missed something, there aren't a lot of restaurants around here."

"You didn't miss anything. These flowers and heirloom vegetables go as far as Seattle and San Francisco via FedEx. They're tender little things that won't last long; they go overnight."

The back acreage was lined with fruit trees and berry

bushes. "The berries come in in spring, finished by the first of August, but the apples come in later. I don't rely on that apple crop for much, except to satisfy the deer. I sell them out on the roadside stands—we have two large ones now. Kelly uses the fruit and berries in her creations; she ships a lot of pie filling, jams, jellies and that sort of thing. I've added to the berry bushes and paid the price—the bears love berries. I have to scare them away. I have an air horn they don't like. Having wildlife in the yard can be fun until you get a sample of their mischief. A mama bear with a couple of cubs will break into the greenhouses or turn a garden mobile upside down. I really can't afford to be welcoming."

"They don't scare you?" Kaylee asked.

"Not really," Jill said. "But I don't get up close and personal. I've seen the size of their claws. And I've seen the evidence of their shenanigans."

"Could you put up a big fence?" Kaylee asked.

Jillian laughed. "Have you ever seen a bear up a thirty-foot tree? There's no fence to keep them out. We do have fences around some of our outdoor gardens to keep the deer out, plus I use a lot of bunny repellant to save my lettuces and root vegetables. The bears, I'm afraid, go where they please. Thus the air horn. It's very loud."

Kaylee was in awe of the terraced plots that adorned the hillsides surrounding the house, separated by narrow roads to make movement easy. Every now and then Jillian would stop the golf-cart-size garden mobile and pick some fruits or veggies and throw them in the back of her little truck. There was everything from apples to tiny potatoes; there were several rows of grapes with only a few still on the vine. She pulled up a few honeydew and cantaloupe from their vines and added them to her catch.

"The pumpkins will be ready for Halloween," she said.

When they got back to the house, Jillian showed her around, and by far the biggest treat was the second-floor sunroom where Colin had his studio. His wildlife paintings circled the large room, and he was at work on a huge painting of a buffalo. "God, that's breathtaking," she said. "Do you sell them in a gallery?"

"Most of them go to a small gallery in Sedona, Arizona, owned by an artist who has become a good friend. I do some special orders and sell some from my website. It's keeping me out of trouble," he said.

There was a third floor that had a couple of guest rooms and to Kaylee's surprise, a staircase to the roof and a widow's walk. "We don't know where the idea for a widow's walk came from, but you can see all of Jilly Farms and beyond from up here. The first year I was here, I came up here all the time. I would call Kelly; we didn't have a satellite connection yet and it was the only place I could get really good reception. And I would watch over my little farm."

When they went back downstairs, Kelly had some snacks prepared for them. They talked for a while about their various artistic pursuits from Kaylee's writing to Kelly's culinary skills. And when Kaylee was finally leaving, Jillian handed her a large plastic laundry basket full of the things she'd picked on their tour of the gardens.

All of them made sure she knew she'd be welcome back anytime. "I can't wait to come back," she said.

She drove directly home from there, and as she pulled in she saw Landry was sitting on his porch steps, holding a bottled water. When she parked in front of her house, he wandered over. She lifted the hatch. "I've been to Jilly Farms. And look what I got!"

"Awesome," he said, looking through the fruits and veggies.

"I'm going to have a veggie dinner."

"Do you have a ham hock to go in the beans?" he asked.

"No, of course not—I wasn't expecting this."

"I do. I'll get it for you. You can't have a pot of green beans without pork of some kind."

"Then you have to join me for dinner!"

And there was that grin. "That would be great. I'll make sure Otis stays home."

5

KAYLEE'S FIRST DINNER WITH HER LANDLORD WAS so easy, she felt as though she'd known him for years. He helped her clean up the kitchen, accepted an after-dinner cup of coffee, didn't stay too late and thanked her profusely. She and Kitty—erm, Tux—wrote eight pages, staying up till almost midnight.

The very next day when she was returning from her afternoon walk he waved to her from his porch and shouted, "What are your plans for dinner?" She gestured that she didn't know, just shrugging her shoulders. He told Otis to stay on the porch and walked down the path to the road. "I thawed some ground sirloin for hamburgers. Care to join me?"

She glanced at Otis. "If you cook them on your grill and bring them over, I'll slice tomatoes and make deviled eggs. And there are leftover beans."

"That sounds perfect," he said. "I'll get a shower and do some grilling. How about six?"

"I look forward to it."

She had her own shower and did a little primping, wondering if he'd notice. Then she wondered why she bothered.

She bothered because he was handsome, pleasant and quite good company. They talked about anything and everything. He gave her the background on a lot of her new friends.

"The story on Jillian and Colin is she was fired from a big executive job and came up here from San Jose to try to get her head together. Colin came to Virgin River because his brother Luke lives here, though why he did that is a mystery. They can't get along at least half the time. I take that back— they're either best friends or enemies. Jilly found the house and its neglected garden and started digging and planting. Colin is an ex-military Blackhawk pilot. He was recovering from a crash and painting was his therapy. He didn't quite know he was any good."

"Any good? He's gifted!"

"I know. He met Jilly, fell in love with her and they've been together ever since."

"And now they're married?"

"No. But they are a permanent couple nonetheless. And, this being Virgin River—meaning it's very small and very nosy—people ask them constantly when they're going to get married. They've been together in that big house for years. I don't know why they haven't married and as far as I'm concerned, it doesn't matter. Kelly, Jilly's sister, is married."

"To a film writer, I was told," Kaylee said. "She's very proud of him."

"Then there's the preacher," he went on, giving her the scoop on how Noah came to town to fulfill the needs of a church he bought on eBay and how he fell in love with the church secretary, a former exotic dancer.

"This town doesn't look nearly as interesting as it really is at first glance," she said, laughing.

Three days later, after only seeing Landry on the porch or in the yard, she asked him if he was interested in joining her for dinner and he readily accepted. They had drinks on her porch at sunset before dinner and then coffee on the porch afterward. She always sat on the swing and he lounged in the porch chair, a rocker, next to the swing.

The next day Kaylee could see that he was busy and she watched as the owners of his three dog trainees came to pick up their pets. Landry spent at least an hour with each of them in the yard, going through the training commands, directing the dogs to heel, turn, sit, down, stay in place. She watched it all from her porch—from a safe distance, while trying to write. She noted that the owners didn't leave without handshakes and hugs. There was such a sense of joy around their well-behaved dogs.

She was surprised when there was a knock at her door at about eight that evening. She opened the door to Landry, who held up a bottle of wine. "Care to see the stars come out?"

"Look at you, armed with incentive!"

"I was paying attention to what you like," he said.

"Then let's open it and watch for the stars. Have you eaten?"

"By the time I finished with the dogs I was starving so I stuffed down a sandwich. Have you eaten?"

"A couple of hours ago."

They took their usual seats on the porch. The sun was just sinking below the horizon.

"I have an arts festival in Oregon this weekend," Landry said. "I'm going to stay over but the following weekend I'll be in Grace Valley for their Art Walk. That's close enough that I'll be coming home at night, but late. You should consider checking it out. You might like it."

"I'll plan on it."

"I have four shows in a row. September and October are my busiest months; there's a lot to get ready and pack up. But with the dogs gone, I hope we can still fit in the occasional dinner. And I think it's time, Kaylee. Time for you to get a little closer to Otis."

"Oh, I bet Otis doesn't mind that I haven't been in his bubble…"

"Tomorrow. I'll make spaghetti. My father's recipe, which is open the jar and heat it up. Can you come over at four? You and Otis will meet and I'll reward your courage with dinner."

Her first thought was that she probably wouldn't have much of an appetite if she was sharing space with a dog.

"Be brave. You'll be so glad you did."

"I wouldn't be too sure."

In the end, she agreed. But she wasn't doing it because she wanted to conquer her fear of dogs. She was doing it because she loved spending time with Landry.

Kaylee knew she was wound a little too tight when she knocked on Landry's door. He opened it and immediately pulled her hand into both of his.

"Sweaty palms," he said. "I think we'll begin to end that now. There is Otis." He pointed to the mat behind him where Otis sat, alert and patient. "I told him you have a nervous condition and to wait on his mat until he's called."

"I'm sure he understood every word."

"Sometimes it seems so. Now I want you to look at him and say his name and that he should come." She was frozen silent. "It's okay, Kaylee. I'm right here."

"Otis, come," she said very softly. The dog slowly walked toward her.

"You might want to give him a soft pat and tell him he's good."

She did so, though her hand shook.

"Try s–i–t," he suggested, spelling it. Before she could get the words out, Otis sat, making Landry laugh. "Okay, here's a better way. I'm going to give him a few training commands and then I want you to do it. Otis, come." The dog sat at his side instantly. "Heel, heel, heel," he said, and Otis walked at his knee, even as Landry turned. "Good boy," he said, petting him. "Sit," he said, and the dog obeyed. "Down," he said, and the dog was on his belly. "Stay," he said, then turned and walked away. From the other side of the room, he said, "Otis, place." Otis went immediately to his mat. "You are good, Otis." He turned to Kaylee. "Have a go."

Kaylee took a deep breath and put Otis through his paces, her voice a little bit nervous, but Otis just looked up at her adoringly and did exactly as she asked. She did that several times. She gave him a pat and told him he was a good boy each time, and when she was ready to be done, she told him to go to his place. But first he lay on his back with his paws up, looking for a belly rub.

"No, Otis," Landry said. "Go to your place." The dog got up wearily, probably disappointed. "You can give him a belly rub if you feel like it," Landry said.

Kaylee sheepishly went to the mat, looked down at Otis and said, "Otis, roll over." The dog rolled over for her. Her eyes and mouth both got big and round. She reached down and gave him a gentle scratch on the belly. Then she told him to stay and went back to the kitchen. "Wine," she said.

"You did great," Landry said with a laugh. "Are you comfortable that Otis won't hurt you?"

"I guess so," she said. "But I'm not going to make any fast moves."

Landry smiled at her. He poured a glass of wine for her and she sat up at the breakfast bar.

"Otis is very smart," Landry said. "Too smart for his own good sometimes. He knows how to open his door, for example. And even though that door opens into the backyard, which is fenced, he can jump the fence. I've pulled up to the house to see him waiting on the front porch. If you see him outside, don't freak out. He might walk over to you but you can tell him to lie down or go home."

"You're sure about that?" she asked, sipping her wine.

"I'm very sure," Landry said. "He's an excellent dog. I take him on visits to hospitals and nursing homes. Everyone loves Otis. Okay, I'm going to boil some spaghetti. I even made a salad and I have some garlic bread."

And she was suddenly famished. The spaghetti was absolutely delicious, the salad was great, the bread was crunchy and wonderful. And the dog stayed on his mat.

Landry's phone rang and he ignored it. "Do you want to get that?" she asked.

"Whoever it is can leave a message. I even have dessert."

They took their coffee and dessert to the sofa and talked. He asked her how the book was coming and she told him it was a little better than it had been in Newport Beach in her mother's house. She was hopeful of finishing it this fall. She'd always loved the fall and would love it even more in the mountains.

Then she stopped talking as Otis's head appeared on her lap. He looked up at her with his big sad brown eyes. She looked back at him. The she put her hand on his head and his tail wagged.

"I might've forgotten to mention, Otis falls in love easily.

But you're not his first and you probably won't be his last. I don't want you to have a broken heart."

The call Landry missed while he was having dinner with Kaylee was from Laura. He hadn't heard from her in a while. They had married eleven years ago. They met in San Francisco in the diner where she worked. It happened to be in the same neighborhood as the warehouse where he rented space to create his art because his small flat was just too small.

Landry had gone to college in San Francisco and loved the city. Three years after college he was still there, working away on his pots, vases, wind chimes, sculptures, whatever struck his artistic nerve. He also worked to keep body and soul together, sometimes working construction, sometimes waiting tables or bartending. Laura was working in the diner to pay for her acting habit—she wanted to be a star. She auditioned for plays, TV commercials, small movie roles, anything that came along. They had art in common and when they met and fell in love it was like a bushfire—burning hot and fast. After a year of seeing each other, they got married in a small, quiet Spanish church in Oakland. They were happy every day. They frequented old movies, galleries, diners that were open late and absolutely any parade or celebration in the city. They were young, carefree, hopeful.

Then Laura was offered a chance to audition for a part in a movie if she'd go to LA. It was a decent part with some potential. She told Landry she'd be gone for a few days for the audition and if she got the part she might be gone for as long as three months. That was the end of his marriage as he remembered it. She got the part and traveled to Portugal for the shoot. She was home in a few months but only for a few days before there was another opportunity. By the time their second anniversary rolled around, she informed him she would have to move. LA would be her base, not San Francisco. But of course she would come to him whenever she wasn't working.

He tried to be supportive; he knew how much she wanted it, wanted to be a star. He thought about how frustrated and unhappy he'd be without his art, but he missed her. This wasn't his idea of marriage. He offered to move to LA, though he preferred San Francisco. "That wouldn't solve our problems, Landry," she said. "At least half the time I might get the part there but we'd go somewhere else for the shoot. The next movie—a made-for-TV movie—we're shooting in Vancouver. I'll be there for at least four months. You can come and visit if you like, but I'll be working long days. Twelve-hour days. I'm going to rent something with some other actors. Something cheap that I won't use much. A flop house, if you will. You wouldn't want to relocate your whole business in the hopes of seeing me less than two days every other month."

For two years she "visited" him, usually for less than a week a few times a year. They still talked on the phone all the time, but not every day. It was after they'd been married three years and he hardly ever saw her that he decided to move back to Virgin River. He could live with his dad in the house he grew up in. "But it's so much harder for me to get to," Laura complained. "I'll have to fly into San Francisco and rent a car and drive to Humboldt County!"

So he saw even less of her. Even though she constantly said she missed him, somehow he didn't think she missed him all that much. She had a rental house in LA that she shared with roommates, two men and two women, some of them on location sometimes. It was nicer than a flop house but less conducive to Landry's possible visits. He did visit once to surprise her and a man with a towel wrapped around his waist answered the door. He was talking on a cell phone when he said, "Can I help you?"

"I'm Laura's husband," he said icily.

"Come on in, man!" he said. Then he ended his call and called out for Laura, who looked pretty flustered by the surprise visit. And Landry knew then that things were over. Laura had two lives and the one she had with him didn't rate as high.

Laura had explained the man in the towel was just one of the roommates. They had a miserable time together because there seemed to be a lot of people around all the time. The house Laura lived in was a gathering place. She liked being surrounded by people while Landry was a loner. He liked being by himself, creating his art. Plus, he never quite bought the roommate story.

She'd been wherever there was work for the last ten years. He'd been in Virgin River for the last eight and they kept in touch from time to time.

He listened to the message on his phone. "Landry, darling, call me back soon! I have some good news."

He thought he knew what that meant. She probably had a new film and would be telling him where she'd be spending the next several months. He wasn't sure why she bothered. But then, they did have a good, compatible relationship for people who had effectively separated ten years ago.

"Landry!" she said as she answered the phone. "How are you! I've missed you!"

"I'm great and Otis says hello. How are you and what's your news?"

"I'm going to be in San Francisco for at least a few days. I'm auditioning for a play. I thought I'd tack a few days on to the audition and visit you. Then if I get the part I'll be living in San Francisco for several months and we can see more of each other."

Damn, he thought. "When is your audition?"

"It's in a couple of weeks. This is a huge sacrifice, Landry.

The work is hard and the director and writer are walking nightmares. But it would be so good to see you."

"Likewise, but you picked an awful time. I have several community art shows in a row. The fall festivals. The fall months are tough. During September and October I'll be out of town four times, four days each time. If you're still in San Francisco in November, there will be more room to breathe."

"Can't you cancel a couple of your fair things? They can't be that important."

There were a million angry replies that jumped to his lips, but he wouldn't let them out. Those "fair things" were important and very good moneymakers. Over the years there were people who followed him from fair to fair just to see what was new. He reserved space a year in advance, was listed in the catalog, and taking and setting up his wares was not quick and easy. Each event was exhausting. But he loved it and he knew many of the people who participated and shopped. They were big events. "I pay for the booth a year in advance and there's no refund at this late date, Laura. It's a huge commitment. I usually use the whole week before an art fair to finish my work and have it ready and three days to take everything to the show and to do the setup. It's a lot of work."

"Well, try to fit me into your schedule," she said. "I haven't seen you in a long time."

"Text me the dates you'll be in San Francisco and I'll see what I can do."

"That would be wonderful!"

They chatted for a while about her play. He knew he'd be calling her back in two days to tell her that he just didn't have any extra time. It was true, the time surrounding these fall town fairs was short and busy. But he also wasn't interested in cutting his time with Kaylee short.

★ ★ ★

The morning after her dinner with Landry and Otis, Kaylee went out for her usual walk. The air was cooling down quite a bit and the leaves were already starting to turn. She saw that Landry's truck was in his drive and Otis was on the porch, but Landry was probably in his shop, madly creating.

When she passed Landry's house, Otis came down the walk, moving slowly and lazily, and just took up the place at the end of Landry's walk. She said, "Heel, heel," to Otis and he trotted to her side and stayed with her. She stopped and told him to sit and he did. She told him to stay and walked ahead of him and he did. There was something about the small amount of power she had over him that made her giddy with enthusiasm.

When she came back from her walk Landry was on his porch. "I thought my dog might be walking you."

"He was very polite," she said.

"Have you had breakfast?"

"A yogurt," she said.

"I'm going to scramble eggs. Interested?"

"You're investing way more in me than I deserve," she said.

Kaylee had developed a very nice routine. She'd walk in the mornings and sometimes also in the afternoons, often with Otis as an escort, and it amazed her how much she talked with Landry. Some days she'd go to the bar for breakfast or lunch; some days she'd show up there in the afternoons when it was quiet. Quiet afternoons were a good time to run into Mel as she took a break.

Kaylee loved Jilly's farm! She tried not to be a pest but she found herself driving out there a few more times after her initial tour. And she always came away with whatever Jilly was pulling out of the ground. In order to balance the scales, she ordered books on the internet to give to Jilly and Kelly as thanks for their generosity.

The first weekend that Landry was away, she heard the Cavanaugh orchard was having a big open house. You could pick your own bushel of apples or buy some of the many apple products for sale from cider to apple butter to pie filling. It felt like the whole town was there. There were people sitting under trees in their camp chairs, playing catch with kids, chasing dogs, just hanging out and enjoying the day. She knew so many of them, it was like enjoying a picnic. She found herself flitting from grouping to grouping of locals, sitting for a while to ask them how they were enjoying the brisk fall weather, and they were full of questions for her.

"What do you know about the remodel of that fire-damaged house?"

"How's your book coming along?"

"How do you like living out at Landry's place?"

Realizing she didn't know anything about the remodel, she called Bonnie that evening and learned that after looking at some pictures Paul provided, they told him to go ahead and get started. He was happy to send them progress pictures every few days. They had to pick out appliances, tile, fixtures, sinks, etc., but they could pick them out in LA and they would be shipped to Paul in Virgin River. "As I understand it, he's getting to work on it immediately because there was a break in his schedule and we wanted to take advantage of it."

"It's so lucky that you didn't have drive all the way up here to meet with him," Kaylee said.

"You can do almost anything on the computer these days," Bonnie said.

"If you need me to help, please let me know," Kaylee said. "It's not that I'm overbooked!"

And at least once every three days she had dinner with

Landry either at his house or hers. Sometimes on those days they didn't have dinner together, they would still meet on the porch for a cup of coffee or glass of wine, maybe in the morning, maybe in the evening. And they always waved to each other multiple times a day.

Although Kaylee was determined that Landry was merely a friend and a landlord, the romance she'd created between Caroline and Landon was growing more intense. When they looked at each other now, there was real longing in their eyes.

The first weekend in October, Kaylee drove to Grace Valley to check out the Fall Art Walk. The main street was blocked off and filled with booths that displayed everything from woodworking to spices, from hummus to paintings. She should have known she'd see friends there. Kelly's daughter was manning a booth that sold many of her mother's salsas, relishes and sauces. People she knew introduced her to people she didn't. She met the Grace Valley town doctor, June, introduced to her by Mel. She met the Grace Valley minister, Harry, introduced to her by Colin. She found Landry's booth and gasped at the beauty of his pots, vases and wind chimes. She had not seen much of his work before, just those pieces that decorated his house and hers. He was amazing and had a large group of people gathered there.

They ate some barbecue together in his booth since he couldn't leave. She had come only to show interest and support but once there, she was enchanted by the bounty of goods and crafts. It was early afternoon when the most beautiful woman she'd ever seen in her life came into the booth, saw Landry and said, "Darling!"

He walked to her and kissed her cheek. "Hi, Laura."

"Look at your wonderful pieces! You just get better all the time. You are the most fabulous artist."

Laura was tall, thin, blonde with intense blue eyes to match his and when they stood side by side, they appeared made for each other. Her teeth were perfect and straight, her figure svelte and buxom. Of course her makeup was professional-looking and her nails were star quality. She was stunning. She wore a midlength white lace skirt, a denim jacket and drop dead gorgeous brown leather boots. And the confidence she exuded was palpable.

"And who's this?" she asked, sticking her hand out toward Kaylee. "Hello there, I'm Laura. Landry's wife."

She did look every bit the actress. Kaylee suddenly felt very short and plump and way underdressed in her jeans and hoodie. "It's a pleasure," she said a bit awkwardly. "I'm Kaylee. I rent Landry's house. The smaller one."

"How wonderful!" Then Laura fluttered her lashes at him. "You look so good, Landry. You've been taking care of yourself. Do you have time to walk me around the fair?"

"I really can't, Laura. I'll be busy here the rest of the day. I'm sorry. Why don't you look around and enjoy yourself and maybe we'll talk later."

"Oh, can't your little friend manage your booth for a while?"

"Of course not," he said, irritation in his voice. "Kaylee doesn't know anything about these things. She just stopped by to say hello."

"And it's really time I get going," Kaylee said, trying out a smile. "I still have more of this fair to see."

She gathered up her purse and left Landry and his wife.

Wife? Hadn't he said he was married but it didn't work out? She must have meant she was his ex-wife. But they certainly had a cordial relationship.

Landry was immediately busy with customers, answering their questions about his wares, explaining his process and helping them choose what to buy. His was usually a busy booth and today was no different. After no more than twenty minutes Laura had wandered off, telling him she'd see him later.

Now, what was this about? he wondered. She never showed any interest in these small-town fairs or the people. She admired his work but in all the years he'd lived in Virgin River, she'd only visited a few times and took no notice of the town or the people. The only time she'd mingled was at his father's funeral.

He had to pack up his things at the end of the day. He put them in the trailer he'd brought along, put a padlock on it and left it in the parking lot. He didn't get home until ten o'clock and there, in front of his house, was a strange car. A rental, he assumed.

A light was on in the kitchen but Laura was nowhere in sight. Otis briefly greeted him, then went back to his pallet in the living room. Landry went to the bedroom to see her in his bed. He turned on the overhead bedroom light and she sat up, startled. It was very bright.

"Landry! You scared me!"

"What are you doing here? I told you it was a bad time."

"I told you, I wanted to see you!"

"And I told you I couldn't break away until November."

"So I came to you," she said, as if that resolved the issue.

He turned and left the room. He went to the kitchen and put four ice cubes in a glass. He got down the Crown Royal from a high cupboard and poured himself a generous drink.

She came from the bedroom, tying the sash on a black satin robe. She stood on the opposite side of the counter. "Can I have one of those?" she asked.

He didn't answer but merely got another glass, added ice and some liquor and slid it across the counter.

"Thank you," she said. "Can we sit down?"

He pulled a bar stool around the end of the counter and sat looking at her.

"You certainly aren't making this easy. I've been wanting to have a serious talk with you for a long time," she said.

"You've had ten years, Laura."

"And so have you," she replied. "Yet here we are. So, did I interrupt something romantic between you and your friend?"

"No, she's my tenant. We're neighbors; we're friendly."

"She's very pretty."

"That wouldn't intimidate you," he said.

"Look, this is hard for me. Be kind, at least. Things are not going as I had hoped they would. I'm not getting the parts I want or need anymore. I'm being cast more often as the mother of the bride than the bride. Or the disgruntled sister or the other woman."

"You've had some good parts. Some good films." And he knew this because he'd paid attention. When she was in a TV series or feature film, he made it a point to see it.

"The truth is that at my status the work is very hard and doesn't pay well enough. I've aged out at thirty-five. I'm getting character roles and TV commercials. Ads. I'm burned out and ready to try something else. I'm thinking of giving up acting."

"Really?" he said, lifting an eyebrow. "After all this time and dedication? There are plenty of good acting jobs for women over thirty-five."

"Not plenty," she said. "There are some, but they're hard to get. I have to be honest with myself. It's not going to take me where I always wanted to go."

He rubbed a hand around the back of his neck. "I have to admit, that surprises me. I thought you had the stamina for the long haul."

"But not the enthusiasm," she said. She took a sip of her drink. "I want us to try again."

His head jerked up in surprise. "Try what again?" he asked.

"Marriage. Our marriage. That year we had together was the happiest year of my life."

"And yet you left it," he said. "You chose acting. We fought it out and you chose acting and career over marriage. For a while there you wouldn't even admit you were married."

"That was just PR bullshit to make me seem more desirable, more available, to convince people I wouldn't flutter off the job and leave them all hanging. That didn't last long. We've had a long-distance marriage, but—"

"We've had no marriage," he said. "We haven't slept together in almost a decade!"

"Well, that was your choice," she said.

"Yes, it was," he said. "When I realized I'd seen you for less than twelve days in a year, it was very clear that you had no investment in our marriage. I didn't want to be a booty call. That might've been enough for you, but it wasn't enough for me."

"And yet we never divorced," she reminded him.

"There didn't seem to be any pressing need," he said. "I had no interest in marrying again. I figured you'd file for divorce."

"But I didn't want a divorce! I wanted to be married!"

"To a man you saw for less than a month out of every year?"

"I loved you," she said. "I always loved you! And you loved me. We were good friends."

"We were friends," he said. "I don't know if we were even really that. We got along. We talked on the phone regularly but it was more like talking to a cousin or sister, not a wife. Take a trip down memory lane, Laura. After two years of your chasing stardom we had a blowout. I drew a line in the sand—we had to either find a way to live together or call it quits. You argued that there was no way to live together, that your work was either in Hollywood or on location, that it was your dream, that you worked hard for it and couldn't give it up without at least giving it an earnest try. I said I was done with the trying. I offered up every compromise I could think of but you wanted me on the sidelines. That's when I came back here to live and work."

"It's not like we've ever been out of touch," she said.

"We talk on the phone!" he said. "We meet in San Francisco if I'm visiting the galleries. We don't even share a hotel room on those occasions. We're not even good friends!"

"We're very good friends! You're my best friend! I've always loved you!"

He took a deep drink. "Laura, you need to raise your standards. Your idea of friendship is really lacking."

Her eyes got teary. "I'm sorry, Landry. I failed at everything. I never should have wasted so much time on acting if it was going to come to nothing. I never should have given you up. I've been thinking about it for a long time. I want us to be together. Please say you'll try again."

"I think that ship has sailed, Laura. No matter how I feel about you, the trust just isn't there. I'd be waiting to see you get out the suitcase every day."

"But wait," she said. "Remember when we used to go to the outdoor movies, to the foreign films, to the galleries and street vendors? Remember our picnics in Union Square? Sitting on a bench and people watching? Our drives up the coast to the fish house? To the Russian River? We were young and carefree and so happy. We can't be young anymore but—"

"I think too many years have passed," he said.

"We can start over," she said. "We have the love. We just need the time together."

"I have a different kind of life now," he said. "I've lived

alone for ten years. I'm solitary and you need a lot of people. I agree, there was a time we had fun; it seemed we were compatible. But Laura, you walked away. And you didn't want me to tag along."

"It was a practical issue," she said. "And maybe I was foolish but I thought once I landed a really good role and didn't have to sell my soul for work, then we could get it together. Please, I'm ready to give it up for us. Will you at least think about it?"

"I can't help but think about it," he said. "But I don't think it would benefit either one of us."

"Take a week," she pleaded. "Please."

"Where did this come from?" he asked. "Did something happen? Are you in some kind of trouble?"

"No, of course not, unless you call complete failure to achieve my goals trouble. This just isn't working. I've given up, Landry. I want a sane life again."

"In a little house in the mountains with a dog? And a guy and his pots?" He shook his head. "There are no theaters or spas or fancy restaurants here. You wouldn't last a month. And it would probably leave me scarred. Again."

"Think about it? For a week? Give me a chance?"

"Are you listening? The last time you decided acting was more important than marriage, you walked away and it hurt. You said you'd be back in a few days and it was months. When you ask me to think about us, what do you think comes to mind? Maybe the guy in the towel who you passed off as a roommate you weren't romantically involved with? I never bought that..."

"It was true! There were men and women sharing that house. There were lots of different houses and roommates; there were lots of starving artists who doubled up because that was the only way I could afford to stay in LA. It can't hurt anything to think about putting it back together."

"I'm exhausted. I can't talk about it anymore tonight. I need some sleep and so do you."

"All I want is for you to give it fair consideration."

"Don't you have a job to get to? A play?"

"It's not even a good play," she said. "I'd give it up in a heartbeat."

"I'll be honest with you, Laura. There's about a one in a million chance I'm going to try to resurrect a dead marriage."

"I never thought of it as dead," she said.

You have a funny way of showing it, he wanted to say. Instead he said, "Time to sleep. I'll take the couch. I have to leave early tomorrow for Grace Valley. I have to set up my booth."

"Kiss me good-night?" she asked.

"Oh, come on," he said. "Love and a desire to be partners isn't a switch you turn on and off! You don't sashay in here and declare you've changed your mind after about ten years and expect me to fall in line! Everything isn't all about you, Laura. All about what you want. I have feelings, too."

"I hurt you," she said. "I'm so sorry. I'd like a chance to make it up to you."

"Not tonight," he said. "I had a very long day. And I'm going to have another one tomorrow. Let's get some sleep."

She left the kitchen reluctantly, but she kept the door to the bedroom open.

Of course, he couldn't sleep. That couch never felt like it had so many lumps before. 5:00 a.m. had never come so early. He used the powder room to wash up and dress. He brewed coffee. He turned the bright overhead light on in his bedroom and she stirred. She sat up, rubbing her eyes.

"I'm leaving for the fair. You should go back to San Francisco. I'll give you a call later this week."

6

KAYLEE HAD NO IDEA WHAT HAD GONE ON AT Landry's house. The sound of Landry's truck pulling into his drive late the night before was unmistakable and she peeked out the window just in time to see the lights go out; she heard the truck door slam. She was up late, as usual, and didn't hear him leave in the morning but when she took her coffee cup out to the porch, the truck was gone. Laura's car was still there, however.

Time to be honest with yourself, Kaylee, she thought. She had developed a bit of a crush on Landry. She thought about him more often than she liked to admit. She looked forward to the evenings, always a little prepared to share dinner. She was thrilled when he suggested she come to the street fair; she thought that meant he liked her in a slightly more than casual way, even if there hadn't been any obvious signs of affection.

She decided it was more important than ever to keep her routine, so she got ready for a nice long walk. When she was past his house by quite a distance, she heard the pitter-patter of feet. She turned around to see Otis sitting at attention behind her. She walked on, then stopped and turned again. He sat at attention, waiting. She walked on once more and looked back again. She chuckled. "Okay," she said. His ears perked. "Come," she said. And the dog smiled and trotted toward her. "What? Were you a little lonely? Well, me, too. Come. Heel." He walked at her side, the perfect gentleman. She was amazed to think that a month ago this simple action would have caused her to shiver and shake.

Every day her walks became more enjoyable because of the changing colors, the aspen, maple, oak and other trees she couldn't identify. The yellow and orange rose up the mountainside, growing more intense as the elevation was greater while the valleys remained green and lush. While she loved Newport Beach and appreciated its beauty, there was something about these powerful trees and mountains that filled her with hope. The air was so fresh up here, it almost shocked the lungs to take a deep breath.

When they got back to the front of Landry's house she told Otis to go to his place. He cocked his head and looked up at her as if hoping for a second chance. "Place," she said again, and she watched as Otis went around to the side of the house, easily jumped the fence to the backyard and presumably used his doggy door to go inside and find his mat. She just shook her head. She was beginning to understand how a person could find good companionship with a well-behaved dog.

She went to town and tried writing at Jack's for a while. It was Sunday and quiet, but it was hunting season so the rest of the week would see plenty of hunters in the bar, just not on Sunday afternoon. She'd come to understand that they did most of their hunting early in the morning, celebrating afterward, the majority of them leaving on Sunday evening. She'd already gotten used to seeing them at the dinner hour, after the hunting was done. Jack wasn't even there now. Preacher's wife, Paige, was working behind the bar, and their son, Christopher, was helping out, wiping off tables and bringing plates and glasses to the back. She ordered a sandwich and just hung out with her laptop open as if she was working, which she was not. Unfortunately, no one interrupted her.

She left Jack's after lunch and stopped by one of her favorite roadside produce stands. It was a little lean, but she bought a pumpkin. She did buy some gourds and dried cornstalks and glass gem corn to decorate her porch for fall. She drove to Clear River and bought some chicken strips and the makings for a Caesar salad. She got a candle for her pumpkin. Why she was doing this was a mystery—Landry's two houses were at the end of a long drive. It's not as though people lived close enough or even drove by; there would not be trick-or-treaters. But it had always been important to her mother to keep their surroundings beautiful, to change up and improve things regularly and decorate for special occasions. Kaylee had inherited a little of that. And she wanted to please her mother, even though she was gone now.

When she got back home, Laura's car was gone. She had probably headed to Grace Valley to spend her time in Landry's booth. Adorning his booth. He must obviously want to spend every available moment with her. She was so breathtaking.

Kaylee carved her pumpkin when she should've been writing. And she took a nap. And ate her solitary dinner. She couldn't quite define if she was a little disappointed or actually heartbroken. She missed Landry at dinnertime but she also had a shot of guilt—he shouldn't be spending so much time with her if he had a wife. Should he? Of all the complications that could impede a growing relationship, *he's married* ran at the top of the list.

It was after nine and she was in her pajamas, lost in writing a tale about Caroline and Landon, when there was a knock on her door. Oddly, she wondered if it was Laura. If maybe she needed help with a burned-out light bulb or something. Then she opened her door to see Landry standing there.

"I saw your light was on," he said.

"It's not exactly late," she said. "Though, I guess for you, it is."

"If you're not heading to bed, can you talk a minute?" He looked her up and down. She was wearing her pajamas, of course. "I apologize for the interruption. I can see you're ready for—"

"It's all right, but what about your wife?"

"She's gone back to San Francisco. She won't be coming back here."

"I have a feeling this really has nothing to do with me."

"It doesn't, except that I think I unintentionally misled you and I'd like to straighten it out. Unless you're too tired."

"For this explanation? Oh hell no! I can't wait. Would you like something to drink?"

"Anything," he said. "As long as it has alcohol in it."

"Talk about a signal that it's going to be a doozy…"

She went to her refrigerator and pulled out a cold beer, the kind he liked, the kind he always brought along with him when he came to her porch. She'd bought it this afternoon even though she had no way of knowing if or when she might see him again. A part of her had been preparing for the wife to stay, take over, maybe invite her to dinner with the two or them or something. Ack. That thought almost made her gag.

"You drink this?" he asked her, surprised.

"Sure. All the time." Then she pulled one out for herself,

though she didn't want it. "Sit down," she said. "Try not to sit on the kitty, I mean, Tux."

He examined the chair before sitting. "Okay, so I didn't mean to mislead you. Laura and I have been separated for ten years. We were married eleven years ago, so it wasn't a long marriage. She had what she thought was a breakthrough acting opportunity, went for what she thought would be an interview and audition. She said she'd be gone for a few days and never really came back. She visited. We stayed in touch by phone. It dissolved. But I never filed for divorce. It seemed to be an unnecessary bother, not to mention expense. I honestly thought the day would come that she would want to be free and she'd initiate the divorce proceedings, but it didn't. And I don't know why I didn't."

"It didn't look like it was freedom she was here for."

"Okay, now that's the complication. After all this time she's decided she'd like to be married after all. She's had it with an acting career that's going nowhere. The joke's on me; I can blame no one but myself. And I promise you I never saw it coming."

"Well, you said you were married and it didn't work out," she reminded him.

"That was true. We merely kept in touch. I know divorced couples who have closer relationships than that."

"And I know divorced couples who hate each other and fantasize about their death…"

"There are those," he said. "I wish her nothing but the best, but—"

"You looked almost angry for a moment, when she showed up in your booth."

"I was angry," he said. "I'd told her it wasn't a good time for her to visit, that I was all tied up with the fairs. I see her two or three times a year. *If* it fits into her schedule. If she needs something."

"And if you were to divorce, would you continue to have these visits with your wife?" She lifted one brow and smoothed her hair over one ear. "Asking for a friend..."

He grinned at her. "You're very funny, Kaylee. I like Laura," he said. "She's entertaining, smart and we have history. I've known her a long time by now. I was angry for a while. I was really pissed, actually. But when my dad died, that was the last thing to worry about."

"It would be pretty convenient and not terribly troublesome, having an affair with someone you're married to..."

"No, no, no," he said, shaking his head. "We don't sleep together; there is no affair. The first thing I noticed was that she wasn't that interested and I suspected she might have... you know..."

"Other relationships?" she asked.

"I guess. So at some point after she'd been living in LA for a couple of years and came to San Francisco for a weekend, I told her I was starting to feel like a booty call and we were over. I told her I was going home to Virgin River and promised her she would hate it, but she was welcome to visit me here. It was a very smooth transition. She told me she loved me but we're probably better as friends."

"Sounds so grown-up," she said.

"It is. I follow her career. I used to follow with resentment and then with curiosity and eventually I hoped her wish would come true. It stopped being about me a long time ago. Frankly, I think she's a good actress. I've seen her in a lot of things and it's not unusual for me to think she should've been the lead. The star. But I'm not in a relationship with her anymore. I haven't been for a very long time. I think you were shocked and startled. I'm sorry about that."

"Why?" she asked. "Why does how I feel or what I think matter?"

"We're becoming good friends," he said. "I look forward to sitting on the porch after a long day. I like it when we have dinner. I've had several tenants in this house—a few days, a few months. I've never had what I'd call a close friendship with any of them before. It's a bad start to a nice friendship when you get caught lying."

"But you weren't lying." She took a pull on her beer and made a face. "You just didn't explain properly. Or thoroughly."

"You lied about the beer," he said, grinning. "You don't drink that beer."

"It's awful. I bought it in case you came over. Want the rest of this?"

"You didn't spit in it, did you?" he asked with a laugh, reaching for it.

She made a face and handed it to him. She went to the kitchen to pour herself a glass of wine. The bottle was open, after all. She went back to the couch and curled up in the corner. "I just don't want to be a complication. This thing you have to work out is with your wife. I'm just a tenant."

"It's not a complication and it's not about you, except for one thing," he said. "I want to sit on the porch, have dinner, enjoy life. I don't have any expectations beyond that right now. But I think we have potential. I think we like each other enough to have potential."

"No expectations," she said. "Me, either." It was a total lie. She'd been having expectations like mad in the form of Caroline and Landon. They were morphing into a nearly perfect couple. The story was growing lush and sexy. She realized she wanted to become lush and sexy with Landry.

"I did have a thought on my drive home. We're ill suited, me and Laura. Opposites. We thought we had a lot in common, given that we're both artists of a sort. But I live a quiet life; I like being alone. I don't like crowds or busy places but Laura craves people. We want different things—she'd like the adoration of millions while I'd rather go unnoticed. I'm not really shy, I don't think. I just prefer smaller groups or maybe just one person at a time. While she wants restaurants and parties, I'd rather train the dogs or go for a walk. I married a woman like my mother. I believe it's true. I was a toddler when my mother left Virgin River to go back to the city. She divorced my father. He was too quiet and solitary for her. She died a few years later. A car accident. Virgin River isn't for everyone."

"I find it much more to my tastes than I thought I would," she said. "Your dog went on my walk with me today."

By his expression, he was shocked. "Was he polite?"

"Very. And I wasn't afraid. I had a moment, you know… But Otis waited for me to invite him. Of course he followed me, but then he waited."

"What a good guy," Landry said. "He has no ulterior motives, he just wants to be a good friend. That's what I love about dogs. They bond and nothing can break the bond. He's always good, but I think he likes you."

"You shouldn't bother with the locks on the doors," she said. "Apparently he comes and goes as he pleases."

"I know," he said. "It worries me sometimes. I don't want him to wander too far or get himself in trouble, like if he runs into some challenging wildlife. Or some hunter mistakes him for a deer."

"A black, brown and white deer? That would be a very stupid hunter."

"How about dinner tomorrow night? We can share the prep."

"It's getting pretty chilly when the sun goes down," she

said. "How do you feel about your house and a fire in the fireplace?"

"I feel good about that."

Kaylee went to Jack's at lunchtime, planning on a sandwich and salad, but she had a double treat when she found Mel there with an adorable little girl. They were sitting at a table rather than the bar and Mel waved her over.

"Kaylee, this is my friend, Mallory. Would you like to join us for lunch?"

"Absolutely! Is this a special occasion?" she asked, sitting down.

"Mallory's mom had an appointment today and there's no school for teachers' planning sessions, so we're hanging out."

"My mom's having her medicine," Mallory said. "Her chemo medicine."

That hit Kaylee right in the gut. "Oh dear, I'm sorry to hear that."

"Don't be sorry," Mallory said. "It's going to make her better."

"That's what we're hoping for, aren't we?" Mel said. "Mallory, tell Kaylee what your favorite subject is."

"Reading. Not math very much, but I read all the time."

"And you will never guess what Kaylee does for her work. She writes books!" Mel said.

"You do?" Mallory said. "Whole books?"

"Whole books." Kaylee laughed. "Do you read whole books?"

"I love books. They're not long like the ones my mom reads, but they're for my age, which is ten. I read my first one when I was six. Before that I read my magazines and books with pictures from the library. We go to the library every Saturday.

Unless my mom doesn't feel good. Do you ever write books with a mystery? Or like a surprise ending?"

"It turns out that's my specialty."

"Could I read one of them, do you think?"

"I think you have to be just slightly older. You're smart enough to read one, but unfortunately I use too many swear words for your age group."

"I could not look at them or pretend I didn't see them," she suggested. "My mom reads books like that, I think. She says I can't read her books because they're too adult, and I think that means dirty words."

"There are plenty of books to read while you're getting to the right age," Kaylee said. "Tell me about your favorite books."

Mallory talked nonstop all through lunch and it turned out to be one of Kaylee's most fun days. When they were finished with lunch, Mallory thanked Kaylee and promised to read some of her books, "When I'm older. Maybe next year."

Landry texted Laura and asked her when she would be free for lunch. He had another fair on the weekend, but any other time he would drive down to San Francisco. The following Monday he left at the crack of dawn for what would be at least a four-hour drive.

Of course she had chosen The Oak Room, one of those fancy restaurants they had loved when they were a couple. They could hardly ever afford it when they were younger, but they did manage to have dinner there with a few guests on their wedding day. She probably chose it for the nostalgia.

And there was an undeniably warm feeling that came over him when he thought about that day. There were just a few people—his father, her mother, two couples who were friends.

And it was one of the happiest days of his life. He had no way of knowing that barely a year later everything would change.

He parked and took the trolley to the restaurant and was not surprised that she made it ahead of him. Her eagerness to resolve things was showing. "I had the waitstaff find us a quiet table in the corner where we can talk."

The rich dark wood and mirrors of the restaurant were not comforting. He had always appreciated the exquisite decor and yet never felt as though he belonged there. He was more comfortable at Jack's. Landry waited for the wine and intended to wait until they ordered lunch before telling Laura how he felt, but she tripped him up. She raised her glass and said, "Here's to new beginnings."

He put down his glass. "It will be a new beginning, Laura, but not the kind you think. I can't give our marriage a second chance. It just doesn't feel right. It took me long enough to get beyond the disappointment before. I've built a different kind of life now, one I'm comfortable with. I'm really sorry your career didn't work out the way you wanted, but it's too late for us."

"No, you're not sorry about my career," she said, putting her own glass down. "You wanted me to fail."

"That's not true. I wanted you to be with me, not fail. I was always your biggest fan. I just didn't want us to have separate lives. You do realize how little time we spent together, don't you?"

"I was working," she said. "You were working! There was no other way. The only other way was for me to give up my career and it was just getting off the ground when we got married."

"I'm sorry, Laura. It just isn't going to work. The cold truth is, I don't feel the same way anymore. I can remember having those feelings but..."

"You pretend that girl has nothing to do with this, but she must. You've never been like this before."

"I don't know if things might have been different if you'd decided to come back to me five years ago, but honestly, I don't think so. I think our relationship died a long time ago. We just didn't get around to burying it."

"It almost sounds as if you never loved me at all," she said.

"Oh-ho, I had such passion for you it made me light-headed. And there was no question in my mind, you shared that passion. I was thinking about it on the drive down here—we had so many dreams. When we married, they were compatible dreams. It never came down to your career or mine. I was excited about your acting, but that first year we were married, you only took jobs that were nearby. And I can't even say that you leaving for work ruined everything. Traveling for work isn't a weird state for most couples. In fact, I think it's common." He looked at her for a long moment. "But you didn't come back."

"I came back!"

"Months later you came back for a weekend. Within a year, nothing of yours was left in our apartment. We still had the paperwork that said we were married, but we didn't have any of the investment. Laura, the longest we've been together in ten years was two weeks last year and that's because you needed a rest after a grueling movie—and you stayed in my rental house next door. We just don't have enough emotion to build a real marriage on."

"I always felt I could come to you... You shouldn't have let me go on thinking I could come back to you."

"And I don't know how you could have thought so. I'm sure you have friends you're much closer to. I don't even know your friends."

"Is that important? Because I don't know yours, either. I'm

sure you have friends in that little town. I'm sure you've had women…"

He shook his head. "I haven't. I haven't been involved with anyone else."

"Not even friends? No social life with women? Not even casual relationships that had potential if you weren't married?"

"Laura, I haven't thought of myself as married in a very long time. But I didn't have any other relationships. If I had, I would have probably taken the next step and filed for divorce. I'm going to do that now. This is as unfair to you as it is to me. It's good that you brought us to this crossroads. We either have to end it or try to breathe new life into it. I'm for ending it like two people who respect each other. If anyone can do it with class, you can."

She just looked away and silently sipped her wine for a long moment. It was at least a full minute before she looked back at him. "I guess if you don't love me anymore…"

"I have very tender feelings for you, Laura. We shared a special, magical time together that was over too soon. We've been friendly for years. Let's not part on bad terms."

"Yet, must we part at all? At least can't we just go on as we are?" she asked.

"I realized something when you came to Virgin River this time. I realized I don't want to be tied to a sinking ship anymore, and by that I don't mean that you're a sinking ship, it's the marriage. Let's let it go. We didn't do the marriage very well. Let's at least divorce well. So we can remain friends."

"I guess I have no choice," she said. "You're obviously done with me."

"Don't do that, Laura. Don't make it sound like the whole thing was my doing, that it had nothing to do with you. At least own your half of the failure of the marriage. That's the least you can do."

"It breaks my heart," she said. "I have so many regrets."

"You're young, beautiful and talented. You don't need to weigh yourself down with regrets. You'll see—there's something better waiting for you. All you have to do is be open to the possibilities." He reached across the table and took her hand. "Laura, we both know it's over."

It was a very long lunch and when it was finished, Landry was exhausted. But by the time he was headed back to his truck, he was beginning to feel free for the first time in years. He hadn't considered a marriage in name only had been holding him back, pressing him down. It was now evident that it had been the worst kind of ball and chain.

He headed back to Virgin River with a lighter feeling in his chest.

Kaylee decided on a second walk for the day and one of the reasons was she really enjoyed Otis's company. She never had to call him. He seemed to know when she was passing the house and darted out to the road, then sat there politely until he was invited to join her.

The leaves were deepening in color and the changing colors were moving lower down the mountain. In another couple of weeks they would be resplendent with the magnificent beauty of autumn and the hillsides would be aflame with reds, oranges, yellows and even deep purple. The air was cool, sometimes downright cold in the mornings and evenings. She had to wear a jacket even in the afternoon, though it usually came off when the sun beat down.

She had no idea where Landry had gone but he did mention he'd be gone all day and into evening. She wanted to ask, was he visiting galleries? Did he have an appointment with a buyer? Was he seeing his wife? Were any of those possibilities any of her business? Absolutely not.

But there was no denying—the time she spent with Landry, however brief, was time she wasn't mourning her mom. For that she was so grateful.

Otis would take regular diversions to the grassy edge of the road to make sure he watered the grass, but then he'd be right back at her side. If she said "heel" he didn't leave her, so she experimented with that occasionally and was amused by the amount of power she felt. But then he did something he hadn't done before. He darted into the trees with a couple of loud barks and disappeared!

She stood right where she was and listened; she didn't know what to do. If she lost Landry's dog she'd be mortified. She didn't want to follow him. She stood paralyzed but in a moment he came bounding back, excited. He barked at her and she had no idea what that meant. Then he ran back into the trees. What if he'd cornered an animal? What if it was a bear? He came back again, jumped around in a circle, then ran again into the trees. "Otis!" He didn't come back. "Otis, come!" she shouted. And she heard him bark.

She took a few careful, slow steps into the woods. Otis barked again and in another two steps she heard the faint sound of squeaking or peeping. Had he found some baby birds? If he found a batch of kittens, they would be going to the shelter. She wasn't sure she had completely gotten used to Tux!

But there in front of her sat Otis. He was sitting beside a large half of a cardboard box and inside she saw the head of a dog peering out. A dog she didn't know. She gasped and took a step back. The dog laid down its head. The squeaking continued and as she braved a step closer she saw that the source of the noise was puppies. She counted four of them. She didn't dare get any closer for fear the dog would leap out of the box and attack her. Weren't all animals severely protective of their young?

But the dog was a mama and she was lying down on her side with those puppies latched to her chest. And then she noticed that the dog was hooked up to a leash that was looped around a tree trunk. That dog wasn't going anywhere. Upon taking another couple of steps closer, she saw that the dog was terribly thin; she could see her ribs. She was blonde, Kaylee had no idea the breed, but she had a long snout and big brown eyes. Sad eyes. She looked around for dishes of food or water but didn't see any. She obviously couldn't get away. Had this little family been left here to die? Now, who would do that with a no-kill shelter in the vicinity?

Kaylee pulled her water bottle out of her backpack and got down on one knee. "Hey there," she said softly. "How are we gonna do this without a dish?" She opened the water, shaped her hand like a cup and poured a little bit of water into her palm. The dog lapped it up in a second, so she poured more. And she crooned, "That's right, that should help a little." After replenishing the water to her palm several times, the water bottle was empty. She tentatively gave the mama dog a gentle pat. "What am I supposed to do with you?"

The mother dog and her four puppies were too heavy in that box for her to lift them, so she went back out to the road. Of all days for Landry to be gone. She wasn't sure who to call, but it didn't take long for her to decide her wisest choice would be Jack Sheridan. He would at least know who could help her. She pulled her cell out of her back pocket and found his number.

"Hey, Jack, it's Kaylee Sloan. I…ah…have a situation. I was taking a walk with Otis and he found a mother dog and four puppies. Tied to a tree."

"You were taking a walk with who?"

"Landry's dog. Otis. And Landry is gone for the day. He said he wouldn't be home until late tonight. I don't know what to do, but I think the mama dog and her babies were left to die. And Jack? I'm a little afraid of dogs. Okay, not a little. A lot. But she seems like a nice dog and I gave her some water. I don't know what to do. Can you help me or tell me who to call?"

There was a moment of silence. "Where are you? I'll come," he finally said.

"I'm on the road that fronts Landry's two houses. Maybe a half mile from his house. I'm standing out on the road."

"I'll be there in ten," he said.

She looked at her watch, then stood on the road for a couple of minutes. Then she went gingerly back to the mama dog. Otis was in his down position, his front paws stretched out in front. He watched the mama dog closely, but kept his distance. Kaylee couldn't resist slowly sneaking a hand into the box to touch a furry little puppy and when she did so, mama dog licked her hand. And then she was very brave—she picked up a puppy and held it close for a moment.

Kaylee went back to the road when it was almost time for Jack to appear. She stood where he'd be able to see her and when his truck came into view, she waved. He stopped and jumped out of the truck. "Come with me," she said, leading him into the trees.

Jack was right behind her when she got to the dogs. "Holy shit," he said. "Where'd they come from?"

"Well, if I knew that, I'd call the dog police and have them arrested," Kaylee said. "Look how wasted the poor mama looks!" Then she became aware of how cold it was back in the trees and she pulled off her jacket, covering the dog, the whole litter and part of the mama.

"I don't think she gave birth here," Jack said. "I think she was neglected by whoever owned her and was moved out here after the pups were born. If she'd been here a long time that box would be chewed or crushed when she tried to get out or tried to get food. Here's what we do—I called Lynne Murphy in Clear River and she's open till six. I'll help you put the dogs in your car and you can take them to her. We can't leave them here. Lynne will have some options for you, but let's make sure they've seen the vet."

It was when Otis was sitting beside the car that Kaylee looked at him and said, "Okay." He jumped in and watched over his find on the way to the vet. For the first time in her life, Kaylee was falling in love with a dog. She wanted Otis to be her own.

Kaylee was in new territory. Having an SUV full of dogs and puppies was a lot more serious than taking Tux to the vet in a little cat carrier. She was afraid one of the dogs would get excited, start jumping around, maybe spill out the puppies, maybe jump on her and cause her to go off the road, in general just disrupt her. Her hands were tense on the steering wheel, her arms stressed tight, and yet she made the whole drive without incident. And when she got to Dr. Murphy's office, she asked for help getting them in from the car. And because it was quite cool, she cracked the windows and asked Otis to stay.

She had a pet registered at this clinic but they wanted to know if these dogs were going to go to the shelter or was she willing to pay for their treatment. She hesitated for just a moment and then agreed to take responsibility, hoping it wouldn't break the bank. Then the waiting began. She checked on Otis several times until the receptionist asked her if she'd like to bring him in and offered her a leash. Otis was very cooperative and allowed the leash and sat with her in the waiting room. Finally she was called into an exam room, where she found a basket full of puppies on the table.

"These puppies are brand-new," Dr. Murphy said. "Less than a week old. Mama is thin, neglected and malnourished but is in otherwise decent shape. The puppies are okay. I think Mama is some kind of Lab mix and actually a pretty girl. I've given her some meds to help with her appetite and parasites. All things considered, she'll be fine with some nourishment and supplements. Are you going to take them home?"

"I don't know," she said. "I'm renting a house from Landry Moore."

"Why don't you check with him and ask him what he thinks you should do," Dr. Murphy suggested. "You can always take them to the shelter in a day or two. This dog has no ID chip and no record of shots."

"Where is she?"

"Oh, Lydia is cleaning her up. She's a mess."

And right then the door to the exam room opened and there stood Mama on a leash, looking almost beautiful. If it weren't for the fact that she was on the thin side, she'd be perfect. "She had something to eat and a bath. I've never seen anyone in bigger need of a bath."

"Look at you," Kaylee said. Then she looked at Dr. Murphy and asked, "Can I just take them home?"

Mama and the babies were now occupying a roomy basket that had handles. That cut-up cardboard box was too torn up and melted down from being wet and trashed. It didn't make it any farther than the dumpster behind the veterinary clinic. When Kaylee got everyone home she found a corner of her living room to put down a soft comforter for the little family. She rolled up blankets as borders for the puppies, but they weren't moving too fast yet. She put a bowl of food she'd gotten from the vet and water outside the barrier for Mama.

The sun was already down and she was starving, but first she texted Landry.

If it's not too late and you're not too tired from a long day, can you stop by my house when you get home? Otis is here and I have something to show you.

In a little while he texted back, Is everything all right?

Sure. Everything is fine.

After she got something to eat and caught Otis eating some of Mama's food, she dimmed the lights in the room, turned on the TV with the volume soft and sat on the floor beside the puppy pile. She picked up the puppies one at a time under the close scrutiny of Mama.

Then Tux wandered over, clawed his way over the blanket barrier and found himself a spot amid the puppies.

It didn't occur to her until after the fact—Otis simply watched and didn't protest the kitten's presence at all.

She brought a couch pillow down on the floor and reclined with a hand in the puppy bin, gently stroking each puppy and a kitten and Mama.

Landry had no idea how taxing the day had been until he began the drive home from San Francisco and had to stop for coffee not once but twice. Most of his tension had come from the grim anticipation of how difficult it would be to talk to Laura about divorce. And it certainly was every bit as tough as he imagined. Before the meeting was over there had been tears. He'd never been worth a damn when a woman cried, especially if he was the cause.

He was so relieved that it was over. He would never have to do that again.

Then he got the text from Kaylee and he wondered what was going on. When he finally got home, he parked his car in his drive and walked next door to her house. He tapped lightly at the door and heard Otis bark. In a moment she opened the door and there was his dog, standing beside her wagging his tail.

"What's going on?" he asked, leaning down to give his dog a little affection.

Kaylee yawned. "Pajama party," she said tiredly. "I think I fell asleep. Come in and see what Otis found today."

He followed her to the corner of the room where Mama and the puppies were sleeping with a little black-and-white kitten curled up among them.

"Kaylee, where did they come from?"

"Otis found them in the woods," she said. "And he wouldn't let me pass until he showed me."

7

THEY CALLED HER LADY. FOR A WEEK THE RES-
cued dog was referred to as Mama, but that wasn't a real name,
so Kaylee stepped forward and declared she would be Lady.
Landry fixed up a cozy pen for her in his kennel. He built a
two-foot-high barrier around a large dog mattress so that the
puppies couldn't wander off but Lady could step over with
ease. He would have put her in the house in a warm corner
of the kitchen, but he didn't really know her and there were
too many opportunities for trouble, so the kennel it was.

Lady liked the kennel and the new bed for her and her family. Right outside the door was the fenced yard and Otis was
willing to run and play a little bit, but Lady was still a new
mother and underweight and had four puppies who didn't even
have their eyes open to take care of. And she did a wonderful
job of keeping them clean and quiet.

It was no longer necessary to sit beside Lady's box and feed her by hand as Kaylee had done in the beginning. Her appetite had returned and she was enjoying a special kibble with a high calorie content. In no time at all she began to look more fit, healthier and, to Kaylee at least, beautiful. But Kaylee still spent a great deal of time sitting beside her, picking up a puppy to cuddle, then another, then another. Lady patiently allowed this. She would often show her approval by licking Kaylee's hand.

"I wonder what happened that made her owner go to such cruel lengths?" she asked again and again. "She's the sweetest thing in the world."

"I think you're pretty much over that fear of dogs you had," Landry said.

"At least with these two, I am. Do you have new dogs coming anytime soon?" she asked.

"I didn't schedule any training sessions for the fall because I'm visiting those fall festivals and I won't be home to be sure they get out, get fed, get exercised. I'll be too busy with pots."

He called them pots but they were really masterful works of art, clay and ceramic and brightly colored designs in every imaginable shape. Since Lady had come to stay, Kaylee spent a little time just watching Landry in his shop. He'd sometimes wear protective headgear with goggles, especially when he was using a blowtorch on glass or metal designs. He had a kiln and a couple of ovens and long metal tables; when he refinished two bedrooms into a shop he left the floor cement, nailed metal and flame-resistant sheets to some parts of the walls and inserted a metal garage door in the back wall. When the weather permitted, he raised that door for a working outdoors effect. Sometimes the heat in his shop could become intense. The door into the shop from the hall was extra large and metal reinforced. He liked making decorative wind chimes of metal, ceramic, glass or clay.

Then there were the sculptures, shaped and molded with clay. He had just finished one that was a partial female torso with an obvious pregnant middle. It was armless and headless, like an old Greek statue. "Are you going to put a head on that woman?" Kaylee asked.

"I don't think so," he said. "I like the look for one thing. And if there's a head and a face, it will be hard for another woman to look at it and imagine herself. Do you want to see some of my earlier work? I have pictures."

She sat on his couch with albums and paged through photos of beautiful sculptures, pots and chimes. One that caught her eye was a bust of a woman with a man behind her, kissing the side of her neck. Her head was tilted to give him access to her neck and the look on her face was rapturous. The man's eyes were closed. It was one of the most romantic things she'd ever seen.

His glass pieces were her favorite, all shapes and sizes and many colors in beautiful designs, especially the vases, which went from round to oval to square. There was a huge clear glass vase with a narrow slit on top with silver, black and gold stripes running through it—it was stunning.

She watched him blow designer glass a couple of times, keeping her distance and wearing dark protective glasses. He would create pieces that a gallery might get six hundred to twelve hundred dollars for. She was mightily impressed with his talent and his success.

Every day was a new adventure. She walked, usually with Otis if he wanted to come along, but with his "dad" at home working, he usually stayed close to Landry. She made it a point to go to town. She might stop at the corner store and grab a few items. She'd spend some time in the bar with her laptop open. If this were a coffee shop in Newport Beach the sight of that laptop would ward people off out of respect for her space as she was working. Not in Virgin River. It was common for everyone who passed through to talk to her, sometimes going so far as pulling up a chair at her table or right next to her at the bar. This, of course, was why she was really there.

"Tell me how those puppies are doing," Jack said.

"They're growing as I watch. Lady is a pretty good-looking dog and two of the pups take after her while the other two are black."

"What are you going to do with them?"

"Landry is working on that. He talked to a friend from the shelter and he's going to work with them. Landry will foster the puppies at his kennel and the shelter will interview any potential new owners. Landry will take care of the shots and neutering and he'll throw in a complimentary obedience training class to make them a little more attractive."

"What about mama dog?" he asked.

"She could be fostered and then adopted, too. But I can't think about that yet. I'm thinking about keeping her. She's very nice to Tux."

"Be careful you don't go home with a bunch of animals," Jack said. "By the way, we're having a town Halloween party on the thirty-first. Starting around two and ending when the fires go out. You don't have to dress up unless you want to, but you have to bring something for the table. Preacher and I will turn some hot dogs and burgers on the grill. We also put out beer, wine and soft drinks and a donation jar."

"That sounds like fun."

"It's fun when the weather holds. One year the temperature dropped and it snowed so we were all driven inside. That got a little crowded."

"I can't believe it's already Halloween…" She'd arrived in

August; she'd been in Virgin River for more than two months. She'd pretty much overcome her fear of dogs and had almost fallen in love in no time. She heard her mother's voice ask, *So, how's that book coming, Kaylee?*

"There are some picnic tables out back but a lot of people bring a blanket or chairs. There will be children and pets everywhere."

"Do you do this for the town?"

"We never need an excuse for a town party," he said. "It's coming into the festive season. Before you know it, it'll be Thanksgiving and then Christmas."

Her mood went south in a hurry. Christmas. Well, she knew Christmas would be going on all around her no matter where she was or whether she participated or not. She was going to try to hold it off as long as possible.

"I'd better get back home and see if I can find some inspiration," she said to Jack.

"You do that, Kaylee. And I hope I'll see you sometime tomorrow."

"You probably will."

Rather than going straight back to her house, she drove by the Templeton place and saw a bunch of trucks, one Bobcat and one flatbed. There was a small construction trailer, a dumpster and a few men standing in front of the house. One of them was Paul Haggerty, the builder. His eyes brightened and he smiled at her. "Hey, you. You here to check my work?"

"I wouldn't know where to start. How's it going?"

"I wouldn't want to brag, but it's looking damn fine. It's going great. We're ahead of schedule, thanks to good weather. We have a new roof on and are working on the interior. Windows go in next and we're doing a remodel of the kitchen. Gerald said it might get some use over the holidays and if not then, definitely in the new year. Have you talked to him lately?"

"I did speak to Bonnie recently and she said she heard the remodel was going well, though she hasn't been here."

"I text her pictures every few days," he said. "Go in and look around, if you like. There's a spare hard hat on the porch."

"Thanks, I'd love to see it." She skipped up the porch steps, grabbed the hard hat and went inside. It was still a mess, construction litter pushed into corners, building dust everywhere, but she was aware of the new staircase and banister. A man came down the stairs and gave her a nod hello, so she went up. The windows were still covered with construction paper to keep the elements out but the walls and floors and ceiling where the fire had done the most damage were all new. There were still wires sticking out of the walls where sockets would be installed and she peeked in the upstairs bathroom— all redone with a beautiful new, modern shower where the old tub had been and except for the finishing decorator touches like paint and wallpaper, it looked complete.

The kitchen had new cupboards and granite countertops and while they hadn't been wiped off or shined up yet, they totally modernized the kitchen. The spaces for new appliances stood yawning and there was a picture of a stainless steel sub-zero taped to the wall. She couldn't wait to see the finished product. The floors she stood on were new and polished to a high sheen.

She stepped out onto the porch and took a deep breath, looking around. The leaves were changing at a rapid pace and in another couple of weeks would hit their peak color, which would be glorious.

"We're going to reinforce the porch with new studs and porch boards," Paul said. "Some of the foundation boards underneath had begun to rot from the damp weather and even though it still has a couple of good years left, might as well do it while we can. It's going to rot out and collapse before we know it anyway."

"I loved this porch. And the back porch, too. We used to sleep out there when we were kids."

"All new durable screens on the back porch and several new doors throughout."

"It's going to be beautiful."

"We'll clean up that stone hearth so it looks fresh and spotless."

She picked up a slight chill in the air and shivered. Fall had not come early here, which she was told was rare. Usually by mid-October the temperature had dropped and the leaves were almost done turning. But this year the air was still comfortable.

She thanked Paul and headed home to feed Tux and check on Lady and the pups. She put away the food she'd picked up at the store and then went to Landry's backyard, opening the gate. She cradled Tux in her hands, holding him against her chest. Otis heard the gate and came bounding outside, tail wagging. The three of them went into the kennel. It was little more than a portable metal annex about the size of a railroad car, but it had heating and air conditioning, a couple of windows, lighting and eight roomy kennels. There were cupboards to hold dog food and supplies for training. And at one end, Lady's little space, walled in to keep her puppies safe.

When Kaylee came in with Otis, Lady sat up and her eyes twinkled. Landry made sure she got out several times a day and that she was fed on a schedule, but other than that, her job was to take care of the puppies. And in that, she seemed to be doing a fantastic job. "Hi," Kaylee said softly. "How's my best girl?" She dropped Tux into the barricade. Tux immediately picked his way through the puppies to Lady and for that he was treated to a generous dog-lick. "I thought you were supposed to be natural enemies, but you're changing all my preconceived notions."

She hadn't been in there long when Landry opened the door and stepped inside. "You get any writing done today, miss?" he asked.

"A little," she said. "I'll write a little more tonight."

He crouched down and gave Lady a little rub under the chin. "This girl is looking better all the time. And this cat is getting fat on mutt milk. You have yourself a real zoo here."

"Did you work today?"

"I slaved," he said with a smile. "The weather is perfect. Let's meet on the porch. It's cocktail time."

"Okay. Your porch or mine?" she asked.

"Come over here. I bought some wine and if you're not too busy, we can have hamburgers. I'm celebrating that I'm caught up for the next two shows."

"That sounds worth celebrating."

"I'll get a shower and meet you out front in twenty minutes."

Kaylee felt a small charge of excitement. She saw him every day so this was not such a big deal, but they hadn't had a drink together at the end of the day in at least several days. He'd been busy getting his wares together for the next weekend fair and she'd been trying to write, despite being very distracted by the new family she'd taken on. She went home and used her twenty minutes to primp, putting on a clean shirt, a light touch of makeup and some lipstick. She fluffed and brushed her hair and gave herself a squirt of perfume.

When he came out of his front door, she was already sitting on his porch. And he was ready for her, handing her a glass of her favorite chardonnay. He held a bottle of beer.

"It must be going very well in there if you're tired and in need of a cocktail hour," she said.

"You can have a look while I cook our hamburgers if you want to. I haven't packed anything up yet and I will tomorrow."

"I'd love to see, thanks."

"Now tell me about your day," he said. "It has to be much more exciting than mine."

"Doubtful. I ran a couple of quick errands, then went to Jack's, where I always go with the intention of doing some writing, and that almost never happens. People are not shy about pulling up a chair."

"That's the beauty of the place," he said.

"I did run by the Templetons' place, however. Paul Haggerty is doing the remodel and he invited me to put on a hard hat and take a look around inside. He put in new floors, replaced walls, completely remodeled and modernized a bathroom, the kitchen has new cupboards and countertops, and it needs to be cleaned, but it's beginning to look better than ever. Better than I remembered it, at least."

"When were you last here?"

"Ten years ago," she said. "I was in my twenties and had just gone through a divorce and although it was the best decision I ever made, I was pretty broken up about it at the time. I think I was more embarrassed than anything."

"Embarrassed?"

"Everyone knew Dixon was not good marriage material, including me. I thought he'd straighten out once we were married. He got worse, I think."

"Okay, what made him bad marriage material?"

"He was irresponsible, flirtatious, inconsiderate, slovenly, had a short fuse, and the second we were married he thought he had a maid and a call girl."

"How old was he?"

"We were both twenty-four. We had dated for a year, got

engaged, and lived together while we planned a big wedding. See, I was an idiot. It was all there—big red flag after big red flag. I even had a few people ask me if I knew what I was doing..."

"There had to be a reason you were determined to marry him."

"He was handsome, had a great sense of humor, and was so sexy women stopped in midstride to look at him. Waitresses used to write their phone numbers on the bill. Plus, we had a lot of friends and we always had fun. He was very good at playing. Boating, paddle boarding, scuba diving, bowling, golf—you name it. We were busy every weekend. But... he was so childish and irresponsible. He was never on time, he stood people up when he got distracted. He dropped his underwear for me to pick up. And if he carried a dish to the vicinity of the sink, he expected a marching band. Plus he was arrogant. It was all about him, you know? He talked about himself constantly. I think he made up half his stories. He was immature."

"He was twenty-four," Landry pointed out.

"Were you like that at twenty-four?" she asked.

"Nah. I was too serious."

She chuckled. "You got over that, I guess."

"It took some doing. I, too, was married at twenty-four. And looking back on it, it probably shouldn't have happened, either."

"Um, lest we forget, you're still married."

"Yes and no," he said. "I mean, yes, I didn't get divorced because it really didn't seem important. But we did have the talk. When I pointed out to her that we never saw each other and sometimes didn't even talk for weeks, she said, 'But when we are together it's so wonderful and I love you!' And I said if we're not going to live like a married couple, why should we be married? It was a very emotional showdown and she said if I wanted to get divorced she wouldn't try to stand in my way. That clearing of the air changed things. I moved up here from San Francisco and moved in with my dad. I had more room to work and when she did visit, which wasn't often, she took the guest room."

"Was your heart broken?" she asked.

"Sure. The thing I couldn't get past was that she didn't love me enough to make a sacrifice for our marriage. I offered to move, to change whatever had to change so we could be together, but she said our living in different places wouldn't last forever. She was wrong—it did last forever. Eventually I got over being mad or hurt. She had a dream and she wanted it so bad, nothing was going to get in her way. So, I kind of let it go. I let her go."

"But you didn't get divorced," she reminded him.

"First of all, I was busy, trying to make it in my little art world. I'll never be world famous, but I do a good little business. Then my dad died suddenly. He hadn't even had a chance to retire, the poor guy. That preoccupied me for a long time. Getting a divorce to make it official was the last thing on my mind."

"But what are you going to do about the fact that she still loves you! It's obvious."

"Kaylee, I might be greedy, but that's just not enough love to keep me going. A phone call every week or two, a little small talk, a visit two or three times a year? Once she came up here from LA to rest because she was exhausted from a really tough movie and she stayed in the guesthouse, your house, and got two weeks of rest. But she went back. She's driven. There's no room in her world for a husband."

"Huh. Well, I'm very sorry that happened to you."

"Thanks, but I'm all right. So, your ex? Is he still around?"

"Sort of. We have a lot of mutual friends so I get the occasional updates. Some have been good. He got married and had a couple of kids real fast and it looked like he found the right woman, one who could make it work. Then he got fired and I heard they'd fallen on hard times. Then he got back to work and I heard they were getting on their feet. Then they divorced and I actually felt bad. I mean, they had kids.

"But back to your original question. My mom brought me up here after my divorce so I could whimper and cry and lick my wounds. We borrowed the Templetons' house and stayed ten days. It took me a lot longer than ten days, but I love it here. My mom loved it here."

"Were you ever tempted again? To get married?"

"Not once. In the past ten years I've dated a few very nice guys. One was my boyfriend for a year! But I was busy with work, lots of travel with my job, I had my mom and her friends and my friends and besides, I liked living alone. And after Dixon, all I'd have to do is remember his rowing machine under the bed and his dirty clothes on the floor and I was over it." She smiled at Landry. "I've seen your house and your guesthouse. I might marry you. You're very tidy. And considerate."

"And married."

"Ah, yes and no."

And they laughed and laughed.

"I saw Dixon last year," she said. "He's bald and has put on about forty pounds. He looks sloppy and pale. That made me so happy."

Landry was taken with Kaylee and he'd known that almost immediately. She caught a man's eye, for one thing, but he was no longer twenty-four and it took a lot more than that to interest him. Despite her admitted vulnerability, still grieving her mother's death, she was solid. Or maybe the fact that she knew she was vulnerable was a strength. He loved hearing her talk, explain things, describe things. She was articulate and intelligent. There didn't seem to be a wishy-washy bone in her body even though she had a lot to work out. She was late turning in a book for which she'd been paid, for one thing. She was worried about it, but she was powering through. That took strength and determination. He knew only too well, as he often made contracts on art that was not yet created.

After they had dinner they were back on the porch. He asked her to tell him about the book.

"A couple of models are murdered and the suspicion is that there's a killer stalking beautiful young women. There are many links between the deceased women, their boyfriends, family members, colleagues, etc. Then an attempt is made on a third model, also linked to the first two, and she not only escapes, she steps up to try to solve the murders before it happens to her. You know, eat or be eaten. Our killer gets by with a couple more signature murders, always putting her closer to danger. And of course she makes friends with a sexy detective who not only wants to protect her, he wants to help her figure it out. And there's an elderly forensics expert also on the case."

"Hm. Sounds interesting. Is it almost done?"

"It's getting closer but it's weeks from done. I'm writing another book at the same time, one that I don't have a contract for, one that I'm more interested in writing. So I'm forcing myself to write six pages a day of the suspense, and then I find myself sitting up very late writing the one I enjoy writing. This is just coping; my ability to concentrate and think creatively took a giant hit when my mom died."

"Tell me about the one you enjoy," he said.

"It's a fictionalized version of me, the character often growing in directions that make her stronger and more together than I really am. It's not unusual to write about characters I admire or wish I was more like. It's about a woman who runs off to the mountains to reclaim her confidence and strength after her husband dies. I decided it should be a husband, not a mother. But as I'm writing, I know the truth. And as I write, I figure things out."

"Is that something you do to get closure?"

"No, it's something I do to understand what I'm feeling. See, when I hear of a problem or have an issue that needs to be resolved, I often don't really know how it should work out until I write about it. Sometimes I interview my characters, asking them key questions about themselves. Sometimes I'll write about situations that confound me. I'll start out writing about how it was and finish up writing about how it should be."

"It must be cathartic."

"Sometimes. I've written a few terrible husbands named Dick or Richard or Rick or Dax." She beamed. "Once he was Zach."

"I bet they had some familiar qualities…"

"Oh yes. Sometimes they died, depending on how I was feeling about him at the time. They always got tripped up by their arrogance and self-centeredness. And it makes me better somehow. Once I write about it, I develop some understanding."

"Does your ex-husband ever redeem himself?" Landry asked.

"Sadly, no. Thus he is forever punished."

"Remind me never to piss you off," he said, laughing.

"Oh, I honestly don't personalize those quirks of plot. If you piss me off, I might name a very bad doctor Dr. Landry. Or maybe just an incompetent pilot. Not an evil person, just a stupid one."

"And I might make an ugly pot shaped like your head."

She laughed happily. "Talk like that and you could end up a serial killer!"

"How long have you been writing these books about killers?" he asked.

"Since I started. It was my favorite genre when I was learning and you should always write what you want to read. I like the edginess of a great suspense novel, like a really good J.T. Ellison."

"Who?"

She shook her head. "You have homework to do."

"I might just read a few Kaylee Sloans."

"There you go. If I'm worth my salt, you'll sleep with one eye open while I'm renting your little house. Oh, by the way, Jack's having a Halloween party on the thirty-first. I'm planning to go. Are you?"

"I've stopped by a few town parties. I'll probably go."

"I suppose you know everyone."

"I did grow up here."

"What was it like, growing up here?"

"It was good," he said. "I had fun. I had friends, although like I said, I was a little too serious. I played ball, went to school things, got good grades. But almost every kid who grows up in a quiet small town can't wait to get to the real life in the city, and that was me. I went away to college, missed my dad and my friends, came home when I could. Then after Laura went to Hollywood and hardly came back, I gave up the city and moved back here and had a whole new appreciation for it. I think it's the people. The air, the quiet and the people who stand up for each other."

"I didn't expect to make friends here," she said. "I expected to be a different kind of lonely."

His brow wrinkled. "Different from what?"

"From the kind of lonely I was in Newport. There were lots of people around but there was only one I wanted—my mother. I ached with loneliness.

"My mom and I didn't live together after I went to college. Oh, there were a few months here and there—while I was waiting for a new apartment to become available or after my divorce while I looked for my own place, just temporary situations. Then when she got sick, I moved home to be with her. After she died, the house became mine, but it was always her house. I couldn't seem to escape the feeling that I'd just lost her, surrounded by her decorating and her things. That's why I looked for a getaway. And I'll go back to that house. It's a wonderful house with an office on the second floor that looks out to the ocean. It has a large backyard and a pool. I can walk to the beach from there. I want to live in that house again. I just hope I'm stronger when I do."

"You seem pretty strong now," he said. "Don't worry too much, Kaylee. That immediate, crushing feeling of loss will pass. You'll always miss her. But you'll start to feel better."

"Is that how it was for you?" she asked.

"Yes. It took a while, but eventually... Yes, that's how it is."

The next day Landry had an appointment with Brie Valenzuela, Jack's sister, and a local attorney with a small practice. She opened the door for him to come in, a smile on her face. "So good to see you. I'm glad you called, but I'm confused. You need a divorce?"

"That's right," he said, shaking her proffered hand. "I'll explain."

He had a seat in front of her desk and laid it out quickly, eleven years married, ten separated. "Laura visited recently and I told her I was done being legally bound and that I'd like it to be official. I've been thinking of her as an ex-wife for years. We're still on very good terms. We're friends. But we haven't lived together for a decade."

"How do you plan to handle the settlement? Will her attorney be contacting me?"

"I doubt there will be any kind of settlement. We've both paid our own way since she moved out."

"You haven't paid any support or alimony?"

"Nope."

"Nothing?"

"No. I gave her a few loans that she never repaid, but I wasn't expecting repayment. Her life as an actress went hot and cold—she'd have a good season followed by waiting for work followed by another role. It wasn't steady. Thus the loans. She'd need money for rent or to get her by till her next check or for some special thing that would help her in her business. Like, once it was dental work. Very expensive. I helped if I could."

"And did you also borrow money from her?"

"No, I wouldn't do that. No, I never asked her for money."

"I suppose that's a demanding and uncertain lifestyle, acting."

"I thought she'd be a star. I thought she was good. When I was over being insulted that she'd choose a career over a marriage, I tried to be supportive."

Brie folded her hands on top of her desk. "Will she be expecting to receive divorce documents?"

"When we last talked about it she said that I should go ahead and do whatever I felt I should do. I don't think she'll be surprised. If she is, it's only because I've done nothing for so long."

"Okay. Maybe it will go smoothly. I can write it up for you. One piece of advice—even couples on the best of terms can get a little weird or strange when the divorce becomes a reality."

"Even couples who have been separated for ten years?"

"Completely separated?" she asked.

"She has only visited a few times in the past ten years. She left some things behind when she first left but over the course of a year they slowly found their way to LA, her home since then."

"So, she also wants the divorce?"

"Well..." He paused. "Actually, on her recent visit she asked if I'd be willing to try again. She says she's frustrated with acting and it's not going as she hoped. I told her it was just too late for that. She was a little disappointed, but she said it was up to me."

Brie just stared him down for a moment. "I'll need some information—birth dates, Social Security numbers, ID, addresses, date of the marriage. I'll have the initial documents ready by the end of the week. But Landry, I suggest you call her, tell her of the progress you've made."

"Probably a good idea," he said. "I wouldn't want to upset her, though she should be aware this is coming. I told her I would get it going."

"The reality is this is a no-fault, community property state. If you two don't agree on the terms of the divorce and decide to each get a lawyer, it can become a very expensive and pro-tracted case. If you can avoid that it will be quick and easy. But don't be too surprised if you run into a little resistance."

"In eleven years we've hardly had a fight. There were a few tense conversations, but no real fighting."

"I hope that record holds," she said. "Now, let's get that information. If there's anything you don't know, you can get it from her and email it to me."

That night Landry called Laura. He had to leave a message, which was often the case. Within the hour she called him back.

"Are you in that play you auditioned for?"

"I did get the part. It's not a big part, but since they're paying for my hotel I decided I might as well take it. San Francisco is a lot closer than LA."

Closer to what? he wondered. "Well, I wanted to tell you that I saw a lawyer today and she's starting the paperwork for a divorce. She'll write everything up and if we don't each have a lawyer, it will be cheap and easy, and since I'm the one who wants to do this, I'll pay for it. I'll have the preliminary documents by the end of the week. Give me your current address and I'll send them to you."

There was no response for a moment. "I see," she said at long last. "I had really hoped you'd think things over and give us another chance."

"I'm sorry, Laura, but I'm afraid I'm past all that. Time to move on."

"Fine. If that's what you're going to do. I'll text you my address."

She disconnected without saying goodbye.

8

OCTOBER 20 WAS AN UNFORGETTABLE DAY FOR Kaylee. It had been a life-changing day. She tried ignoring the significance of the date, but it snuck up on her and left her feeling melancholy and fatigued. She didn't go for her morning walk, nor did she check on Lady and the puppies. Instead she got out the special suitcase she had brought along with her from Newport Beach. This was only the second time she had opened it since she'd been in Virgin River.

This was her treasure chest. Her secret garden. Inside were artifacts of her mother. Nothing valuable by monetary standards but priceless to her. Inside were sentimental things that helped with the remembering.

Folded neatly on top was her mother's favorite wrap. It was pale blue, knit with fine, thin yarn, and she'd loved to put it around her shoulders first thing in the morning and sometimes late at night. It was perfect for keeping her from getting a chill. Meredith's sister, Beth, had made it for her. And with it, the scarf that she loved, Armani, that she had tied around her bald head.

There was a framed picture of Kaylee and Meredith, cheek to cheek, smiling and holding on to each other, their hair blowing in the wind. She loved that picture. She had other favorites, she had filled a small plastic bag with them—in the swimming pool, her first dance recital, snowboarding in the mountains, on the beach, Disneyland and later more recent pictures—out to dinner, a trip to Turks and Caicos, a trip to London, San Francisco and many from Las Patios, which was their joke name for evenings on the patio of Meredith's house.

There were copies of two books her mother loved—*Eat, Pray, Love* and *Rosie Colored Glasses*. She caressed them and decided she would reread them because Meredith loved them. There were some magazines; people didn't subscribe so much anymore but Meredith and her company had been mentioned in several and the articles had included photos, so into the treasure chest they went. There was a cell phone; Kaylee kept it, kept it charged, checked it often to see if any messages had been left, people she should notify. And she turned off the ringer but called that number sometimes just to hear her mother's voice answering. She paid the monthly bill to keep the account active. Her mother's voice was worth fifty dollars a month. Meredith's Kindle was in the suitcase. It was the most recent record of what Meredith had read. Kaylee intended to read everything her mother had read.

Her mother had a picture of Kaylee as a flower girl that she kept on her bathroom shelf; that went in the suitcase. And she had found in her mother's desk drawer several cards Kaylee had given her over the years. There was a card from Art, the man Meredith had dated for quite some time, a couple of years maybe, until Meredith had decided to end the relationship because they had too many disagreements on crucial issues—like, he wanted them to live together and Meredith didn't. In fact, he thought they should marry and Meredith declined. He was constantly giving her advice about how to run her business when perhaps he could use some advice on how to run his. They argued and Meredith wasn't interested in arguing. "Do I need to get into a power struggle at this late date?" Meredith had said. "I don't think so."

Meredith showed Kaylee what Art had written in the card. *I'm very disappointed and sorry for whatever I might have done to cause this rift, but if you've made up your mind, I guess that's it. I will always love you.*

At the time Kaylee had said, "That's so sweet."

Meredith had agreed that it was very sweet. "But he doesn't know what he might have done wrong. He doesn't know why we're breaking up. That's a huge red flag. All that talking and arguing and he still doesn't know what he might have done differently." Then she had smiled and said, "Maybe he should have asked. And then listened to the answer."

Kaylee wanted to be like Meredith. Strong and fearless, independent and confident.

She spent a couple of hours with her memories, gloomy and sad and lonely, and then she cried. She threw herself into the crying and wondered if there would ever be a day she wouldn't long so much for her mother. At about three her phone rang, but she didn't answer. She looked at it and saw it had been Landry. She might call him back later, after she'd pulled herself together. Then she fell asleep for a while. At five she woke up with a puffy face that cold water didn't improve one bit.

The sun was setting much earlier and soon they would be turning the clocks back. Right now it was growing dark by six and in a couple of weeks that would be five o'clock sunset and it would stay dark much later in the mornings.

There was a knock at the door. She didn't move. Landry knocked and yelled, "Kaylee! Are you all right?"

With a heavy sigh, she went to the door. "I'm fine. Just having one of those days."

He looked alarmed and pushed inside. "Kaylee, what is it?"

Her eyes welled with tears because she hadn't quite shaken it off. "I'm just having a sad day. I'll be fine in the morning."

"But wait, what's wrong? You've been fine! Did something happen? Everything all right with your publisher? Tell me."

She shook her head. "It was one of those memory days. I couldn't stop it so I let it take me. It'll pass now, I think. But I'm not likely to be good company."

"What was significant about today?" he wanted to know.

"It's not that important..."

"Yes, it is." He reached for her and pulled her close. "I can't bear to see you hurting. It's too familiar. I remember those feelings."

That was all it took for her to lean against him and sob. He murmured that it was okay, he rocked her in his arms and she cried for what seemed like a long, long time but it was probably only five minutes. She finally pulled away and looked up at him. "It was this day a year ago that the decision was made. The doctor said they had done all they could with the chemo. She was weak and thin and bald and at the end of her endurance. She was done. That's when we moved to Hospice care. From that day on, the focus was on quality of life rather than curing her cancer."

She cried a little more.

"I was just going through some of the things I saved, things that were special to us. You know—artifacts. Her shawl, her scarf, some pictures and books." She glanced over her shoulder at the open suitcase on the sofa.

He had the most gentle smile. "Tell me about her."

"Aww, I don't know..."

"No, really. Tell me all about her. I have a feeling you take after her."

"If only..."

"Let me make us some coffee. Tell me everything."

They sat on the couch together, holding their coffee mugs, when Kaylee began. "She was the most awesome woman. She was so strong and fearless. When I was a little girl she worked for a decorator in the LA area and after years of that, she began to design beautiful patio furniture. When I was a senior in high school she opened a company that manufactured high-end patio furniture. Sunshine was the name she gave her company. I didn't pay that much attention at the time but I knew she took out loans, did all kinds of special promotions, had to do some part-time design to make ends meet, but eventually, Sunshine took off. She joined with a partner and they doubled in size. She designed the most beautiful, luxurious outdoor furniture, very heavy so the high wind we're famous for wouldn't blow it away, and she became successful. She sold a lot to resorts and hotels. She was in her early fifties and it all came together. She was featured in so many local design magazines. She worked long hours and we almost never got to spend days off together, but she was so happy. She was so proud of herself."

They moved to the porch swing for a while with a second cup of coffee and unsurprisingly, Otis found them and lay down on the porch.

"When I was small and my father had left us, it was hard for her to work and keep all the mommy commitments from parent-teacher conferences to attending special programs and do her part to host playdates and sleepovers. I remember that I wanted a sleepover and she was up to her eyebrows in work and just couldn't, so I pitched a fit and made things even more difficult. And she was furious, but she forgave me, and then we had a long talk about how it was just the two of us and we were going to have to work as a team or we just wouldn't make it. I'm not sure I tried hard enough to hold up my end."

"It sounds like she did very well even with all her duties. Was she fun?"

"Oh God, she was always fun. She had close girlfriends, some from as long ago as high school and some she had met later, but when the women were getting together I was included most of the time. Once I was out of college and teaching, I was always included, as were some of my friends. We were usually a group of four to eight and divided into two generations. We went on a few weekend trips together, to wineries or art walks in small towns, and we had a ball. It was so fun—we would gossip and laugh till we cried. There was one time when we were in a small restaurant in Half Moon Bay and we, mother and daughter, got hit on by a father and son. Oh God, our whole group found that hilarious. I was a little interested, to tell the truth, but my mother said, 'You can have them both, I'm not going there.' Then there were those times of crisis when we had to be there for each other as support and there might have been less laughing. Like when Janette went through a divorce and her pain was so awful and we propped her up."

"And when you went through a divorce," he said.

"Oh, that was classic," she said. "My mother always knew it wouldn't work. She could see right away that Dixon was self-centered and lazy and she really tried not to say anything. Then there was an incident—he stood me up for dinner on my birthday! He had an excuse, but it wasn't a great one. And he wasn't sorry. And my mother caved and broke her own rule. She asked me what I was thinking and had I lost my fucking mind. And yes, she said 'fucking.' And of course I said, 'But I love him!' and she stopped talking. She said she just had to do it once in case there was some sanity in my head."

"Her rule?" he asked. "Do what once?"

"She said when you're the mother of a young woman and you don't think the boyfriend is good enough, you dare not say so or your daughter will marry him before morning. It's more of a challenge than advice. So she always tried to be welcoming to any boyfriends, to be accepting. I strained her willpower with a few of the guys I brought around, but the thought of me marrying such a selfish egomaniac just wore her down. And of course I married him! He came on to the maid of honor and I still married him. And when I divorced him she never once said she told me so. Instead she was totally sympathetic."

"You came up here together, after the divorce," he said.

"That's right. A quiet getaway. I told Dixon to get his stuff out of our house and that I was filing for divorce." She grew quiet. "He never asked for another chance. Now, of course, I can see that I dodged a bullet. I'm so much better off. But at the time I felt abandoned and lonely and devastated."

"We need to eat before there's more story," Landry said. "And I know there's more story."

"I can't even think about eating," she said.

"Even more reason." He went inside and she followed him. He opened the refrigerator and took inventory. "There's lots of stuff in here. How would you like an omelet? A veggie omelet with sausage and potatoes on the side?"

"Sounds delicious, but I don't have sausage and potatoes."

"I do. I should go check on Lady, make sure she gets out

for a break. I'll bring the rest of the stuff for a breakfast for dinner when I come back. You can go take a shower, see if it makes you feel better. I'll be right back and I'll cook. How's that sound?"

So that's what they did. She showered while he was dealing with Lady and gathering up his groceries. When she came out of the shower he was slicing and dicing in the kitchen. Of course showering, blowing out her hair and having a nice dinner made all the difference. The storytelling went on while they ate and continued through the washing up of dishes. Then they moved to the sofa with glasses of wine, Tux on her lap and Otis curled up on the floor at their feet.

"My mom was very smart about life issues. When I wanted to write she encouraged me to make it happen. On a teacher's salary it was hard to afford everything and some of the writer's conferences I wanted to attend were prohibitively expensive. I think money was still kind of tight then for her, but she found ways to help. My birthday gifts were plane tickets or conference fees. Then she listened to me for hours after I came home. For a long time I had to write and teach—even my first contract was barely enough to keep me for a month. She would bring dinner to me a couple of times a week."

"Any reason you didn't live with her?" he asked.

"We wanted to be independent. I wanted to be independent, especially once I recovered from Dixon. But I chose a town house very close to her house. We talked at least twice a day, but we only saw each other two or three times a week. There were a few times we'd get together, kill a bottle of wine and I'd stay overnight rather than drive. We'd have a sleepover. That didn't happen very often, not even once a month, but we were very compatible even though we didn't live together by choice. We had our own routines; we needed our own space."

"How was it when you eventually moved back in?" he asked.

"It wasn't very long after she was diagnosed. She stopped getting around as well. She was fatigued. Maybe a little depressed. I didn't think I'd lose her. But I wasn't going to let anything happen to her. She didn't need me as a caregiver; there was home health care. But I needed to be there, to go to doctor's appointments, to make sure she wasn't ever left lonely or afraid. She fell once in the bathroom in the night, and she wasn't badly hurt, but I was so glad I was there. It was what was in my head, not hers. She was never afraid. She was all courage to the last. But I gave up my town house in October, moved some things into her garage and rented a storage unit for other stuff and moved into what had been my old room. I set up my office in a guest room. My mom still tried to work, to at least watch her company if she couldn't run it. She hung on to that to the end, too."

"And then...?"

"In December she had a meeting with her partner and the lawyers, finalized her will and her trust, arranged for her partner to buy her out. She said she was too weak to even advise and that she wanted to spend what time she had left with her family. By that time she had informed my father and he was starting to get in my way, wanting to be around all of a sudden. I told him to go spend all this newfound time and energy with all of his other families. That's when I learned those other families had pretty much washed their hands of him. Apparently my mother was gracious and forgiving. She was classy. I'll never be as classy. I'm kind of mean. I hold a grudge."

He smiled at her. "You don't have to."

"Tell that to my grudge!"

They refilled the wine once and kept talking about the late, great Meredith, and Kaylee yawned a couple of times. Her lids threatened to close. He pulled her closer and asked a few soft questions while she leaned against him. What was your mother's favorite celebration? Restaurant? Beach? Holiday? What was her favorite food? When were you most in awe of her? When did she make you angry?

She answered but she yawned.

"Kaylee, time for you to go to bed."

"I'm sorry," she said. "I guess it was the wine…"

"It's the emotional exhaustion," he said, standing and pulling her up, disturbing Tux, who looked unimpressed. "Let's get you to bed. You're going to sleep like a rock tonight."

He held her hand and escorted her to the bedroom. He kissed her brow. "Thank you for sharing all those special things with me."

She gave a huff of laughter. It had been so wonderful to have someone ask! She had wanted to talk about her mother and it always felt so awkward. She didn't want to force her discomfort on people. "It felt good, I think."

"It will feel good to sleep now," he said.

"It also felt good to be held. Want to lie down here and hold each other a while longer?"

"That would be good." He sat on the edge of the bed and took his shoes off. He lay down on the bed and pulled her closer. "Cuddle up here."

She put her head on his shoulder and snuggled close. "This is much better."

"Do you want to tell me one of your favorite memories? Or maybe tell me a story? Like the story of the book you're writing?"

"I'll tell you tomorrow," she said, and she burrowed in. Her head rested on his shoulder and her leg was draped over his thighs. He had an arm around her, under her shoulders. She let a hand drift across his chest. "This is very nice. You cuddle very well. I'm sure you've been complimented many times."

"Not that many."

"Is there anything you need to talk about?" she asked.

"Not tonight," he said.

She softly snored and he laughed.

"Sorry," she said.

"No, please just let go. This is nice."

So she did, floating off into a blissful nothingness. It was soft but blank. In her sleep she remembered her mother saying, *Don't worry. I have enough morphine in me to sink a ship. I'll just go to sleep. I'll always be with you, but I'll be watching from a new perspective.*

It was dark and Otis was snoring at the foot of the bed. *Or maybe that was me*, Landry thought. It might have been what had awakened him. But no, that wasn't it. It was the movement of Kaylee's hands, gently rubbing his chest. She was as close as she could be without lying right on top of him. He turned his head and his lips found her temple. He inhaled the fresh scent of her; it was soap, water and that which was Kaylee, the special scent that could belong to no one else.

He pressed his lips there. And damn, he sprang to life.

She squirmed against him and, lifting her lips, found his neck and then his chin and then his cheek. And he groaned.

They moved around a little bit, turning on their sides, and Landry found her lips. His arms were around her. His large hands grabbed her bottom, pulling her closer against him. Her arms mimicked, her hands on him. Her response was to open her lips slightly and his tongue explored. It brought a deep sigh from her. That just fueled his passion and he went after her mouth like a starving man. It had been so long and he had craved a deep taste of her from the first day he saw her.

He pulled away enough to kiss every last part of her face—her neck, her chin, cheeks, forehead, neck a little more. She put her leg over his to get closer, pushing against him right where his bulge drove them both a little crazy. He plunged his hands into the soft silkiness of her hair while he kissed her and loved the little sounds she made while he touched her and pressed against her.

"Okay," he whispered. "Okay, are you sure you don't just need a little comforting?"

"I'm sure I do," she whispered. "And I also need a little of this."

"You might regret it later," he said.

"Why? Aren't you planning to be good to me?"

"Oh, I'd like a chance to be very good to you. Listen, I don't have protection."

"I do," she said. "Condoms. A little on the mature side. I keep a couple in my cosmetic bag, just to be careful, never really expecting to... They've been there quite a while. I don't think I'd regret it. Will you?"

"Kaylee," he said, brushing her hair back. "We've been good friends and I want to stay good friends. You have to be sure."

She smiled at him. "I'm sure I'm not letting you go. You feel too good."

"Okay, if you're sure."

"You aren't going to make me beg, are you?"

A deep and low laugh rumbled out of him. "Go get those condoms. And make it quick."

She rolled right over the top of him and was back before he had his shirt off. She put the packets by the side of the bed and climbed on him, straddling him. He rolled with her until they were again on their sides, clutching each other desperately, their mouths locked together in the never-ending kiss of lovers. Without breaking free for even a second, they pulled at each other's clothes and when they were down to boxers and panties, they slowed. Their hands explored more carefully. He touched her whole body gently, tenderly, hungrily. She touched his, caressing his chest and flat belly, a hand sliding underneath the elastic waist of his boxers.

"Oh my God," he said in a breath. And then he made her panties disappear. With great care, he parted her legs and touched her in her most vulnerable spot. It was amazing that that caused her to tighten her hand around him. "God," he said again, going after her mouth, plunging his tongue deeply. His fingers moved slowly and more deeply into her. "Yeah, I think this is what you want."

"I can't remember ever wanting anything this much," she said.

He rolled away, found one of the condoms and quickly applied it. Then he took her in his arms again. "I'll try to slow down."

"Don't," she said. "You can slow down later."

He grinned into her pretty eyes. "In a hurry, are you?"

"No more talking," she said. "Just doing."

He laughed at her. She was cute; she was fun. He was on fire. He didn't laugh anymore. He went to work on her with his fingers, with his tongue, more fingers. Then he rolled her on her back and took his place between her legs, entering her slowly. He groaned and she sighed. He held her hips and rocked with her, slowly at first and then a little faster but not too fast. He went deep and strong and he couldn't keep his eyes open. He stroked her, giving it all he had, and when he felt her come, he held her tight against him. She made a gasping sound, clutching him desperately close.

They exploded together, holding on for dear life.

It was quite a while before their breathing calmed and their clutching relaxed. He rose above her. "That was amazing. You are amazing."

"It was. I think that was probably the best sleeping pill I've ever had."

"Think you'll be able to rest now?" he asked.

"No question. You have to stay, of course."

"I get up early."

"I know."

"Otis may request a trip outside and you don't have a doggy door."

"I understand. But don't leave me until you absolutely have to. Even if I'm sleeping."

"I'll hate leaving you. If you need me for any reason in the night, just tap my shoulder," he said.

Somewhere in the depth of night, she reached out to him and gave that shoulder a tap. He pulled her to him at once. Without a word, the only sounds their breathing and sighing and shuffling in the bed, he made love to her again. Again, it didn't take very long before they were exploding together, left shuddering in satisfaction.

"This is the best night of my life," he whispered.

"Same," she said. And she fell back to sleep in his arms.

Like a poem or a song, the morning sun was brighter than ever before. The birds were more melodious. The sky far bluer than she'd seen. And her heart was exploding. Kaylee was filled with feelings that didn't hurt.

She felt Landry slip from her side and heard him leave with Otis in the predawn. She smiled and allowed herself to go back to sleep. She wasn't sure how much longer she slept but when her eyes opened, the sun was struggling to rise and shine, and Kaylee smelled coffee. She wrapped herself in a robe, brushed the knots out of her hair, pulled it back in a scrunchie and found her lover in the kitchen. He was drinking a cup of coffee and looking at his laptop. He put down his cup and held out an arm for her.

"Mm, I slept very well," she said. "Very."

"It was my pleasure," he said. He tapped his laptop. "My morning news."

"How's the world looking this morning?" she asked.

"Despite the dire condition it's been in lately, it's never looked better."

She poured her coffee and sat down across from him. "Funny, I woke up with just that feeling. Thank you for last night. For all of it, from the storytelling to the lovemaking. I feel brand-new."

"You're beautiful in the morning," he said. "I wanted to be here when you woke but I don't want to be a pest. I fed Tux and he's already asleep. Can I make you some breakfast? And we can talk about our days?"

"I think I just had breakfast last night," she said.

"Which is why I brought pancake mix. You have some berries. How does that sound?"

"Hm, I could get used to you," she said.

"Let's have some breakfast and go to our corners. I have a little work to do, you have work you're supposed to do. And this afternoon I thought I'd drive over to the coast and around the hills—the leaves are at their peak. And it's going to be a beautiful day. Want to come?"

"I do," she said. "What time?"

"How does two sound? Does that give you enough time to get some work done?"

"Of course," she said. But she thought the last thing she wanted was to work.

She felt the urge to burst into song.

When Landry had gone and the kitchen was cleaned up,

she called Janette, the first person who came to mind. "It's possible I'm falling in love," she said. "With my landlord."

"Well, now, that's interesting. Is he falling in love right back?"

"I think so, yes. It's early. Time will tell."

"You have nothing but time, cookie," she said. "Can I suggest you use that time to enjoy life? It seems you've been having some trouble doing that for a while. Obvious reasons."

"Obvious," Kaylee returned.

9

LIFE TOOK ON A GLOW FOR KAYLEE. EVERY DAY was a bright and sunny day even when there were clouds in the sky. She saw Landry every day but not all day. They had coffee inside in the mornings now because it was getting very chilly outside and they drove around the countryside at least once a week, sometimes twice. They went to dinner on the coast, watched movies on his big-screen TV, had dinner together frequently and breakfast most mornings. They slept together every night. One of them always made the first overture: Do you need a night alone? Would you like to spend the night? Even if they didn't make love like a couple of sex-starved bunnies, they held each other and murmured sweet, soft words during the night. But they also made love like sex-starved bunnies.

They had long, meaningful talks about everything from

philosophy to great books; they had read many of the same authors. Thanks to digital publishing, they would often download each other's recommendations so they could discuss more of the great books they loved. They talked about religion, politics, travel and even the possibility of space aliens. They told each other about their friends, family, people they worked with or people they had known who left an impression.

One day they drove down to San Francisco. Jack agreed to check on Lady and the pups, let her out a few times, and to feed Tux. He took Otis home with him for the night, much to the joy of Jack's kids and the annoyance of his border collie, Ralph. The purpose of the trip to San Francisco was to visit some of the galleries that Landry liked to work with. Some of his finer glass creations were on display and Kaylee was bursting with pride. They had a nice dinner at Fisherman's Wharf and stayed overnight at a lovely hotel. Kaylee was a little nervous that they might run into Laura but Landry said, "It's a very big city. And besides, it doesn't matter if we do."

They only stayed the one night, both anxious to get back to their pets.

Kaylee told her closest friends about Landry, about his art, his tenderness, his dogs, his kindness and his passion for her. She told Michelle and Janette and her aunt, Beth. No one seemed concerned that this could be a bad idea. In fact, everyone was thrilled to hear some joy in her voice for the first time in so long.

She even told her mom, though of course her mom had no reply. She wished her mom could meet him, get to know him, love him as Kaylee did. The feeling she got when she communicated with Meredith was that her mom would be so relieved to know that Kaylee had someone special in her life, someone to love. Someone to take a little of the weight of her grief off her back. It had been quite a while since she'd had a boyfriend.

She ran into Mel at the bar and Mel said, "You look so great. Have you been getting a little extra sunshine on your cheeks? Did you get a new haircut or something?"

"No change that I'm aware of, but I'm feeling great. Maybe it's just time. Maybe I'm finally learning to live with losing my mom. I still miss her like mad. Nothing has changed there. But lately I've been spending a lot of time with Landry. We've become pretty close and it's making me happy."

"Maybe that's what's glowing on your pretty cheeks," Mel said. "I don't know if you heard this through the grapevine, but Jack is my second husband. I was widowed when my first husband was killed. He stumbled into a robbery in progress and was shot. It was a terrible ordeal. I came to Virgin River for a fresh start, too."

"I'm sorry, Mel. That must have been so horrible."

"Very hard, but it's a process. I wish I had some advice on how to survive the grieving process, but all I can say is, there's no shortcut. You just have to plow through it. One suggestion is to just weather the year of the firsts without your loved one—first birthday, first anniversary, first holidays, etc."

"I'm working on that," Kaylee said.

"Like I said, there's no shortcut. But are you coming to the Halloween party?"

"Yes! And thankfully that's not a memorable holiday that my mom and I shared. There should be no dark clouds hanging over the day."

"Then it could be total fun. It's supposed to be a chilly, sunny day."

On that Saturday, Landry and Kaylee arrived in town at about three and had to park all the way down at the edge of town, there were so many cars and trucks lining the road.

They walked to the picnic area behind the bar and it looked as if the entire town was there. People were camped out at the picnic tables, in lawn chairs, on blankets and just standing around in clusters or leaning against trees. Kaylee had made a big platter of chicken wings and Landry's contribution was a large bowl of fruit and nuts mixed up with Cool Whip. Once they added their contributions to the table, they held hands. That was how they were linked as Landry began to introduce Kaylee to people she didn't already know.

Paul Haggerty introduced them to his wife Vanessa and their five children. "I'm glad I ran into you, Kaylee. You should give Bonnie and Gerald a call. They're planning to come up in a week or two to check out the house. It's nearly finished. I figured you'd want to see them."

"I can't wait to see them, and the house!"

Landry had a beer in one hand and passed a cup of wine to Kaylee so he could shake hands with Paul. "I'm going to drive over and take a look, too, if you don't mind."

"You're always welcome. It turned out just right," Paul said proudly.

They made the rounds, visited with the minister and his wife. Kaylee met Luke and Shelby Riordan, of course she already knew Colin and Jillian, and another brother was visiting so she was introduced to Sean. "How many of you are there?"

"Five Riordan boys—Patrick and Aiden are missing. When we all get together you can hear the noise shake the rooftops."

"It's a good thing Colin lives in a very big house," Shelby said. "It gets to be quite a crowd."

Kaylee visited with Jack, Preacher, Paige and Mike Valenzuela and was introduced to Brie, Jack's sister. Then she found her way to the table Mel occupied with some other women. There were pony rides for the children, a big inflated bounce house for the smaller kids and all kinds of games taking place around the grounds. A lot of the kids and several adults were wearing costumes; Jillian was wearing a very inventive witch costume complete with shoes with curled-up toes and a blacked-out tooth. And the food! She looked at the long table covered with dishes that seemed to go on forever. "This is food porn," she said to Landry.

They stayed for several hours, visited with most of the town, ate themselves silly, and Kaylee hated to see it ever end. But the temperature dropped as the sun was going down and Landry whispered in her ear, "I think you should come home with me and we should light the fire."

"That sounds perfect," she said. "Maybe I should go to my house first and take a shower."

"Kaylee, I have a perfectly good shower. It's big enough for two."

"My life is wonderful," Kaylee told Janette. "I almost feel guilty for being so happy."

"Please don't," Janette said. "You know if your mother is watching, all she wants for you is that you feel happy and fulfilled. Remember that she was. Till the last day, she was happy all the time, even in the hardest times. She had some major struggles with the company, but she was positive and grateful for every day. Just be thankful that you were blessed with such a fantastic mother and role model."

"Yes, I know. Sometimes losing her is so hard I forget to remember how lucky I was to have had her as a mother," she said.

"That was one of many things that stood out about Meredith," Janette said. "She always said the cure for the blues is gratitude. It works."

"I have some good news and some bad news," Kaylee said to Landry. He was just lighting the fire in his living room and she was sitting on the couch. He looked over his shoulder at her and lifted a brow. "The good news is I'm going to finish my book in four weeks."

"Good for you," he said.

"The bad news is, I'm going to have to get serious and hit it hard. I'm going to work at my house every day for at least six to eight hours a day until I can send it in. This book has been like a monkey on my back for over a year. I can't separate it from losing my mother so I have to finish it and send it away. And until I can get my writing back, a part of me is missing."

"That's not bad news, Kaylee. I'm glad you're going for it. If you wanted to give it up, I guess I'd understand, but I'm glad you want it back. It's who you are."

"Have you ever had trouble with your sculptures?" she asked. "Like when your dad passed away?"

"It was hard to concentrate then, for a little while. I can't remember how long it took for me to feel like myself again. But I'll tell you when I really choked. When I realized Laura was probably gone for good, I was disoriented. That's when I decided to move back here and concentrate on the one thing I had some control over—my work. It wasn't quick, either. And I spent a lot of time building the little house rather than being creative. But it all came back."

"Even with Laura's visits distracting you?"

"She didn't visit that often, but sometimes she'd call and ask me when my next visit to the city would be and she'd meet me there for a couple of days. I insisted on separate rooms and separate checks and so those visits were less frequent. Her visits to Virgin River were rare unless she needed something. Laura didn't have that big an impact on my work. If I was upset about her absence, working helped. If I was upset about her presence, working helped. So I know how you feel. We need it;

it defines us. Just tell me what I can do to help. Except don't tell me I have to ignore you 24/7. I won't be good at that."

"I will use you for my reward," she said, grinning.

They had not yet said those three magic words, but Kaylee felt them. She wasn't holding out, she was just getting comfortable. She wasn't sure what she was supposed to say after that. Let me stay here forever? No, that wasn't what she wanted. Come to Newport Beach with me? She didn't feel ready for that, plus he admitted he didn't like Southern California. How about I see you every couple of months? Oh, what was the point? That's what he'd had with Laura. That didn't sound like real love, it sounded like an inconvenient convenience.

"Did I mention I have a house in Newport Beach?" she asked him.

"Twenty or so times," he said.

"It's very nice," she said. "My mother had admired it for years, like twenty or so years. When her business started doing well the one thing she wanted was a house that would hold her tight, make her feel safe and comfortable till her last day. She didn't expect to be only sixty when that day came, but that's what it was. It has a large patio and backyard and pool. It has a view of the ocean, too bright at sunset so she put up custom outdoor shades. It's on a hill in a very nice neighborhood. It's not a huge house, but the rooms are generous. It was all hers, that was the important thing. It's beautiful and comfortable. Have you ever been to Newport Beach?"

"Can't say that I have," he said. Then with a curl of his lip he added, "I have some pretty negative impressions of my few visits to LA."

She remembered his telling of his feelings for LA, the place Laura wanted to be and didn't want him to join her there.

"I don't think I'm a Southern California kind of guy," he said.

She was glad she hadn't said, "But I love you! We should be together somewhere!"

"Let me take you to bed, Kaylee Sloan, and see if we can work up some book ideas when I rock you to sleep."

Which was as good an idea as any.

For a few days, Kaylee stuck to a very rigid schedule. She did take her walk with Otis, spent some time with Lady and the puppies, and took her laptop to Jack's, but when she saw that she'd only written a page the whole hour and a half she was at Jack's, she hustled back home. She worked as hard as possible but still was doing more rewriting than writing. She had wanted to have thirty pages after three days but she had nine. She redoubled her efforts.

Her book about Caroline and Landon, however, was growing. They had fallen in love and fallen in bed and it was delicious. That book made her heart sing; poor Caroline had been a lonely widow in need of a fresh start when she found Landon and her world was suddenly twirling. It was certainly reflective of Kaylee's experience, but she had learned it was also very like Mel's and Vanessa Haggerty's. She learned from Mel that Vanessa had been pregnant with her first child when her marine husband was killed in action, and Vanessa ended up marrying his best friend. Whew. And now they had five children.

Her autobiographical fiction was getting more fulfilling by the day and she wondered if she'd ever be brave enough to show it to anyone. She wasn't very confident of her ability in this women's fiction genre. But even though she was struggling, she knew what she was doing in suspense. She was surprised to find herself finally closing in on the end and called her editor.

"Simone, it's Kaylee," she said. "Are you in the middle of something?"

"Everything can wait for you! How are you? I think about you all the time!"

She used to talk to her editor at least every other week. They had a great rapport and had become friends. Kaylee had worked with her for eight years now and Simone was not her first editor.

"I'm in good shape, actually. I'm going to be sending you this manuscript before Christmas."

"So your getaway is paying off?"

"I love it here," she said. "In a perfect world I'd have a house in Newport and one up here, in the mountains." And she told Simone about the weather, the leaves, the giant trees, the Halloween party, the people she'd met and had developed friendships with like Mel, Jilly, Jack and Preacher. And eventually she told her about Landry. Before she knew it, they'd talked for an hour. "And there's this other thing," she said. "While I was having trouble getting into the book, I dabbled around a little bit on a different story. I was just doing it as an exercise, something to get me moving. And now that I've written quite a bit of it just for fun, I kind of like it."

"Do you want to tell me about it?"

"You know what I'd rather do?" Kaylee said. "I'd rather just send it to you. I think it's a romance, not a genre I know that much about. But you know romance and women's fiction very well. Maybe you could take a look and tell me what's missing."

"I'd be happy to."

"I'll concentrate on finishing the suspense as a priority. Am I still on the schedule for next fall?"

"Of course," Simone said. "But you know you have time if you need it. I don't want you to feel pressured. We can drop you out and put you back in a few months later, depending on how slammed we are. Kaylee, I don't want you to worry—you have a publisher and when a good writer has an emergency, we don't kick them when they're down. We're here to work with you."

"You've been so good that way. Please know how much I appreciate your patience and understanding."

"As long as you know how much we love publishing you."

Kaylee put in a tough week but produced forty pages that she liked, and the protagonist was getting closer to discovering that it was her photographer's jealous brother who was murdering models. But she was exhausted. At the end of a hard writing day her neck and shoulders ached. Sometimes Landry would give her a nice shoulder rub in the evening and revive her spirits.

They were sitting in front of his TV, the fire roaring against the cold night, when her phone rang. She looked at it and declined the call.

"I don't mean to be nosy, but you've done that a lot lately," he said.

"It's my father," she said. "I really don't feel like dealing with him now."

"Do you know why he's calling?" Landry asked.

"Yes. He's hoping we can get together sometime around the holidays. You know how I feel about the holidays."

"Like you wish they weren't happening," he said.

"Exactly. I know there's no avoiding them but I really don't want to try to add Howie to that stress."

Landry frowned. "Did he do something really traumatic that makes you want to avoid him at all costs?"

"He did absolutely nothing. Nothing at all," she said. "Can we just not talk about him?"

He gave her silky hair a soft stroke. "We won't talk about

it if you don't want to, but I'm here for you if you do. I'm a good listener. And I care."

"I know, that's very sweet."

"Because I love you, Kaylee."

She felt the tears begin to gather in her eyes. Then they spilled over and there was a catch in her voice when she said, "I love you, too."

"I'm no expert, but shouldn't that make us happy?"

"It does make me happy, but what about us? I came here to get away and try to ignore the whole Christmas thing, but then there's you and you live here and I live there and what's going to happen to us? I'm supposed to go home after Christmas. I want to be in my mother's house again but you don't like Southern California and I can't stay here, this isn't my home. I have a home. You have a home! What am I supposed to do? We haven't talked about—"

"Kaylee, you can do whatever you want to do. I know the landlord here. I can fix it for you to stay. Or go and come back. Literally anything that works for you."

"That's just it," she said. "I don't know what will work. I can't stay, I can't go. I can't ask you to come to Newport, we're not ready for that kind of commitment. I can't stay here much longer, I don't have my things around me. I'm only sure of one thing and it's huge. I want my mom to not have died!"

He pulled her close and held her for a moment. "I know," he said. "It's going to be all right. Just stick to your original plan. Get your book done and get through Christmas. Everything will look better on the other side."

"It would break my mother's heart to think I'm dreading Christmas. She always worked so hard to make it nice for me."

"I think she would understand, and I understand."

Landry didn't have any deadlines or pressing work—he wasn't showing anything and he sold some of his pots from his website, but he was ahead of schedule. Still, he kept mostly to his shop working and designing because he didn't want to get in Kaylee's space. After having a good cry, she'd snapped out of the blues for a while, but she was hard at work and a little more serious than usual.

She'd had a call from Bonnie Templeton and asked Landry if he wanted to go with her to see the house, so they drove across the mountain to the other side of Virgin River and he was the witness to an emotional reunion. Kaylee, whose feelings seemed to be on a trip wire, cried as she embraced her old friends. It took a little while to get it under control and then they walked through the house with Paul and Landry.

"You're going to want to start a list of things that aren't quite right or damaged or any imperfections you find," Paul said. "As far as I can tell, there's nothing to prevent you from staying here. Everything has been tested and passed inspection."

"I can't believe how beautiful it is," Bonnie said. "Better than when we originally bought it!"

"I think over the past twenty years it got a little run-down," Gerald said. "It was past due a little facelift, but I wasn't sure we were going to keep it."

"Were you thinking of selling it?" Kaylee asked.

"We'd always intended to keep it in the family," Bonnie said. "We thought the boys would want it, but they're undecided. They're scattered all over the place—two in California, one in Oregon, one in Arizona. They vacillate on whether they'll actually use it. Each family has other ideas, their own vacation spots, closer to where they live. We might keep it a couple more years, then sell it if it doesn't see much use."

"It'll be easier to sell in its current condition than before," Bonnie said. "I'd offer it to you for the rest of the year but I suspect you're settled where you are."

"I'm pretty comfortable," she said with a slight flush. "Plus, there are important dogs there."

"You? Dogs?" Bonnie said.

"She's come a long way," Landry said.

"Will you break away from the writing long enough to join us for dinner? I haven't been to Jack's since last summer."

"Sure," she said. "And he would love to see you."

Landry felt his phone buzz, pulled it out of his pocket and read a text. It was from Brie, asking him to come by her office at his earliest convenience.

"Kaylee, can you go with the Templetons to Jack's and I'll meet you there? I just got a text from a friend asking me to drop by. I shouldn't be long."

"Sure," she said. "Take your time."

Landry left while Kaylee and the Templetons continued to look at and praise the renovations on the house, much to Paul's satisfaction. Landry wasted no time texting Brie that he was on his way.

It had to have something to do with the divorce. It could all be over in no time. Surely Laura had signed off on it. They had agreed long ago, if one of them wanted to divorce, the other would not make it difficult. And they had no common property.

When he repeated that to Brie she said, "Oh, but you do. Any property you acquired during the marriage or jointly own is considered part of the divorce settlement."

"As I said, we don't have any jointly owned property."

"Don't you have a house? Land? Maybe a retirement account? Equipment that you use in your business?"

"It's not jointly owned. I inherited the house and land from my father a few years ago and Laura has never been a part of my business."

"It would very likely be considered part of the marriage

assets, since you're still married. Just as her assets would be considered part of the marriage assets."

"Unless she's keeping something from me, she doesn't have anything. In fact, I told you that over the years she's had to borrow money from me, not that I was fool enough to consider it a loan. I think Laura spends whatever she has when she gets paid and isn't much of a saver or investor. She lives well when she's working and not as well when she's not."

"Explain your situation to me again," Brie said. "You haven't lived together in ten years, you discussed divorce due to your separation eight years ago and agreed on the terms—"

"There were no terms," he said a little hotly. "I didn't have anything but my art supplies, she didn't have anything. We agreed we weren't going to live together. We were friendly and she visited sometimes."

"Define *sometimes*," Brie asked.

"I saw her three or four times a year. I haven't sent her monthly money or slept with her in eight years. I didn't support her. I gave her loans because she was short. I knew they weren't loans and I did it anyway."

"I received a very polite email from her lawyer that said she'd be happy with half of your house and land and support payments."

"She never lived in that house! I'll call her and get to the bottom of this!"

"As your attorney, I advise you not to make contact with her. She has an attorney, you have an attorney. I'll recommend mediation supervised by family court and you can lay it all out."

"And just because I didn't divorce her a long time ago, I'm going to lose my home and half my possessions?"

"I do think under the circumstances we'll get out better than that, but there's no question that now that lawyers are involved, it'll be more expensive. Listen, the law is the law and believe it or not it's written that way to protect the innocent. No-fault divorce means it doesn't matter who does what to who and community property is simply half or whatever can be negotiated. Right now, feeling like you're being robbed, you don't have much empathy, but this is meant to protect men or women from falling at the mercy of powerful spouses who want to turn their backs on their responsibilities. That is not your situation. So—we'll try mediation and fight it. Your marriage was over a long time ago."

"I'm still going to call her and ask her why she's doing this."

"If I were you I'd probably ignore my lawyer's advice and do that, too. Try very hard not to give her more ammo. Okay?"

Landry was so angry that he didn't wait long. He called Laura on his way to Jack's. Of course she didn't answer. Now that he thought about it, she rarely did. She almost always returned the call. On the other hand, if he saw that it was her and he wasn't in the middle of something important, he would answer. But clearly Laura's life was more important than his. To the voice mail he said, "I've just heard from my lawyer. My lawyer heard from your lawyer. So you're going to make this difficult and you're asking for half my father's property? Property that you visited maybe six times in as many years? Property that you never shared with me, but now you want it? What the hell is going on, Laura? We agreed years ago that we'd chosen to live separately and if the time for divorce came, there would be no altercation! This is altercation, my wife. I've given you patience, kindness, money, and now that I just want to end it, you're going to drag every dime you can get out of my kicking, screaming body? If you'd come to me and told me you need a little help… Haven't I always been willing to help you? But this—after you left me—"

By the time he got to Jack's, he could barely conceal his

cranky mood, though he tried. They had dinner and he hoped he'd come off as a little quiet but not much worse. Fortunately Bonnie and Gerald were talkative enough to cover his silence.

But on the way home, Kaylee said, "I get the feeling that something is wrong."

"It's nothing much," he said. "I'll fill you in later. Right now I'm stewing."

"I hope it's nothing I've done."

"Not at all," he said, reaching for her hand. "You're perfect."

When he and Kaylee went to bed, he turned off the ringer on his phone. He slept poorly, of course. He was consumed by the unfairness of it all. In the morning, he didn't look at his phone until they'd had breakfast and gone to their separate work spaces. Then he looked and saw there were six missed calls from Laura, the last one coming in at 1:00 a.m.

He was not fooled. He couldn't remember when she'd ever called him so late. She wanted to know if he was alone.

When he finally called her in the late morning, she actually answered.

"I take it you got my message," he said. "Do you want to explain what it is you're doing and why?"

"I just want a chance," she said softly. "I want you back. Obviously you're doing this because you have someone else now. And you know I know who that someone is."

"I'm not even going to respond to that," he said. "It's not relevant. I made a life for myself. I've lived alone for ten years, I built myself a house and a business and you took off to pursue your dream. I helped you. I gave you money when you were behind on rent or whatever. A couple of times I took out loans for money that you were never going to repay. If you think I'm going to buy my way out of a nonmarriage, you're crazy. I won't give up easily and I won't pay you off.

Damn you! I would have helped you, but you had to get a lawyer to fight me!"

"You said you'd always care about me."

"I'm not likely to care about a person who uses me. Taking what little I have, Laura? That's not generating a lot of goodwill. Think about it."

He disconnected and sat in his shop, seething. Eventually he got out his clay and began to sculpt. By midafternoon he was feeling better and he had the beginning of a small statue of an old man, then wondered what the significance of that was. He carved and shaped the old man's head with his loop and ribbon tools, wet it down with sponges, bent his stooped frame and added detail to the old man's shapeless sweater with modeling tools.

He heard his front door open and realized he'd pretty much used up almost a whole day. The sun was sinking. Kaylee came into the shop and he smiled at the sight of her. She was tired. And beautiful. He lifted his arm to her and she came to him, standing beside him.

"Wow, Landry, look what you've done. That's unbelievable. Someone you know?"

"Me, I think. In about forty years." Or four years, depending on the stress level in his life, he thought.

"It's magnificent," she said. "Oh, what I'd give for your talent."

"You don't need my talent. You have your own."

10

IN HER SUSPENSE NOVEL, THE MODEL-DETECTIVE
was being held captive by her photographer's jealous brother
and no one knew where she was or that she was missing—
a very stressful scene. In the other book, Caroline and Landon
were madly in love and couldn't keep their hands off each
other, kind of like another couple Kaylee knew intimately,
but Caroline and Landon were having a little trouble in one
department—they didn't know where they were going as a
couple. Or if.

Kaylee was getting her contracted book closer to the end
but she was addicted to her love story. Both her own and her
fiction.

There was a knock at her door and she wondered what time
it was. She hardly ever wore a watch; looking at her computer
she saw it was only three. It was not likely to be Landry. He

respected her work time and space to a fault. He waited for her to come to him.

She opened the door and there stood her father. "Howie, what are you doing here?"

He winced. "I wanted to see you," he said.

"I'm on a deadline here!"

"I know that. I also know you'd say that even if you weren't. Look, this is my problem and not yours, but you've been putting me off for months. I know we both miss your mother terribly. I thought maybe we could lean on each other a little bit. I'll do whatever it takes to make amends, Kaylee. We're family."

She turned from the door and walked into her house. She picked up Tux and held him close. "You have more family than you know what to do with."

"I have two ex-wives, both have remarried, but I'm working on mending things with my kids as best I can. It's not the same with them, though. They didn't lose their mother, for one thing. They don't really need me and I don't blame them, but I'm trying. I see them, at least."

"You should," she said. "But Howie, I don't say this to be cruel, but I don't really need you, either. Not that you're such a bad guy, it's just that you were never there for me before. I got over the fantasy of having a daddy a long time ago."

Howard had three other children. Two with his second wife—they were now in their twenties and one was engaged to be married. There was a third child, also a daughter, with his third wife. She was in college. Kaylee didn't keep up with them and they hadn't made any efforts to have a relationship with her.

"You've made that pretty clear. I'm going to keep trying. With you and with them. I've wasted enough time."

She sat down on her couch. "Do you have a terminal disease or something?" she asked.

"What a thing to say!" he said.

"Not to be mean, but it's like you never worried about your relationship with me until my mom was literally dying. What's the deal?"

"Kaylee! I care about you very much. I wasn't such a good dad after your mother and I divorced, but I still cared. And I came around when I could." He stepped farther into the room. "May I sit?"

"You should have called," she said. "How did you find me?"

"I called the Templetons," he said. And he sat. "Bonnie told me where you were staying, though she didn't have an address. I had your landlord's name. The guy at the bar in town gave me directions."

"Well, that's good for security," she muttered.

"I hope you're not unsafe. Do you feel safe here?" he asked.

"Of course, or I would be somewhere else."

It was obvious why Howard had had so many wives and girlfriends and girlfriends who became wives. He was a good-looking man. He had a full head of silver-and-black hair, was sixty-five, very fit, and about six-foot-two. He was tan from hours on the golf course. He was still working as an account executive for what was once a phone company and was now a "communications corporation" that produced everything from wireless services to cell phones.

"I know the holidays are especially hard for you," he said. "They are for me, too."

"Why so?" she asked. "You and my mom haven't had a holiday together for thirty years."

"There was the last one," he said. "We weren't exactly together, but I was there almost every day at the end."

She almost said *too little too late*, but stopped herself. "Just out of curiosity, why were you there so much at the end?"

"Kaylee, I loved your mother," he said. "She forgave me for hurting her. And I couldn't let you go through that alone. I was worried about you."

"You loved her?" she said, but her lip curled.

"And she loved me in her own way. We mended our fences the best we could. I hurt her very badly and my apology came far too late but believe me, it didn't take all that long for me to realize that giving her up was the biggest mistake I ever made. I just didn't come to that realization in time to make a difference. But despite that, after some years and the fact that I hadn't done anything to improve my life by marrying and divorcing, we had formed a nice friendship. Talking to your mom... Even though we'd never again be a couple, I loved talking to your mom. She was brilliant and funny and probably the strongest woman I've ever known."

"Which begs the question...why?"

"Why other women?" he asked. "Your mother said I had a weak ego. I suspect she was right. I never tired of having beautiful women tell me how fantastic I was, even when I knew it was a lie and I'd regret it."

"Yeah, she said you had half a brain," Kaylee said.

"I'm not entirely stupid," he said, straightening his spine. "Not entirely."

She smirked and just shook her head. He was pitiful. He lost the most wonderful woman in the world because he liked being flattered by pretty women. He was quite successful in business, at least in his forties and fifties, but he was clearly an idiot who thought with his little man.

"Your mother, on the other hand, was incredible. The way she started that business from practically nothing and made it into one of the best furniture companies in the area. You must be so proud of her."

"I didn't pay that much attention to it at the time, to be honest. It was patio furniture. And it ate up so much of her time. I didn't realize until right before she got sick how much she'd achieved, and against all odds. Once I understood, I did tell her how much I admired her. But I admired her for so many things. She was a good person. She had great compassion. She was always kind. She cared about people in a genuine way. She forgave you!"

"How are you going to spend the holidays, Kaylee?" he asked. She noticed that he was a little misty-eyed.

"I'm going to write, lie low, let it pass. I really need to get through Christmas, and then maybe in a year or two I can endure it again. Last Christmas was the worst day of my life."

"What about Thanksgiving? Have you made any plans?"

"Sort of," she said. "My landlord and I have become good friends and he's alone, too. We talked about maybe getting some fresh seafood in Eureka and having the meal together. Also, knowing I'm alone, the cook at the bar in town said I'm welcome to join them. I guess they cook for their families at the bar and keep space open for anyone who wanders by. He says no one goes hungry in Virgin River on Thanksgiving and he prepares a feast. I am going to help the local midwife with her charity baskets—just a couple of afternoons of stuffing them full of food and helping to deliver them before Thanksgiving."

Then she got a little melancholy. "Last Thanksgiving is a holiday I never want to forget. It was the best ever."

"I don't remember anything about it," he said.

"You weren't there," she said with a laugh. "Mom had given up on the chemo, had some pain meds, was feeling pretty good, and we had a girl party. Mom was too weak to put the meal together, but she felt good enough to eat and enjoy the day. She even had a little champagne. It was Janette, Michelle, Korby, Maggie and Terri. We had a blast. We had a pajama party. Lots of food, everyone but Mom had lots of drinks. We played cards, ate desserts, watched movies." She was quiet for a moment. "We talked about all the best old times. Memory gathering."

"I know Janette and Michelle," he said.

"Korby, Maggie and Terri are my friends—one writer, one florist, one teacher. They all ditched their families for the day, knowing it would be Mom's last Thanksgiving. And instead of being dark or sad, it was awesome. I didn't sleep that night, even though I had a full stomach. I just wanted to be with her till the sun came up. She did great. She totally had a good time. A few days after that she began sinking. Her last three weeks were pretty hard. You remember."

"I remember."

She stroked Tux. "She wanted to talk about it and I wouldn't let her."

"What do you mean?" he asked.

"Oh, she said things like, 'You know, when I'm gone, you should...' And I would cut her off and say, but you're not going, so don't say that. I kept begging her to be positive, to fight it. But she had been fighting it and didn't have any more fight in her. I wish I could have let her talk. Who knows what she had to get off her chest?"

"Don't worry about that, Kaylee. I think she was at peace. She told me she'd been proud of her life, that it was a good life, that she had very few regrets. And why should she have regrets? She was nearly perfect." He glanced at the kitty she was holding. "Is that the stray you found?"

"Tux," she said. "He's not the only one I found. I found a dog and her four puppies tied up in the woods not far from here. My neighbor is a part-time trainer and has a kennel and lots of supplies so she's over there, her puppies safe from predators. I go visit with her; we call her Lady. She's very well behaved and there's just no reason for a person to treat her that way."

"I'm impressed; you always avoided animals."

"Not all animals, but I was always scared around big dogs. Especially big dogs I didn't know, until I rented a little house from a dog trainer. He helped me get past my fear. When I found Lady, my heart melted. I'm thinking of keeping her."

"I worry about you being alone out here," he said.

"Actually, one of the reasons I came up here to finish the book is because people were dropping in at Mom's house all the time. Friends, neighbors, even the UPS guy came to the door to see how I was doing. If I didn't have someone drop in, the phone was ringing. Add that to living in my mom's house and I couldn't escape the overpowering grief—it never left me. I fell asleep to it at night and woke up to it in the morning. I'm anxious to get home, but even though I sorted through Mom's things and gave a lot of stuff away, I'm afraid it'll be just too familiar again. It's a very contradictory feeling—don't want it to go away, I don't want it to be so constant in my life. It can be overpowering."

"Why don't you make some changes?" he suggested.

"I've thought about that," she said. "I feel like I'm cheating on her. She loved that house and decorated it from floor to ceiling."

He shook his head. "That house should reflect your taste. Maybe a few choice things to remind you of Meredith tossed in. You should hire one of her decorator friends to help you. I can help with the cost, if you need me to."

"It's not necessary. I have what I need. And the house is mine now."

"Then if you find the memories aren't letting you move forward, you can always sell it."

"I know. I do love the house, I just loved it better when my mom was in it."

"I feel the same," he said. "Sometimes I drive by to look at it because I miss her."

"Just out of curiosity, when did you realize you missed her so much?"

He chuckled, but it wasn't an amused chuckle. "It didn't take me too long to realize I'd made a mistake in leaving my marriage to your mother. It took a long time beyond that for her to decide she didn't hate me for it. My second marriage was difficult and my third was a freak show. The kids seem to be good and well-adjusted in spite of that. Those marriages were supposed to make everything better, but they only served one purpose—to make me realize what a fool I'd been. Why do men who have everything blow it off and lose it all? When you can answer that one, you should write it up and charge a million dollars for it."

"Weak ego?" she suggested.

"Half a brain?" he said. And they both laughed.

They spent another hour talking about Meredith, what a comfort she was to each of them. Over the years, Howard continued to talk to her about his business problems or work frustrations. But never his family problems. "She flatly refused to listen to any of that. She said I had made my bed and I should lie in it." And she never mentioned any romantic problems of her own because, as she told him, that was not his concern. "But at least we were friends."

Kaylee talked about how encouraging her mother had always been, how supportive when she wanted to change careers from something as stable as teaching to something as unreliable as writing fiction. "But she always encouraged me to take a chance. That's what she had done with her business."

It was growing late in the day when he said, "Is there any hope we can have a closer relationship?"

"I don't know, Howie. Like I said, it's been a long time since I fantasized about having a daddy."

"Where would we have to start?" he asked. "Because I'm willing to do whatever it takes."

"I don't think we can recapture that father-daughter thing now. You just don't know what it's like."

"Tell me, Kaylee."

"I'm not sure you really mean that," she said with a rueful laugh.

"I do mean it. Tell me where I failed you."

She shook her head. "I don't think you can possibly understand. Try to picture your six-year-old daughter whose daddy is coming to pick her up. She's in her favorite outfit and even has a purse, and of course that stuffed rabbit that went everywhere with her." Kaylee paused for a moment and took a deep breath before continuing. "I sat on the chair in the foyer for what seemed like hours. You didn't come." She shook her head sadly.

"You took me to your new house when I was about ten and there were so many people there, I sat on the sofa until it was time to go. Your wife wanted me to call her Mom; your mother-in-law wanted me to call her Mimi. I'd never met them before and they had a big fight in the kitchen before we left. Then there was the father-daughter dance when I was in junior high. You weren't available for that. I spent most of my childhood either waiting for you or being stood up by you."

He frowned. "I remember going to your house to see you on a regular basis," he said. "I walked you down the aisle at your wedding."

"Most of the time if you came over I would go watch a movie in my room and you and my mom would talk in the kitchen. As for the wedding, thank you for that. And thank you for not bringing your third wife."

"You must feel you never really had a father…"

"No, what I felt was that I had a father and my father left us. I'm sorry if you were unhappy, but I learned at an early age that I couldn't make you happy. And Howie, I'm having a little trouble being happy right now myself. So if you're counting on me to make you happy now…?" She shook her head. "My mother asked me to be kind to you because despite all evidence to the contrary, you love me."

"I do. And I think there's hope for us. Maybe down the road a bit. I'm going to keep trying."

"Maybe. But I can't help you with your grief over losing my mother because my own grief is just so heavy."

"If there's any way I can help you, will you tell me?"

"Of course. Thank you for asking. But I need to be alone to finish my book now."

The Monday before Thanksgiving, Mel called Kaylee to remind her about putting together the charity baskets. At that precise moment Kaylee felt like she should stay home and write like the wind to get her book finished. She was close and it was finally going quickly. But she liked Mel and didn't want to let her down.

When she got to the bar, she saw an assembly the likes of which she had never seen before. The tables were all lined up against the walls, forming a big circle around the room. In the center of the room were boxes and boxes of groceries. Huge boxes of groceries. The place was full of men and women, mostly women, many of them she knew or recognized. Jilly and her sister Kelly, Vanessa Haggerty, Paige Middleton. She saw the pastor's wife, Ellie Kincaid, and Nora Cavanaugh, the wife of a local orchard owner. There were also a few townsfolk she'd met, Connie from the store and a couple of the Riordan men. And Mel was standing at the center of the room, barking orders.

"We have lists of what goes in each box. Some of our families have six kids, some are widows or solitary men, and we've stocked their boxes accordingly. We have turkeys and hams, cooked and frozen, and the rest is nonperishable. Take a list, fill a box, and check it off my master list. And Vanessa and Paige have made plates of cookies and bars and those are a sweet treat for us! Let's do it."

Mel saw Kaylee and came over and gave her a hug. "I'm hoping you'll come with me to do a little delivering, some today and some tomorrow," she said.

"How many boxes will you fill?"

"Oh, I think fifty. At least as many as we can."

"Is the poor population so high around here?"

"No, it's not too bad. But we do have working families who feel the strain and we want to help them as well. The very poor get assistance from the county, but it's never quite enough."

Mel handed her a list and she got to work. She wrote the name of the recipient on the side of the box and began to gather the groceries. She learned that Jack and Colin Riordan had gone to one of the big box stores on the coast and filled up their truck beds with supplies. And the gift boxes weren't limited to food—they also had soap, toothpaste, feminine hygiene products, diapers, baby wipes, bleach and shampoo.

While she was loading the boxes with essentials, Kaylee became profoundly aware that all her life, even in the leanest of times, she had always had what she needed. Her mother, a single mom, had managed not only to feed and house Kaylee, but there were also lots of those special things. A new outfit for a party, a day at Disneyland every now and then, a prom dress, a wedding. They'd never received a box of food over the holidays because they were in need.

And she made a silent pledge to remember that Howard had contributed to her well-being and education, which had been costly. She might have a grudge because he left, but he had been there with the checkbook when it counted.

Of course, the women were all talking and laughing. She got Vanessa's recipe for lemon bars and fudge; Ellie started them singing Christmas carols and oddly enough, Kaylee survived a little Christmas spirit. The men were joking around, making the women laugh or scold them. And the thing that Kaylee noticed most was the affection that passed between these couples. Even the preacher leaned close to Ellie to give her a little squeeze and kiss on the cheek. Every couple, it seemed, took a moment for a touch or a hug or a whisper. As if they were all still madly in love.

Kaylee realized that's what she wanted. Not just a boyfriend or lover. She wanted a future. Permanence. Something that lasted and endured. She wondered if that was even possible.

Preacher put out a buffet of sandwiches and salads and the women took breaks to eat and chat. Kaylee heard about the kids, how they were doing in school, what they wanted for Christmas, how the local football teams had done this year. A couple of women were knitting and talking while others were eating. A great stack of big boxes was lined up in the middle of the floor, ready to go.

After lunch, some of the men began carrying them out.

"Kaylee, would you like to come with me?" Mel asked.

"That would be great, since I don't really know my way around these mountains yet," she said.

"I'm going to deliver five, as long as I can get them all out before dark. And I'll do it again tomorrow."

They bundled up against the cold and once they were in Mel's SUV, Kaylee asked who paid for the food baskets. "We take donations. We've been passing the hat since spring. Whenever we have a town party, Jack puts out a jar just for holiday food baskets and it's amazing how well we do."

"Can I make a donation?" Kaylee asked.

"We will never turn down money!"

They drove out of town to a tiny isolated house in the mountains. The road to the house was not well kept or smooth and inside the little house they found an old man wearing long johns on the outside of his jeans. "Well, aren't you looking good, Cyrus," Mel said.

"You're looking mighty good, too, miss."

"And how have you been feeling?"

"Just fine, ma'am, thank you."

"I'm going to put this right on your table and you can go through it. Is there anything you need? You need a doctor or a pastor?"

"No, ma'am." He laughed. "I don't wanna see both of 'em at once, that's for sure. That usually means bad news."

"How's your firewood holding out?"

"Plenty good."

Those same questions were asked everywhere they went. There was a young woman with three small children in a small house out on the ridge, no man in sight. There was an elderly couple in the lower valley in a little weather-worn house with a barn behind it. There was a family with four children near Highway 36. And their last delivery was to a mother and daughter—the mother was in her eighties and the daughter in her sixties and they occupied a very small, very old house that was scrubbed clean as a whistle even though the wallpaper was peeling and the linoleum was cracked.

Kaylee felt good down to her toes to be doing some good

for others and said so to Mel once they were finished their deliveries.

"It usually gets everyone stirred up and ready for the holidays. Have you decided what you are doing about Thanksgiving dinner yet?" Mel asked. "We have room at the table in the bar if you're interested."

"I'll be cooking and eating with Landry," she said. "The two of us are alone out there and he's going to drive over to Eureka and poke around the seafood market."

"Fantastic," Mel said. "And what about Christmas? You'll still be around here then, won't you?"

"Yes, I'll be leaving after Christmas."

"And do you have plans for Christmas? Do you know about our tree?"

"No, I don't believe I do."

"We put up a huge tree in the center of town and decorate it with military unit patches that we've been collecting for years. Some of the guys chop it down, put it up—it usually falls down at least once in the process and they do a better job of putting it up after that. Jack rents a cherry picker so he can string tinsel and hang lights and ornaments, and half the town turns out to watch because there's a lot of swearing and a lot of laughing. But it is always a magnificent tree. We have to borrow a flatbed truck from Paul Haggerty to bring it out of the forest." Mel grinned. "You should put bows around the necks of those puppies and display them around the tree at Christmas."

"Will they be ready?" Kaylee asked. "They have to be eight weeks and get their first shots, right?"

"Something like that. So, will you be having Christmas dinner with Landry? We would love to have you both if you don't have other plans."

Kaylee sighed. "I haven't made any commitments for

Christmas Day. To be honest, I'm not looking forward to it. I'll probably lie low. Maybe read a good book. Or take a couple of long walks. I knew for sure I didn't want to be in my mother's house on that day."

"Is this because of your mother's passing?" Mel asked.

"Yes, I'm afraid so. I'm doing much better with that, however. I think it's because of my new experiences and new friends in Virgin River."

"I hate to think of you alone on Christmas Day. Wouldn't it take your mind off things to be with friends?"

"It's complicated," she said. "My mom was very sick. We had Hospice care the last weeks of her life. And she died on Christmas Day." She was quiet a moment. "I just don't know how I can manage Christmas. I don't know how I can face it."

"Oh, Kaylee, how difficult that must be. Think about what I can do to help," Mel said. "Anything that would make you happy or even just take your mind off the sadness of the experience. Maybe it would be a good day to celebrate her life. I bet she didn't die in sadness."

"She definitely did not," Kaylee said. "She was never afraid and never angry and God knows she had enough morphine in her to make the passage smooth. But that was the day I lost my best friend and I'll never get her back."

Mel was quiet for a moment. When she pulled into the bar parking lot next to Jack's truck, she asked, "Have you had some counseling, Kaylee?"

"Yes, right after she died, for several months. I'm not sure it helped."

"But this will take time. Of course it will take time. I'm not a religious person but I bet your mother is not very far away. I bet she's your guardian angel. I bet she helps put the right people all around you so that you can feel her love even from a distance."

Kaylee smiled. "Sure," she said.

Mel patted her hand. "I'm never sure of the right thing to say. But knowing you a little bit now, I believe you'll get through this difficult year and find joy again."

"That might take a miracle," Kaylee said.

"Miracles happen around here all the time. It will come, I'm sure of it. As your world gets bigger than your grief. Anything I can do to help, just say the word."

"Thank you, Mel."

"Don't thank me yet," she said. "Will you help us again tomorrow?"

"Absolutely! It was a very good day."

Landry did ask Jack if his help was needed in the filling and transporting of holiday food boxes, but Jack said, "We're good. If you come around, you get cookies, but we're covered."

So instead, Landry made an appointment to speak with Brie.

"I've been thinking. Do you have any suggestions as to how I can move forward on this divorce with the least difficulty?"

"Have you talked to Laura? Do you have any inside knowledge as to why she'd hire a lawyer and ramp up her settlement demands?"

"I did talk to her. She said she wanted another chance with our marriage, but that's out of the question. Especially now that she's trying to hold me hostage."

"Well, the fastest and least cumbersome way is to offer her half the value of your property. I don't think that's the smartest way, but it is probably the quickest."

"That wouldn't leave me in a very safe place," he said. "I owe money on the house and land. I took out a mortgage so I could 'loan' her money."

"Do you have records of those transactions?"

He reached for the papers in the inside pocket of his jacket and passed them to Brie. "Here's what I have. I never asked Laura to sign a loan document, but here are copies of checks I made out to her and I did write 'loan' in the notes section. I'm emotionally tied to the property. I grew up there. It was all my father had when he died. He had a pension from the communications company he worked for, which is a fancy name for a phone and cable company. My dad was a hardworking cable man. I can pull together some money, if it would help. I can get a loan using my property as collateral."

"Help what, Landry? Get the divorce settled?"

"Yes, before I hate her. I should have done it years ago, when I realized she'd chosen something else over our marriage. I should have done it when my net worth was a bunch of pots and a kiln. I should have done it before my father passed away. I thought she was as unmotivated as I was but I think I was naive. She asked me for money quite often. She said she wouldn't contest or argue against a divorce, but here she is asking for money."

"I could find out from her attorney what it would take to end it on good terms," Brie said. "If they want to go the distance, we can take your case to the mediator. Usually abandonment factors in the bottom line. She left you. She never lived with you after that. She might only be successful in getting half of your net worth at the time of separation and nothing more…"

"It wouldn't be much," he said. "I'm a pack rat. A tidy pack rat, but I have all the old tax returns and bank statements. I'm self-employed; I kept very good records."

"Let me give it a go."

"I think that would be a good idea," he said. "Thank you."

11

KAYLEE HELPED WITH THE HOLIDAY BASKETS ON
the Wednesday before Thanksgiving and again it brought her
great pleasure. Her mother used to always say, *Feeling a little
sorry for yourself? Do something nice for someone else. Particularly
someone you don't know. That will put you right.* She hadn't done
it intentionally but it never failed to be completely true. And
it wasn't a case of seeing people who had it worse and thus
making her feel better. It was about giving. Her mother was
right. Giving fed the soul.

When she got home, she fed her kitty and then went straight
to Landry's house. She found him in the shop, working on his
sculpture. "Did you go to Eureka and get seafood?"

He grinned at her. "Shouldn't you kiss me before you ask
if I've done my chores?"

She hopped right into his arms and kissed him long enough and lovingly enough to convince him of her gratitude.

"Can I see it?" she asked.

"First we have something important to do. Go pet your dog and then I have somewhere to take you. I have something to show you."

"What?"

"A surprise. You're going to like it. Let's not waste a lot of time with you trying to figure it out."

"I'm not that crazy about surprises."

"No arguing for once!" he said. "If you don't like this one I promise I'll never do it again!"

"Fair enough," she said, running out to the kennel to check on Lady. The new mother was looking so good. She'd filled out, her coat was clean and shiny and thick, her puppies were getting big and playful. Lady looked to be a yellow Lab with the most beautiful American head, a long sleek nose, and deep, soulful brown eyes. Kaylee learned all this by looking through a lot of Landry's books about dogs. When Lady saw Kaylee she seemed to smile. She wagged her tail and shook off four puppies and went directly to Kaylee, putting her face right against Kaylee's face.

"I'm happy to see you, too, but I hear there's a surprise of some kind. Such a pretty girl; such a good girl. You have to stay here. I'll see you later. Stay."

Kaylee ran back to Landry. "Okay, let's do this. I'm so hungry I could eat a horse."

"There could be food involved in this surprise," he said.

"I hope so."

She told him about her day of delivering food boxes with Mel as he drove right through Virgin River. "We're not going to Jack's?" she asked.

"Not this time," he said. "Haven't you had enough of Jack's after the last two days?"

"Probably, but did I mention I'm starving?"

"A time or ten," he said, laughing at her.

Just a few minutes later they pulled up to the Templetons' house.

"What the heck, are the Templetons back in town?"

He parked his truck right in the driveway. "Why don't we have a look?" he said. "This is your surprise. Go ring the bell. I'm right behind you."

"You're so cute," she said. "What a nice surprise. They must be here for Thanksgiving and you set this up."

She ran up the stone walk to the front door and rang the bell, but it wasn't a Templeton who answered. It was Janette. "Well, hello, cookie," she said. Right behind her was Korby. "Hey, girlfriend." And crowding in were Michelle, then Terri and Maggie. And then there was a group hug and of course, tears.

"Oh my God, my God, my God, what are you doing here? You're here, you're here," Kaylee exclaimed. She couldn't stop crying.

"We're going to have a replay of last Thanksgiving, our last one all together and one of the best ever!" Janette said.

"But how did you get this house?" she asked.

"I got a call from Bonnie Templeton and she said it was all arranged. There's not quite enough room at your place, so we needed something larger. This place is great! I may never leave."

"But your families?" Kaylee asked, wiping the tears from her cheeks.

"Everyone is taken care of," Janette said. "It was a little last-minute, but sometimes the girl squad has to step in and make it happen. Now, don't you be expecting a reunion every year, but this was a good idea."

"I'm blown away," Kaylee said. "Wait! Where's Landry?" She pulled out of her girlfriends' arms and saw his back as he was leaving.

"Hey, you!" Janette called. "Where do you think you're going?"

He turned and waved. "You girls have a good party. I'll get Kaylee's bag."

"I have a bag?" she said to Janette.

"I asked him to throw a few overnight things together for you. Anything he missed I'm sure one of us has. But don't you let him get away. He doesn't have to sleep over but he stocked the place with food for us and he's very cute so he stays to eat. And I won't hear any argument."

"You won't hear one from me," Kaylee said.

When Landry handed over her small duffel, she said, "You have to stay. At least through dinner."

"And come back for the feast tomorrow," Michelle said. "You can be our mascot."

"I should probably be your chaperone," he said.

And there was a loud pop as the champagne was opened in the kitchen. Six women shouted, "Woo!"

Landry flipped burgers on the grill for the sisterhood, who put together the side dishes. It was cold and dark outside and he stood alone, but the women were not far away and he thrilled in hearing the talk and the laughter. They got a fire going in the big stone fireplace right away and lit candles all around the great room. "Be careful of those," he heard Kaylee say. "This place already burned down once." He chuckled and shook his head. She was pretty bossy. He loved it.

Janette had contacted him. She'd had a call from Howard

Sloan, Kaylee's father. He wondered what it would take to bring all of Meredith's friends together for Thanksgiving for Kaylee. Janette then called Landry and the Templetons and of course she called the tribe together. Only Korby had kids around for Thanksgiving and her husband happily agreed to take them to his parents' house for the holiday. Janette's kids were married and spent their holiday with in-laws, so it all fell together. She had explained the plans a half-dozen times as he scribbled notes because there was no way he'd remember everything.

Then Janette texted him a shopping list. All she really needed him to do was buy that seafood in Eureka, but he'd done much more. Every one of them threw extra groceries into their cars. All of them lived on the West Coast; they met at Janette's and drove up in three cars, packed to the brim with food, drink, extra blankets and their bags. They also brought poker chips, cards, board games and a five-thousand-piece jigsaw puzzle.

"We may not get to it all, but there is a diversion for everyone," Janette announced with a smile.

They set the table in the dining room, put the sides of deviled eggs, a relish tray, baked potato slices and condiments on the table, and sat down to eat together through laughter, teasing, poking and praising. Landry sat next to Kaylee and all through dinner he learned how Kaylee and Meredith had been both mother and daughter as well as the best of friends, but they each had these other units of friends closer to them in profession or interest and certainly age. And then over time the groups had blended. Now they were a group that ranged in age from thirty-five to sixty-five. They were all healthy, energetic, scary smart and hilarious. And also very insightful.

He realized he had never seen Laura in a group like this. When Laura was in a group, she was the center of attention.

She held court. It was a struggle to get to know the others because she dominated them.

But in this group of friends, who were all gathered to remember Meredith, there were many differences and yet complete equality. They bounced off each other so nicely. Korby was a little loud and the most hilarious, though they were all funny to some degree. Terri was a middle school teacher and the bossy one.

Janette had been Meredith's closest friend since high school. She'd been a teacher who transformed herself into a counselor, was part of a small counseling practice, and frequently worked for the county in the school district. She was divorced, her children were grown and she lived alone. There was something about her that made her the leader. The others seemed to defer to her in a way that suggested she held the wisdom card. And it became clear right away that she was fiercely independent.

"How is John?" someone asked her.

"He's good," she said. "He's working a lot but he's spending Thanksgiving with his son and daughter and their kids. These patchwork families manage to piece together one way or another."

"You two aren't living together yet?" Kaylee asked. "Haven't you been a couple for years?"

"Six years," Janette said. "But we've both already had spouses and kids and we're a little set in our ways. Honestly, I'm not looking for someone to share a house with, I just want someone to share a life with. Our arrangement is very satisfactory. We do spend a few nights a week together. And he's a great travel companion."

"I want a man with a tool belt to move in with me as soon as possible," Michelle said, making them all laugh.

"That sounds good, but every time I consider the prospect

of being lonely in my house, one of my adult children moves home for a while, usually with kids and dogs," Janette said.

"You mean when they leave, they don't stay gone?" Terri asked. "So, you're saying counting the days till the empty nest is a waste of time?"

"Even I only lived with my mom when I was between apartments, or when she was sick. We liked our own space, yet we were very close," Kaylee said.

The dinner conversation went that way for an hour until someone finally said, "What about you, Landry? Do you have family? Ex or otherwise? Kids?"

He cleared his throat as if he might be giving a speech. "I was an only child who was raised by my father and my parents are both deceased. No kids but a soon to be ex wife."

"Really?" Terri said.

"You're going through a divorce?" Korby asked.

"Yes. But we haven't lived together for years. I was just too busy or preoccupied to do the paperwork. Same for her, I guess." He lifted his drink and peered at Kaylee. He hadn't mentioned any of his plans to her. "It's all just a formality now."

"Tell us about your ex," someone said.

"You don't have to unless you want to," Kaylee said reassuringly.

"I don't mind. Laura is a very interesting person. She's an actress who has been chasing the limelight for years."

"She's the most beautiful woman I've ever seen," Kaylee said.

"You've actually met her?" Janette asked.

"I went to one of the town fairs where Landry was showing his work, and who should stop by but his wife!" Kaylee said.

"She was auditioning for a play in San Francisco," he explained. "She came by because it was close. I hadn't seen her in almost a year. We've managed to maintain a friendly relationship. We'll see how that goes now that I've actually filed for divorce. I'm told that sometimes the most agreeable couples find a lot to fight about during a divorce."

"That would seem logical," Korby said.

That opened up the table conversation to divorces. Only two of the women were still married and two had never been married. Landry was much happier talking about someone else's divorce.

There was more conversation around the table but they left Landry alone, except for the occasional question about his work or his dog training. When they started to clean up, they refused to let him help, but he hung out in the kitchen anyway.

This was not what he expected, this band of women who all knew each other so intimately, drawing him in and making him feel almost like family. He liked each one of them and also liked them as a group. It was a great idea, doing this Thanksgiving almost like a tribute to Meredith.

When people started staking out their places in the great room after a big meal, he pulled Kaylee aside and said, "Time for me to go. Walk me out?"

She grabbed their coats. Landry thanked everyone for the meal and conversation and said good-night, and he and Kaylee stepped outside. Once they stood on the porch, he opened his jacket so she could step inside, pressed against him. He closed his jacket around her.

"That was the best surprise I've ever had. Did you plan it?"

He shook his head. "You should get the details from Janette. She called me, but it didn't originate with her."

"Really? This should be interesting."

"Kiss me like you're going to miss me tonight," he said. "We hardly ever spend a night apart anymore."

She accommodated him, stretching up onto her toes, arms

around his neck. He didn't wonder if she'd miss him for long. It was so good to see her happy.

When she was back on her heels, she looked up at him. "I didn't know about the divorce."

"I didn't want to bother you with it," he said. "It's not really about you, not because of you or even my feelings for you, which are pretty hot, by the way. It is true that when I found myself with a woman like you in my house and in my bed, it begged the question, why the hell am I legally married?" He ran a knuckle along her cheek. "But no matter what happens with us, I'm ready to cut ties with Laura."

"She still loves you, Landry."

"No, she doesn't," he said. "She loves me when it's convenient. That's a pretty poor excuse to stay married."

"But do you love her?"

"Sure," he said immediately. "At least, I hold the memory of a love I had for her. But it's way different from what I feel for you." He kissed her softly. "Have fun tonight. I'll see you tomorrow."

By the time Kaylee went back inside, the women had all changed into their pajamas or lounging night wear. A couple of logs had been added to the fire and a few of them had fresh drinks or mugs of tea. They were scattered about the room on couches and chairs.

"Well," she said. "Did you like him?"

"He's adorable," Janette said.

"He seems very sweet," Maggie said. "If you aren't keeping him, I could get to know him better."

"I haven't made up my mind about that yet," Kaylee said, plopping down on the couch. "He told me this reunion wasn't his idea."

"No, it wasn't, but he was very cooperative," Janette said.

"Actually, it was Howard who set it up. He called me and asked if I could round up some of the girls. He talked to the Templetons and arranged to borrow the house for us. He offered to pay for everyone's transportation and for the food for the holiday. In the end, no one wanted or needed his offer of money, but I think it's worth acknowledging—he did this for you."

"He came to visit me a couple of weeks ago," Kaylee said. "He really wants us to work on having a father/daughter relationship. He's pestering me to death. I just don't know what to do with him."

"He's trying, Kaylee," Michelle said. "Do you really want to be so angry with him?"

"Nah, not really," she said. "But he's let me down so often. I don't want to trust him to be there for me and be let down again."

"This is a whole new Howard," Janette said. "In fact, he became a whole new Howard a long time ago. Remember, I've known him since he and your mother were engaged. He had a short attention span, thought only about himself, was fixated on making sure he was deliriously happy all the time, and was easily bored. And let's be honest, doing nice things for others was never one of his gifts. But he's changed. I guess I noticed the change about the time I was going through my divorce—for the first time since I've known him he became kind and caring. He was always charming, that's how he racked up so many conquests. But he went beyond charm and began to act as though he actually cared about people. He was very supportive of me when Carl left me and I was in a bad way, at least briefly. I think it was all his failed marriages and relationships. It took its toll. I think he took stock of his losses."

"He really started acting wounded when my mom got sick," Kaylee said.

"We all noticed that," Terri said.

"But it was about the time you graduated from college that he began to change. He was married for the third time and it wasn't going well. You weren't around that much. You were busy with your job, then Dixon, then your divorce—you know. Life. And he started visiting with Meredith more, talking to her more. They went out to dinner now and then. Not a lot, but a few times. She said he was a little lost. Don't get me wrong, she didn't feel sorry for him or anything. But she said that underneath it all he was a good man. She also said they would never be anything but friends and even that was a miracle.

"And she said he really cared about you," Janette added. "But you were a stubborn girl, just like your mom. You said that was fine, that he cared. A little late, but what the hell."

"Yeah, I was not impressed," Kaylee said. "She asked me to be kind to him. She kept reminding me that he was my father, as if I needed reminding."

"Can I tell you, cookie? People will hurt us. Disappoint us and let us down. Sometimes we just can't forgive them. I'll never forgive Carl, even though I am in a much better place since he left me. Of course, Carl never asked to be forgiven, either. But my son has let me down several times. He can be such an ignoramus, and I'll give him as many chances as I have in me. There's one thing—when they say they're sorry and ask to be forgiven, that's a big step. I may be a fool, but that's a step worth acknowledging. I put on my body armor, remind myself of the truth of their character, stay cautious and alert, and give them a chance. An apology and an effort are both rare and valuable."

"The queen has spoken," Korby said.

"You can make fun of me if you want, but I didn't just fall off the turnip truck. I've been studying this for a long time. I see clients who are angry and unforgiving. I see them trying not to be when they're certainly entitled. And sometimes I see them when they're moving on, no longer fueled by the anger. I always hope I'll see them by then so I can remind them to protect themselves by maintaining boundaries.

"If Kaylee asked my advice I would say, see Howard on your terms in your time. And if you think there's a reason he might offer some comfort, take it."

"How can Howard possibly offer me comfort now?" Kaylee asked.

"There are some ways. He went to a lot of trouble to set up this little party, thinking it would make you happy. Which it did. And you can probably share memories of your mother together. You might even learn some things about her that you weren't aware of. There is no question in my mind, Howard loved your mother. He told her he regretted ending their marriage, and I can see why. I doubt she told him but she came to be grateful because she landed in a better place. She told me that was how she felt. It was the same with me. I was devastated when Carl left me, but a year later I saw how much better my life was as a single woman than the wife of a man who put himself first, who never worried about my happiness. Of course neither of us, your mom or me, felt inclined to thank the bums for cheating and abandoning us."

"I suppose a lot of women come to you when they've been abandoned by their spouse," Korby said.

"That's who mostly comes to me. Some of them are left in impossible situations—no job, no money, kids to take care of. There's so much to overcome. I get to watch them gain their independence and blossom. Meredith and I did all right; our exes paid some child support."

Getting a master's in counseling was one of the gifts Janette gave herself after divorce. Kaylee remembered her struggle, with a couple of kids in high school and Janette working and going to school. She also remembered when Janette completed her program and took a job as an associate in the counseling office that got regular contracts from the county. Meredith had just started her own business, also a struggle. "I remember you and my mom sat on the phone late at night, talking…"

"Talking each other off the ledge, mostly," Janette said with a laugh.

For the next couple of hours the women talked about their relationships with each other, with Meredith, with their families, jobs and other friends. They had all staked out their sleeping spots, and one by one they drifted off to bed. When Kaylee closed her eyes on the day, she was smiling. It wasn't just because she was with her tribe, she was with her mother's tribe. It was a wonderful reunion.

Thanksgiving Day dawned bright and sunny with a light dusting of snow on the ground. A couple of women were busy in the kitchen putting out a breakfast. A couple had bundled up and were sitting on the porch, taking in the view of the snowy mountains. Kaylee made sure to take her morning walk.

Then they began to get their meal ready. King crab legs, mussels and oysters were the main course, but Janette brought a brisket as well. The red meat was in a marinade and she flipped it regularly. They made twice-baked potatoes smothered in cheese and sour cream and sprinkled with bacon. They had corn casserole, broccoli mixed up with onions, peppers and mushrooms, and a giant loaf of soft French bread. They prepared dishes of butter for dipping and Korby made her specialty of pot stickers. Janette prepared an appetizer of snails; she brought the shells and special plates from home. There was enough food to feed an army and dinner was scheduled for four o'clock.

Michelle put on a movie—*An Affair to Remember* followed by *Sleepless in Seattle*. Two favorites guaranteed to give them all an excuse to cry.

"Like a purge," Michelle said. "Some good old tears will clean out the pipes."

By the time Landry showed up late in the afternoon, they were all dabbing the tears from their eyes but were ready to eat. Kaylee had to explain what they'd done—prepared food all day, watched a couple of tearjerkers and set the table.

They had already started the brisket on the grill, but Landry was more than happy to take over. The mussels were cooked indoors, the crab was thrown on the grill, scattered around the brisket, the oysters were served chilled, the potatoes, casserole and vegetables all warmed for the table. Dinner was scheduled for four but it was promptly at five that they all gathered around the big dining room table and lifted their glasses in a toast.

"To Meredith," Michelle said.

"And to Kaylee," Janette added.

Then, except for regular comments about the food being out of this world, there was very little talking. In fact, Landry did most of the talking when he said, "Oh my God," and "Are you kidding me right now?" There was very little additional comment from him. He was too busy chewing.

"Landry, you don't seem to be uncomfortable partying with a bunch of women," Michelle said.

"Are you kidding me?" he said. "I haven't eaten like this in at least a hundred years. This is amazing." He lifted his glass and added, "And never have I had such beautiful and brilliant company for a holiday dinner."

"Very slick, Landry," Terri said. "You seem to know who to flatter. We like having you, too."

"I would travel far for another day like this!" he said.

"Unfortunately, we leave in the morning," Janette said.

"I'm sorry to hear that," Landry said. "The day after Thanksgiving is a big day in Virgin River."

"What's going on?" Kaylee asked. "We've already handed out all the food baskets. They're having Thanksgiving dinner at Jack's."

"The tree, Kaylee!" Landry said. "The tree is going up in town. A huge tree between the bar and the church. Appropriate, wouldn't you say? And it's not just that it's incredibly big, it's that the men from town have to make it happen while the women from town are giving advice and directions and bossing them a lot. Hardly anyone misses the tree raising and trimming. It's not like you have to stay all day but if you stay into the afternoon, you'll see some of it. And... Well, if you're interested in meeting Kaylee's rescue dog and her pups, it would be great to have you all come out and see where she lives. Kaylee brought that dog out of the woods, saved her life, and now Lady lives for a smile from Kaylee."

"I would like to see where you are living for now," Korby said.

In the end Michelle and Janette decided to head back to their homes first thing in the morning while Korby, Terri and Maggie stayed on until afternoon. And the day did not disappoint.

They raved about Landry's pots and sculptures and other art; they loved the little house he had rented to Kaylee. Lady completely charmed them and Landry had to nearly arm wrestle them to keep them from absconding with the puppies. Otis and Tux got a fair bit of attention as well.

Then their trip into town paid off. They got there at about

noon, just as the big flatbed was pulling in with the tree, and they were all stunned by the size of it. The raising of the tree was exciting and great fun. People were already lingering around what could almost be called a town square, waiting for the tree, and when it arrived, cheers roared. Then people kept coming as the tree was lifted with pulleys and positioned to be raised.

Kaylee was so glad that her friends had decided to stay a while longer; she wouldn't have missed this for the world. She introduced Korby, Terri and Maggie to Mel and a few of the other women she knew, and they all admired the collection of ornaments and lights that would adorn the tree.

In the early afternoon the cars kept coming, people gathering around the tree to watch the complicated process of raising it. By midafternoon the tree was standing and Jack claimed possession of the cherry picker.

"We have to be going," Korby said. "It's going to be a very long day of driving. But I feel so good about you being here. This place—it's a little magical."

"Not what I was expecting at all," Kaylee said. "I expected to be hiding out here, not having the time of my life."

"Not having a new boyfriend…"

"That was the last thing I expected."

"Well, I like him. I hope it works out for the two of you."

"Thanks, I'll be sure to let you know how things go."

"Kaylee, you must be crazy about him. I see the way you look at him."

"I might have fallen for him," she said. "At least a little. And now I'm going to fall for that book, finish it and see what comes next. Please text me when you're home safe."

Her friends left with hugs and thanks, but Kaylee and Landry stayed for the afternoon, watching the decorating of the tree. They were in no hurry to leave, didn't want to miss anything, and had a light dinner at Jack's. When they realized the decorating wasn't going to be finished in a day, they decided to head home to their dogs, planning to come back the next afternoon to see the tree lights come on.

"It's like a circus," Landry said. "I'm not very social, but I always drop by to watch the tree go up."

They checked on the dogs, made sure Lady had a break from the pups and Tux got a bowl of food, and then fell into each other's arms like lovers who had been apart for years. Their mouths were glued together, their arms clutching, their hands roving. "Damn, I missed you," he said. "I'm glad your friends came, but I missed sleeping with you."

"Seeing them again, especially on this particular holiday, I think it was just what I needed. But I missed you, too."

"They're fantastic," he said, kissing her cheeks, her lips, her neck. "And now I'm glad they're gone and I have you to myself again."

"Aw, that's very selfish."

"Kaylee, I've found that when it comes to you, I am selfish. Thank you for including me. It was like meeting your family."

"They are my family. The only other family I have is my aunt Beth, my mother's sister. I talked to her yesterday. She lives in Seattle and was very busy, having a ton of people for Thanksgiving. I love Beth but I'm closer to Janette and the girls."

"That's kind of how things go," he said. "Our close connections aren't always planned. They grow. Sometimes they surprise you. Look at us. You rented my house and now—I'm closer to you than anyone I know."

"Did you talk to Laura?" she asked. "Oh, I'm sorry. That's none of my business. I didn't mean to pry."

"It's entirely your business and you don't have to apologize. She called me yesterday and asked me what I was doing for the holiday and I told her I was spending it with you and some of your friends."

"How'd she take it?"

"She asked me if I loved you."

"Ew, that was direct. You don't have to tell me. Okay, what did you tell her?"

He chuckled. "I told her the truth, Kaylee. Maybe not quite as much truth as she really deserves. I told her we were the best of friends and that I hoped it worked into something more for us. I also told her we didn't have any future plans and no matter where things go from here, I'm ready to be unmarried. A decade is long enough to test the waters, to think about it. I said I hadn't changed my mind. And yes, she was emotional. She asked if she was too late."

"Oh, Landry…"

"Laura is used to having her way. She's having trouble accepting that it was too late a long time ago," he said. "There's no going back for me."

"I hope you don't regret it," she said.

Late that night, while Landry was getting a shower before bed, Kaylee called Howard. "I hope I didn't wake you?" she said.

"No," he said sleepily. "No, not at all. I mean, wake me anytime. It's good to hear from you."

"I wanted to say thank you," she said. "I had a wonderful Thanksgiving with the girls. That was very thoughtful for you to suggest it."

"In the end I didn't do much but make a few phone calls. There are no plane tickets to be had on the Wednesday before Thanksgiving. Did you know that's the busiest travel day of the year? So a couple of them had to drive a huge distance, but they were good sports about it. I'm going to send out some fruit or dessert baskets as a show of my appreciation." He paused and started to cough.

She suddenly felt a chill. What if Howard became gravely ill right as she was beginning to not hate him anymore?

"It's obvious, they love you very much," he said. "They seemed happy I suggested the idea even though it was last-minute and a lot of trouble. Was it fun?"

"So much fun," she said. "We ate like pigs, drank a little too much, watched movies, talked till we went hoarse. It was wonderful, Howard. If I'd thought of it myself, I wouldn't have wanted to impose, so you doing that meant even more. But you know what was the best part? That you seemed to understand my relationship with those women. The relationship I had with Mom and those women. That you respected it and didn't try to include yourself."

"No, honey. I realize that's yours. I'm so glad you were able to be together."

"So, maybe if you're willing to travel again, we can get together? Not on Christmas because I don't know how I'm going to feel on Christmas. Probably like crap, considering. But maybe we can have a nice dinner before Christmas. A week or ten days before. How does that sound?"

"I would like that very much."

"Landry has a guest room. You can stay at his house, which is right next door to my house. Would that be acceptable?"

"It would be wonderful. Just let me know when."

"I'll give you a call. And thanks again. Dad."

"You're welcome, honey," he said, a slight catch in his voice.

12

BY THE TIME LANDRY AND KAYLEE RETURNED TO town on the second day of the tree raising, it was almost fully decorated. There weren't as many people there as Kaylee would have expected. She found Mel sitting in a corner of the bar at a table, her laptop open.

"This is usually my position," Kaylee said.

"Oh, hi. I was just working on a special project," Mel said, closing her computer. "I barely talked to you yesterday. I was busy bossing Jack around most of the day. Sometimes I don't know how he stands it."

"I hear some men like it," Kaylee said with a laugh. "I don't know any, but that's what I hear."

"So, I met a couple of your friends and Landry said you had quite the Thanksgiving party…"

"Is that all he told you? Because my father arranged for my

best friends to come up for Thanksgiving. There were six of us plus Landry, and it was amazing. We borrowed the Templetons' house. It was a very special day. See, last year, we had my mom. She'd decided to discontinue chemo because she wasn't sure what was worse, death or chemo, and she'd run out of time. By Thanksgiving she was feeling a little bit better so her best friend and I put together a girls-only Thanksgiving dinner. We knew it could be my mom's last and we had the most wonderful time. This was almost a reunion."

"And your dad arranged it?" Mel asked. "I thought you didn't get along with him very well."

"He started putting it together with Janette's help and the generosity of the Templetons. And Landry. He picked up the crab legs and oysters and he certainly stocked the place with wine. He didn't expect to share it with us but the girls wouldn't let him leave. He had a wonderful time. It was perfect and just what I needed. That was the last time I saw my mom feeling good and having fun. This group of women—we blend just right. In fact, I think my friends like hanging out with me because they love my mom and her friends."

"That sounds fantastic. And how's the book coming?"

"I actually like it," she said. "I'm closing in on the ending and should be finishing up in the next week."

"That will be such a relief, won't it?"

"You have no idea! I think coming up here saved me in a dozen ways. Getting that book done is at the top of the list."

"Oh? I would've put my money on Landry being at the top of the list," Mel said.

"He's right up there, that's for sure. What a guy."

"So, will you two be staying in touch after the holidays pass?"

"I certainly hope so," Kaylee said. "I don't know when or how, but I hope so. I can't imagine not having him in my life."

"Have you made any special plans for Christmas?" Mel asked.

"Nah," Kaylee said. "I'm just going to let Christmas wash over me. Maybe after this year I'll be able to consider having fun on Christmas again, but…"

"Your mom?"

"She passed away on Christmas morning," Kaylee said. "She'd been lingering. I don't think she was in a great deal of pain at that point, thanks to Hospice and their drugs. I don't know if I was relieved or devastated, but she left me while I was holding her hand." She glanced away. "I try to hold on to the sweet memories, but then I get to feeling sorry for myself…"

"I bet you have many sweet memories…"

"It was usually just the two of us for Christmas. Sometimes we'd include friends—we had a lot of friends between us. But Christmas morning it was just the two of us. I've been writing for a dozen years or so and our joke was that I'd work in my pajamas, so every Christmas I got a new pair. Really nice, classy, soft and beautiful pajamas. She gave me other things, too, but the pajamas… They were always a treat. And last year, after she passed, I found a box under the tree and there they were, my annual pajamas. Red and silky and perfect. I'd been so preoccupied and distracted I didn't even notice them and I have no idea how or when she got them. She must have ordered them online. She must have had the Hospice nurse wrap them."

"Aw, that's so touching. I understand your feelings completely but if you decide to make plans or join us, I bet it would make your mother happy."

"I'm sure she wouldn't want me to be all sad and depressed, but it's kind of hard to be otherwise. That's the day she left me. You know, she loved getting her nails done and while she was so sick that last month, the Hospice nurse would do her nails. After she had passed, I went to the kitchen to make the calls and when I went back to her bedroom, the nurse was doing her nails. It was the most tenderhearted thing I've ever seen." She smiled at Mel. "I wish you could have met my mother. She was so funny and smart. You would have loved her."

"There's no question in my mind," Mel said. Then Mel's cell phone rang. "Excuse me a second, Kaylee," she said. Then she answered the phone. "Hey there, Marjorie, how's it going? No, I'm afraid I haven't made any progress and I've checked with everyone I know. Well, I'm not going to let the child go into foster care before Christmas. We'll make room for her if we need to, but she's not going to be alone at Christmas. I'll let you know if I get anywhere."

Mel hung up the phone and rested her head in her hand for a moment, rubbing the bridge of her nose with her thumb and index finger. Then she looked at Kaylee. "Sorry."

"I take it you have a heavy load right now," Kaylee said.

"It's very sad. My terminal patient. She has a child. It's not unlike what happened with your mother. She was diagnosed less than a year ago. And she will leave behind a daughter. Oh, that's right—you met Mallory. She's only ten and there is no father in the picture. She's the sweetest child I've ever known."

"I love Mallory! Remember our lunch? It was like a book club. Where will she go if she loses her mother?"

"I think to the neighbors. They have a ten-year-old daughter and they're good friends. The problem is, the neighbors are a family of eight pressed into a small house. But they're good and generous people. We're working on details. Mallory's mother is single and there's no family that I know of." She shook her head. "If it gets to the county, they will put her in foster care."

"Surely they'll find a good family," Kaylee said.

"Eventually. We suffer a shortage around here so they usually begin with emergency foster care and that often results in moving the kids around a bit. A few weeks here, a few weeks there, until a permanent home can be found that is right for everyone concerned." Mel smiled and patted Kaylee's hand. "Maybe her mother will make it till Christmas, but I highly doubt it. I'd give her another week at the most."

"Wow, and I thought I had it bad. At least I was thirty-five and able to look after myself."

"Yes, a lot of kinks in the road of life," Mel said. "I'll do my best. Now, are you staying a while? Because Jack is going to light up the tree at about six. You really should see it. Even if you don't think you're in the mood."

"I wouldn't miss it."

Landry was talking to Colin Riordan across the street from the bar, watching as the last of the lights were going up on the tree. He saw Brie wave from the porch of the bar and he waved back. Then she walked across the street to join him.

"How are you doing?" she asked.

"Excellent, and you?"

"Very well. Getting ready for Christmas and all the hoopla. There's a Christmas pageant that all the kids are involved in, a couple of parties, and Mike tells me it's going to snow for real tonight, no more of that little dusting. I hope you have your snow tires ready. What's going on with you for the holidays?"

"It'll be quiet. I'm going to offer to cook for Kaylee."

Colin excused himself and walked away a bit to talk to one of the guys on the tree crew.

"I couldn't have planned that better," Brie said. "I have some news. Would you like to meet in my office or do you want it now?"

"Now is good, if it's not real complicated," he said, bracing himself.

"Your offer of a hundred thousand with no support payments has been accepted. If nothing more comes up to complicate the situation, I can write this up and get it before a judge before Christmas. It'll take a few weeks to finalize things. And we should be prepared for your wife to change her mind or ask for more or..." She shrugged. "It doesn't usually go so smoothly, but then yours is the first divorce I've handled where there's been a ten-year separation."

"Wouldn't it be nice if it just sailed through," he said. "I talked to Laura on Thanksgiving. She was very emotional but she didn't offer any arguments. And she didn't mention she'd received my offer."

"So, you're sure, then?"

"Absolutely. I talked to the bank about a mortgage on some of the land."

"I'll keep you posted," she said.

The tree lighting was nothing short of amazing. The bar was overflowing with townsfolk, gathering to see the tree. It was so bright, Kaylee wondered if it could be seen in the next county. There was some carol singing, children running around wildly, lots of laughter, and then it began to snow. That thrilled the kids much more than the adults, since they wouldn't have to drive in it.

Kaylee saw Jack's family all together around the tree and noticed that David and Emma had a little friend with them. It was Mallory. She was a beautiful little girl with almost blond pigtails trailing out from under her knit hat. Kaylee was relieved to see her laughing. But Kaylee knew how hard it was going to be for her when her mother died. The loneliness could be terrible.

★ ★ ★

As the days passed, of course little Mallory's situation weighed on Kaylee's mind, though she tried to shake it off. She turned her attention to her book and exercised all her willpower to focus. And at night when she was in Landry's arms, she found at least temporary peace of mind. A few days later she called her editor.

"I have some news, at last," she said. "I'm sending you the completed manuscript."

"That's wonderful news," Simone said. "I'll give it a read as soon as possible. I think I can get to it right away. Congratulations."

"I'm sure it needs some revision," Kaylee said. "There were moments when I was so distracted, but that's getting better inch by inch as time passes."

"It's probably better than you think," the editor said. "You just need some distance from it."

"Definitely. And I'm going to send you that other manuscript we talked about. I think it's a romance or maybe women's fiction."

"Just where did that idea come from?" Simone asked.

"It started out as a kind of therapy for me. I was writing about making a fresh start in a small town. Hardly a new concept. I think every third book on the shelf starts with that trope. But then instead of writing about what's been happening in my own life, I started writing about how I wished it would be, and that ended up with a love story. I like to read romance but I'm not confident I know how to write one. All I can say is it's been a long time since I've had so much fun writing."

"I can't wait," Simone said. "Are they both coming today?"

"Yes, I'll email them to you when we finish our call."

Her editor laughed and said, "My favorite overachiever.

After I've read and we've both had time to relax, we should talk about a new contract."

"I'm not in any great hurry," Kaylee said. "I want to get through the holiday and see if my life takes on anything that resembles normalcy."

"Me, too," Simone said. "I've come to the conclusion one should never make a major business decision while trying to survive Christmas. In your case, the challenge is even greater. How are you feeling these days? About coping with the loss of your mother?"

"Sometimes I feel like I've come light-years and sometimes I feel like it's fresh and raw. The latter comes slightly less often now. Let me tell you about my Thanksgiving, which was a dream."

Kaylee told her the whole story, starting with last year when her mother was experiencing some of her final positive days, to this year when the same group of women shared the holiday together. She could detect a little bit of emotion in her editor's voice, noting she was touched by the event. "Oh, my heart," Simone said. "What a beautiful story."

"It's easier when I don't have to miss my mother alone," Kaylee said.

After hitting the Send key, Kaylee did what she often did when a book was finally finished. She gave the little house a sound cleaning, answered the emails she'd been putting off for God knew how long, called Korby and Janette so they could celebrate with her for a little while, and drove to Clear River to hit the store. There hadn't been any locally grown fruits and vegetables in a couple of months, but there was plenty of organic produce in the grocery, probably shipped in. She wanted to have a celebratory dinner. Knowing that Landry was a red meat kind of guy, she grabbed a couple of steaks and big potatoes along with some broccoli, mushrooms, onions and peppers.

Then she showered, primped and walked next door. She went to his shop.

"Well, look at you. Do you have a date tonight, miss?" Landry said with a sly grin.

"I hope so. If you'll do the steaks on the grill, I'll make the rest of our dinner. And I have a bottle of champagne."

He made a face. "I'll definitely toast the finished book with you, then you can have the rest of the bottle."

She laughed. "That's exactly why I bought a small bottle. I'm going to go see the puppies while you finish up."

"Those puppies are big enough to go outside for a little while with Lady as long as you can keep an eye on them."

"Otis, want to help me babysit?" Kaylee said and Otis joined her immediately.

The puppies were probably about six weeks old and had gotten to that chubby, adorable stage where they would knock themselves over just trying to bark. She watched them wrestle and nip and roll around while Lady just wandered the yard in bliss, free at last, ignoring them completely. The germ of an idea was trying to break out, but Kaylee was a little too busy chasing puppies to let it come through.

When Landry joined her in the yard, he began to pick up the puppies, one at a time, blowing in their faces, snuggling them and laughing at their cuteness.

"Will they be ready to leave Lady by Christmas?" she asked.

"I think so, but the shelter and I have decided, no Christmas puppies. They'll post pictures and take applications for the new year. Too many people get puppies for their kids for Christmas and then when it doesn't work out, they're neglected. They can go to their new homes after Christmas, if the offers hold.

And speaking of going home..." He looked at her over the head of the puppy he held. "We've avoided that subject..."

"Not intentionally," she said. "Let's talk about it over dinner."

They settled the puppies in the pen with Lady and chose to have dinner at Landry's house since he had the barbecue. She finished cooking in his kitchen while he grilled the steaks.

When they sat down to dinner, he raised a glass to her and said, "Here's to your finished book."

"At last," she said.

"And, here's to a divorce," he said.

In shock, she didn't lift her glass. "What? It can't be all done!"

"No, not for weeks yet. But Laura and I have settled on the terms, she signed and notarized the settlement agreement and it's sitting in a big stack of cases waiting for a judge. It might take as long as three months, but probably not even three weeks, if there's no counteroffer or contesting. The important thing is, it's been negotiated and it's ready to be approved."

"How do you feel about that?"

"I feel surprisingly good with it. I gave up hoping she'd miss me years ago. I don't have any regrets. It was time."

"She'll blame me, of course," Kaylee said.

"She can't really blame anyone but herself," he said. "But I take equal responsibility. I didn't try that hard. Not only did I let her run away, I realize that I ran away, too."

"Even though you don't seem to be upset, I'm sorry this happened to you. I remember being very angry and torn up by my divorce. Slightly different circumstances, maybe, but it was no day at the beach."

"The big question is, what about us?" he asked. "What do you want to happen with us?"

"I want us to stay in love forever," she said. "It's just that

I don't know what to do with our reality. My home is in Newport and I love it there. Plus, it's my mother's house and I wouldn't even consider giving it up. And while my work is pretty transportable, yours is not."

"So, the question is, can two people who love each other maintain a close relationship when they have separate lives? Separate homes?"

"You already tried that once, Landry."

"No, I don't think I did. Trying would have had us a lot more balanced—winters in the south, summers in the north? Every other month? Three or four days here, three or four days there? I think there are many options. As long as we both have the same goal. But first, the priority is getting through Christmas."

"I'm sorry, but I just want Christmas behind me."

"Don't apologize, Kaylee. I understand. I do have one suggestion. Why don't you try writing about it? Write the Christmas that would make you feel better."

"That would involve impossible and magical things," she said.

"Don't rule it out," he suggested. "Write it in."

Kaylee wasn't at all surprised that her thoughts were constantly tuned in to the loss of her mother and often to Mallory as well. She kept wondering how she was getting along. She'd heard from Mel that Mallory's mother had passed away and while arrangements were being made, she was with the next-door neighbors—the family of her friend—who had taken her in. Mel hoped that would work out for another couple of weeks, at least through Christmas. But if there was a problem with that, Mel was going to find room for her with their family.

In the dark of night when she couldn't sleep, lying in

Landry's strong, comforting arms, there were times Kaylee couldn't hold back her tears. She tried to keep her crying silent, but he always knew and would pull her close and whisper soothing words. "It's going to be all right." She often thought that if she could have just five minutes with her mother, she could live on happily. She was astonished by how desperately she still missed her.

Then one night she was startled to wake up on the front porch. She was sitting on the porch swing and saw that someone had put a small Christmas tree in the corner of the porch. It had twinkling lights and silver ornaments. And there, leaning a hip on the porch rail, was Meredith. She wore her royal-blue robe, the one with the stiff, arched collar. It was such a beautiful robe, Kaylee had kept it.

"Mama," she said in a breath. "Oh, Mama!" Even though she wanted to run to her and embrace her, she couldn't seem to move.

"My darling girl," Meredith said.

"You're here!"

"Not entirely, but I did tell you I'd never be far away. I think we should talk."

"Yes!" Kaylee said. "We should talk! Did you bring the tree?"

"It's Christmastime," she said. "You don't have to bake a plum pudding or roast a goose, but the whole world is honoring Christmas. You remember what the spirit of Christmas does, don't you, Kaylee? The least you can do is put out an ornament or two. It's all right if it brings a little emotion to your day, but try to remember, it's not all about you. And if you can't bring yourself to celebrate Christmas, consider letting Christmas celebrate you. Think about the people you know who deserve some happiness. Have you done anything special for your boyfriend? He seems so loving and sweet."

"He is," she said. "Am I dreaming you?"

Meredith shrugged. "Are you cold?"

Kaylee looked around. There was snow on the porch and her feet were bare yet she was not at all cold. "Even if you're only a dream, I'll take it..."

"You've dreamed of me many times and usually it makes you happy. I know you feel cheated, Kaylee; I know you feel that you're the only one who feels loss and sadness. And I know that you know that's not true. I'm not suggesting you ignore your grief—grief is personal and runs on its own calendar. But remember. There are lots of people feeling lost and alone. It's time for you to take stock of what you have, not of what you may have lost."

"I can't help it. I miss you so much."

"I'm here. We may not get to talk too often, but you know where to find me. You know where I will live until we have each other again. Remember the spirit heals. Remember that the spirit of Christmas is about giving. Turn your heart to the needs of others—it will help you get through the days that seem too long and the nights that feel too lonely. You know what to do because you've done it before. And remember that I'm very proud of you. Of your strength and your resilience. I so love your abundant joy. If you need me, just whisper. I will hear you."

"Please don't go," she said, tears gathering in her eyes.

"There are things you can do. Don't forget all the things we talked about. There is an antidote to sadness—it is gratitude. There's a great trick to escaping the pain of loss, and that is giving. You may still cry at 11:04 a.m. on Christmas Day. But then you should be grateful for all we had. We had so much. We were so rich, figuratively and literally. Accept the gifts that heal."

"Stay!" she said. "Please! Just for a few more minutes!"

"I love you so much," Meredith said.

"I love you more!" Kaylee said.

Suddenly she felt cold. Her feet were like ice, her hands were stiff and frozen. Even so, she didn't move for a few minutes, willing her mother to come back. This was not like other dreams. This was so real.

"Kaylee?" Landry said, turning over and sitting up in bed. "What in God's name...?"

She was in the bedroom, sitting on her heels in the bed, shivering and weeping. "She was here," Kaylee whispered. "She was on the porch and she brought me a Christmas tree!"

Landry grabbed her hands and rubbed them. "Have you been outside? You're freezing!"

She nodded. "She wanted to talk to me and while we talked I wasn't cold. But then when she left I could hardly stand the cold. She was here. On the porch. I sat on the swing and we talked. I've dreamed of my mother a hundred times, but this time was different. This time it was so real. She reminded me of things we talked about. It wasn't just her talking and me listening. We agreed on so many things. One of the things was that being kind was a sure cure for loneliness."

He was rubbing her hands briskly. "Kaylee, how long have you been outside?" he asked.

"She brought me a tree," she said. "It's on the porch."

He jumped out of bed. He wore only a T-shirt and boxers but he went to the porch and looked out. Then he closed the door and came back to the bed. "There's no tree," he said. "And there are no footprints. And there's no impression in the snow from someone sitting on the swing."

Her eyes grew round. "What?" she asked. Then she jumped up and ran to the front door. She looked out and saw for herself that there was no tree. And the snow hadn't been disturbed on the swing or the porch rail. Then she started to cry in earnest.

Landry led her to the bed, got her under the covers and pulled her close, warming her with his body. "It's all right, love. It was just a dream. Just a very nice dream."

"It was so real," she said. She turned her face into Landry's chest and cried. But it wasn't very long before she slept.

When she woke the sun was high in the sky; her bedroom was bright. Landry was not beside her. She grabbed her robe and went into the other room and he was sitting on the couch, having his coffee. He looked over the rim of his mug and smiled at her.

"How did you sleep?" he asked.

She sat on the couch beside him. "You know how I slept," she said. "You must think I'm a lunatic by now."

"Go look on the porch," he said, throwing a glance over his shoulder.

She got a wide-eyed and suspicious look and dashed to the front door. She opened the door and looked outside to see a very small decorated tree on the front porch, right in the corner where she'd dreamed it was the night before.

"Did you do that?" she asked.

He shook his head. "No. And I didn't hear a car. And what's more astonishing, Otis didn't hear a car. Is it like the one in your dream?"

She stepped out onto the snowy deck, freezing her poor feet. She got a little closer. "I'm not sure. Very similar. But last night I was more focused on my mother. I'm not crazy, I know she's dead. But Landry, I think she paid me a visit last night. Really."

"I've heard of stranger things," he said, walking toward her. "All I know for sure is there was no tree there last night, there's a tree there now, and you had quite a meltdown."

"I'm sorry about that, but it was overwhelming. It was so good to see her. She wasn't like the last time I saw her. Her cheeks were plump and rosy and her hair was thick and dark. She looked healthy. Restored. And she had things on her mind. She said, 'I think we should talk.' That's what she always said when she thought I needed advice. And when she was a little unhappy with me or when she thought I'd better get a grip."

"What did she say?"

She thought for a moment, trying to remember everything. It was pretty clear, not like usually trying to remember a dream, which wasn't always easy. But yes, she remembered everything her mother had said. "I need a little time to sort it out. Let me get a cup of coffee."

"By all means. Then when you're ready, how about some breakfast?"

She filled her cup. "You and Otis didn't hear a car, huh."

He shook his head. "Maybe angels don't drive."

13

KAYLEE TOOK HER LAPTOP TO JACK'S ALMOST OUT of habit. She'd finished her book, had sent it to her publisher, and the deadline was gone. But she wanted to be there, and Jack had good Wi-Fi so she could at least check and answer her mail. She fully expected her editor to call or write and ask her to do more work on the book. She was convinced it was finished, but not good enough.

"Sorry, Kaylee, the Wi-Fi is out," Jack said.

"Oh no! How are you getting by?"

"Me?" he asked, then laughed. "I'm just barely off the clip-board. I gotta say, I'm not that crazy about computers. I'm getting along fine as long as I have Preacher to help me out if I get myself in trouble, but I am no geek. To me, it's a tool, like a hammer. I am not romantically involved with my computer."

"Well, that's good to know," she said, laughing. "What's going on around here?"

"We're in full holiday mode," he said. "We're doing more food baskets if you're interested in helping out. There are a few needs a little beyond food—children in need of a visit from Santa, some more than others. The volunteer fire department is taking on some of that. Mel and Paige and a few other women are making a run on the big box stores over in Eureka."

"Oh, if I'd known, I would have volunteered to help! I finished my book and I'm ready to do more volunteer work."

"That's sweet, Kaylee," he said. "Congratulations on the book. Did you celebrate?"

"I called a couple of friends and drank a toast with Landry, but then I forgot about it and it never occurred to me I could be useful in town. I should have called Mel. She's probably not calling me to help because she thinks I'm bogged down with work."

"She's due back in an hour. Why do you have your computer with you if you're done?"

"I don't know," she said. "Because I never go anywhere without it? Because I feel so vulnerable if I'm not writing a book? Because I can always read something on the computer if I have no one to talk to?"

"Here? No one to talk to?" He threw back his head and laughed. "I don't think you wrote a single sentence in this bar. No one would let you work. That's not how they roll."

"You noticed that?"

"Kaylee, they won't let me work! I can be counting bottles and someone will say, 'Yo, Jack, you hear about that eight-point buck sighted out on Cummins Pass?' And then we have to talk about it a while even though it's pretty clear I'm counting bottles." But as he finished, he grinned. "Congratulations, Kaylee. You going straight back to the south? Where is it? Newport?"

"Newport Beach," she said. "Not straightaway. I rented out my house for the rest of the year. I haven't talked to them lately, but as of a couple of months ago they were planning to move out right after New Year's. Like, maybe the third. Or fourth. I told them to give me a couple weeks' notice."

"What are you going to do with Landry? Because if you'll forgive me for having eyes in my head, the two of you hit it off."

She couldn't help but laugh at him. "We've been talking about how we can arrange to visit each other. Often. But we haven't made any real plans yet. Landry was a great surprise. I wasn't expecting to meet someone like him. Well, as you know, I was expecting to stay in the Templetons' house through Christmas..."

"Yeah, that's right. And look what happened. You ended up with a guy, a kitten, some puppies, and God knows what all..."

"All I really wanted was to avoid Christmas..."

"You mentioned that early on. I can't quite remember why. Did you tell me why?" he asked.

"I lost my mom to cancer last year. She passed on Christmas Day. I don't think I told you. I did tell Mel..."

"She never tells anything," he said. "And I'd have remembered something like that. I'm so sorry, Kaylee."

"It's not a secret, it's just one of those things. I couldn't quite bring myself to plan a celebration, you know? It's hard to even think about it." *You may still cry at 11:04...*

"I can imagine," he said. "It's gotta be hard. But there's a forty-foot tree decorated to the hilt right outside. That's gonna serve as a reminder. Kind of hard to avoid Christmas with that tree right out there..."

"True. Hey, you didn't by any chance put a little decorated Christmas tree on my front porch, did you?"

He shook his head. "Is there a note or a card?"

"Nothing. It wasn't there at two in the morning. I...ah... just happened to look outside then. It was there when I got up. Landry said he never heard a car, and what's more mysterious is that Otis never heard a car. Otis would have made some noise. I just wish I knew who—"

"People around here surprise me all the time. There was a decorated tree above the highway in Fortuna for years. No one ever took credit for it and in January it would disappear. A couple of years ago it stopped appearing. We all went into mourning, wondering if the tree fairy passed. I bet someone was trying to make sure you have a nice holiday, knowing you're by yourself even if they don't know the circumstances."

"I'm really not so all alone anymore, Jack," she said. "I spend most of my time with Landry. We've become very close."

Jack's smile was broad. "Was bound to happen," was all he said.

Kaylee started thinking about what her mother had said to her, about the antidote to sadness. As she recalled from growing up as Meredith's only child, there were countless discussions about how to dispel self-pity and a feeling of hopelessness.

That night, after having a nice long talk with Landry and filling him in on all the goings-on in town, Kaylee called Mel. "I stopped by the bar today and Jack told me you have a lot happening."

"It's my busy season," Mel said. "And I heard the book is done. You must be thrilled. And bored senseless."

Kaylee laughed. "I haven't had time to get bored yet. I did call to say I can help with some of your projects. You're doing food baskets again, right? I could help with that."

"That would be great! I'll take you up on that offer."

"And I wanted to know how Mallory is doing."

"Pretty well, considering. She's coping very well, getting a lot of support from her best friend's family—that's the neighbor she's been staying with. Accommodations are a little tight. She has to share a bed, but they're kids, they've done it before. There just isn't room for her things, that's all. But Jack and I will bring her to our house. It'll be a full house—one of his sisters is coming with kids and grandkids. But we'll manage."

"Well, I was thinking about that. Do you think Mallory likes puppies?"

Mel brought Mallory over the next afternoon. "Mel said you wanted me to see something," the little girl said.

"First of all, I'm sorry to hear about your mother," Kaylee said, giving her a hug. "Did Mel tell you we have that in common? I lost my mother last year. I think I know how you're feeling."

"How I'm feeling is not that good," she said. "But I'm taking it slow. My mom said, just take it slow because you can't hurry your feelings. I don't know what that means, but I'm doing it the best I can."

"You're doing fine," Kaylee said. "Mallory, I was out for a walk and I found a mama dog. She was tied up to a tree and had four puppies with her. Someone left her there, abandoned her. So I brought her back here. I thought maybe you might want to see them?"

"Yes! Were they hurt?"

"No, just hungry. Landry has them in his kennel. I'll show you," she said, taking Mallory's hand.

"I have a few phone calls to return," Mel said. "Can I stay here and do that while you see the puppies?"

"Of course. But we might be a while." She pulled Mallory along to Landry's house and then through the house to the back door. Otis came out of Landry's shop and greeted them. "Mallory, have you met Landry?"

"Yes, I'm pretty sure," she said. "What are you doing in there?"

"Making pots and statues and wind chimes and all sorts of artsy things," he said. "I bet you're here to see the puppies. When you're done I'll show you everything if you're interested."

"I'd like to see it, if Mel says it's okay."

They found Lady in the backyard, sniffing around. "Lady," Kaylee called, and the dog pranced right over. "This is Lady, Mallory. When I found her she was nearly starving but she's looking so good now."

"Why was she starving?"

"I don't know because I don't know what happened to her. I suspect her owners neglected her, didn't feed her, didn't take care of her. But she's very well taken care of now. Let's look at the puppies."

Mallory gasped with pleasure when she saw the puppy pile inside the kennel. She immediately got down on her knees and reached into the space to touch a puppy. Then she pulled a hand back and looked at Kaylee. "There's a cat in here," she said, shocked.

"I know," Kaylee said with a laugh. "That's Tux. I found him, too. He was so young when I found him and when Lady and the puppies came here to stay, he crawled in and never wanted to leave. The puppies are going to outsize him pretty soon. He thinks he's one of them."

Lady joined them and got into the dog bed, lying down for the puppies to nurse. "I don't think they're going to be nursing much longer. They're getting big and they need real food. Landry has started feeing them puppy kibble once a day. Lady will decide when she's done nursing and just quit on them. Then we'll have to try to find homes for them."

Mallory picked up a puppy and cuddled him. "I guess that's going to happen to me, too."

"Are you worried about that, honey?"

"A little bit. I'd kind of like to just stay with Ali's family. I know them, they're nice, they like me, but…" She shrugged. "There's a lot of kids. I don't think there's room. Maybe not enough food or something."

"What did Mel say?"

"She said I don't need to worry because she's going to keep an eye on me and everything." She kissed the puppy's soft fur. "I'm a little scared of going to some house I've never been to with people I don't know. I hope I don't have to do that."

"I would be scared of that, too."

Kaylee changed the subject and asked Mallory when was the last time she'd been to the library. It turned out it had been weeks, which made absolute sense because her mother had been very sick, died, there'd been a funeral, there were probably details with the house and furnishings. "Maybe we can go next Saturday," she said. "Would you like me to take you?"

"Well, yes, but I'm not sure where I'm going to be," she said, and Kaylee could see the poor thing was feeling all uprooted, confused and worried.

"I will find you, no problem. And I'll take you."

They sat on the floor by the puppy pen and held them one at a time, including Tux, then put them back. They talked about books because of course Kaylee had looked up the most appropriate books for well-read ten-year-old girls. Mallory was very interested in how long it took Kaylee to write a book.

Then Mallory said, "When did your mother die?"

"It's been a year now. Almost a year."

"Do you cry every day?"

She shook her head. "Not anymore," she said. "At first, when it was new and hurt so much, I cried a lot. But my mom used to always say, 'A good cry will help you clean out the pipes so you can breathe easier.' Sometimes it felt like I needed it. You know?"

"I know. And I dream about her," Mallory said.

"So do I! Sometimes it feels real!"

"I think it is sometimes!" Mallory said. "When I'm older I'm going to write a book about a girl whose mother dies and she comes to her in dreams."

"That would be a wonderful book," Kaylee said. "We're going to have a good time looking for books." And she thought, *This little girl needs an iPad for books and movies and pictures.* In fact, she probably needed a lot of things. What she had started out thinking could be an experiment was growing in her mind, and she was bonding with her over the loss of their mothers.

She asked Mallory to tell her all about her mother and the girl did, talking about when her mother was working at a motel in Fortuna. "She was a manager," Mallory said proudly. "She was the boss of people." And on she went, describing her mother's beautiful long hair, her exercise suits that she wore to yoga, her friends from work and her friends from the neighborhood. She had a grandma when she was little, but she passed away. "I don't like when they call it 'passed,'" she said. "I think when they die they die and they wait for you to come later."

"Much later," Kaylee said. She felt that her mother, however, had definitely passed. Or maybe slipped away. Quietly and with so little fanfare. 11:04.

Before long, she looked at her watch. It had been two hours. "If you want to see some of Landry's pots and his statues, we better go. I don't think Mel plans to be here all day."

They visited Landry, and Mallory loved the idea of playing with the clay and painting and molding. He showed her some of his molding tools and demonstrated. Then he showed her a pot that had just come out of the kiln. He explained the danger of the super-hot kiln and the blow torch, and she held her hands tight in front of her, careful not to touch anything.

When she took Mallory back to her little house next door, she broached the subject that had been on her mind for days. "I have an idea and if it doesn't sound perfect, you should say so. I have a spare room in this little house. It has no furniture in it, but there is plenty of room for your things if you think you'd like to come and stay with me."

"Just for a little while?" Mallory asked. "Like with Ali next door?"

Kaylee smiled. "At least through Christmas, so you can be here in your town, near your friends and your school, until the right place is found. We can play it by ear; it can last longer if we like it. I want you to always have choices. If it doesn't feel right, you should tell me. Or Mel. But I have a feeling you're going to like it. Let's try it through Christmas and New Year's. We should try to have a nice Christmas for our mothers. If you want to."

"Does Landry say it's okay?"

"Absolutely. I asked him first. This is his property and it's where he grew up. I thought maybe we could help each other get through that hard part of losing our mothers. And we can do it with trips to the library, watching movies, reading together and training the dogs. Lady is very well behaved but she could use a little training. We'll have our friends nearby. Your friends are welcome to come over, too. You might want to invite some of them."

"Do you want me to stay with you?" she asked.

Kaylee nodded. "I do. I think you're very good company.

But the most important thing is if *you* want to. If you don't, I understand. This is a tough time of year for some people."

"I could try it," she said. "I could see Landry make pots."

"And if you ever feel uncomfortable, you can call me," Mel said. "I can always think of something. Your mom asked me to look out for you and I promised I would."

"I think this would be okay," she said.

"Then Landry will bring your bedroom furniture from your house and put it in the spare bedroom. And we can start to dream up what kind of things we want to cook and bake for the holidays, and I bet you'd like to do some shopping. I think we're going to be very busy."

"Will we bake cookies and things?"

"Would you like to?" Kaylee asked. "I have to admit, I haven't had much practice…"

Mallory gave her an impatient look. "If you follow the directions, it comes out good. If you cheat the directions, not so much."

"I'll be sure to remember that," Kaylee said.

If there was one thing Kaylee hadn't expected, it was how the people in Virgin River, her new friends, responded when they heard the news that she'd taken in Mallory. The generosity they displayed was unimaginable. It was almost as if they were showing their appreciation. Jack was probably responsible for getting the word out because he and Mike and Preacher helped Landry move Mallory's bedroom furniture the very next morning. Mallory spent one more night with Ali until then.

Kelly Holbrook brought over a large basket of scrumptious baked goods, and Jillian brought some squash and onions and peppers from her winter garden. Paige and Preacher hand-delivered a large basket of brisket and salmon, prepped for the freezer, for their future meals together. Vanessa and Paul brought two pies and a dozen cookies, which was a lifesaver because Kaylee's first attempt at baking Christmas cookies didn't go that well. Then there were many packages left on the porch with no card. There were gifts of banana, zucchini and cranberry breads and a tray of cinnamon rolls. Not only were the gifts of food plentiful and in a great variety, there were other gifts—hand-stitched Christmas place mats and napkins, garland left decorating the front porch rail, a wreath for the door and a holiday basket filled with ornaments.

"I guess we'll have to put up a tree," Kaylee said.

"That shouldn't be too hard since we live in a forest," Landry said.

Kaylee called her father and surprised him by inviting him to Christmas Eve dinner. "Really?" he asked. "Of course I'd like to come! What can I bring? Where should I reserve a room?"

"Life has become very interesting here," she explained. "I'm fostering a little girl who just lost her mother, she's ten, and she's staying with me. Landry said you can have his room."

"Where is Landry going to stay?" Howard asked.

"I'm sure I can make room for him somewhere in my little house, but he has the larger dining room and kitchen, so we'll be cooking there."

"I guess things are progressing nicely," Howard said.

"There's a gathering in the town at Jack's Bar and it spills out around the tree. I hear there's food, drink, carol singing and in general a town party. I'm told it usually starts around six when the sun goes down and the tree lights up. Can you get here early enough for that?"

"I wouldn't miss it."

The week leading up to Christmas was consumed with volunteer duties. Mallory decided she was ready to go back to school and that freed Kaylee to shop and help with the food baskets. Every evening she read with Mallory and it thrilled her. Since all her books were back in Newport, she downloaded the first book in the Harry Potter series and if Mallory enjoyed it, she'd buy her the set. But for now, having this sweet little girl tucked up next to her, the two of them taking turns reading every other page, was sheer bliss.

Kaylee could see that when children suffered a loss like this, they could be resilient, at least in the moment. Mallory could be easily distracted by the puppies or other children, laughing and playing one moment and then a bit later, morose and feeling a little lonely. Kaylee was there for her when her spirits were down.

Every day was packed with activity. Every evening Kaylee was busy getting dinner ready or spending time with Mallory. Most nights the dogs joined them for at least a little while until one of the puppies made a mess. Kaylee found that Lady curled up beside her, leaning against her, as if Lady had chosen Kaylee as her everything.

Not only had she gone over to the coast to do a little shopping, but Landry had run a few errands for her as well so that Santa would not miss this house. There were gifts wrapped and hidden at Landry's house, ready to be put under the tree.

In the dark of night when Kaylee and Landry held each other, they whispered about the turn of events. "I never would have seen this coming," Landry said. "I'm glad you decided to bring Mallory home."

"How could I not?" she asked. "I know exactly how she must be feeling."

"And for you, this whole idea of ignoring Christmas seems to have changed focus," he said. "You're the kindest person I know. I fall more deeply in love with you every day."

But she thought he was the kindest, most giving person in

the world. "I don't know how long we can have this gift. A foster home might be found for her."

"Unless we tell Mel to ask them to stop looking," he said. "I could live like this. Actually, this is how I always thought my life would be."

She couldn't help but think, she never imagined her life like this. She thought she would grow old with her books, her mother, her friends. But this new routine seemed to suit her as well. "There's still Newport," she reminded him.

"This is not a tragedy," he said. "We each have a house and there's plenty of room in both. We each have a little money set aside, thanks to our parents. All we need is a plan and a little patience."

Kaylee's editor called and raved about both of the manuscripts she'd submitted. "The suspense is right on target and I have a long list of things I love about it, and the women's fiction is a wonderful bonus! I want to buy it, but first we should talk about whether you want to make a change in genres or add a genre to your booklist. For someone who didn't feel confident about writing women's fiction, you nailed it." They talked for an hour then decided to shelve the rest of their conversation about how to proceed until after the first of the year.

Landry helped get a spaghetti casserole ready to put in the oven to eat on Christmas Eve, after they'd been to town. In the afternoon, Howard arrived and was greeted by yipping puppies and barking dogs. And his laughing daughter hugged him. "Dad," she said, giving him a kiss on the cheek, "I want you to meet Mallory and Lady and Lady's kids, and I believe you know everyone else."

Howard just stood stock-still and let the tears well up in his eyes. She knew it was because she'd finally called him Dad rather than Howie. He hugged her fiercely for a long moment and then, wiping his eyes, he said, "Well, what've we got here."

Landry crouched to the floor and said, "A puddle, for one thing." He pulled a thick wad of paper towels from his pocket. "Merry Christmas, sir," he said. "I think it's time for the children to go to bed. Can I have a hand, Mallory?"

"You bet," she said, scooping up two puppies.

"We'll go into town and join the party, then come home for dinner. Dad, let's get your bags into Landry's house and then we can all go in one car. We'll eat at Landry's."

"Sounds good," he said. "Are we ready to go?"

"Just about," she said. "Once Landry gets the dogs settled."

"Will they be all right with no one home?" he asked.

"They'll be in the kennel. Lady is an excellent mother."

He just shook his head. "This is such a wonderful surprise, seeing you around dogs and children."

"It's all been a whirlwind," she said. "Would you like something to eat before we go? I have cookies. Home-baked."

"You made cookies?"

"Yes, I did. But, fortunately for you, these were made by someone else."

The street through Virgin River was crowded with cars and trucks, and there were people milling around the tree, on the porch at Jack's, in front of the church, everywhere.

"Good God, look at that tree!" Howard said. "How'd they ever get it into town and standing up?"

"It was quite a show, I'll tell you that," Kaylee said. "Half the town was here watching. People were hanging around, waiting for it to fall down at least once, and Jack didn't disappoint them. It took a giant flatbed truck, pulleys and winches and a lot of anchoring ropes. Then came the decorating, which required a cherry picker. I couldn't tear myself away."

"I'd love to watch something like that," Howard said with a laugh.

Mallory touched Kaylee's arm. "There's Ali," she said softly.

"I'm going to stay right around the front steps here so please don't go anywhere else without telling me. Okay?"

"Okay."

"And try not to eat too many cookies. We have dinner waiting."

"Okay," she said. Kaylee leaned down and gave her a kiss on the forehead, nudging a smile out of the girl.

"It's almost like you two were made for each other," Howard said.

"I met her for the first time a couple of months ago," Kaylee said. "I knew her mother was sick but I never imagined it would come to this. She's been with me a week and I can't imagine her ever leaving."

"Does she have to?"

Kaylee shrugged. "Mel said that Social Services will conduct a search for family members, but Mallory doesn't know of any. What we need right now is time. Even with the best of intentions, I'm not going to be selfish. I want Mallory to have the right home. One where she can count on staying through her teenage years."

"I hope it turns out to be with you," he said. "I don't know anything about situations like this but it feels right to me. Kaylee, I'm very proud of you."

A warmth spread through her and she was a little bit surprised by how good it felt to hear that. This father who had not been there for her suddenly filled her full of pride and affection.

"I'm going to go inside and see what's available to drink. Would you like something?" he asked.

"If they have anything hot, that would be great," she said.

She scooted out of the way of people who would be going to the porch or inside and also those coming out and wandering over toward the tree. She saw so many familiar faces and waved to a few friends. It was almost as if she'd lived here for years, she felt so comfortable among them. She wondered which of them had brought the tree, who decorated her porch rail with garland. For someone who didn't want Christmas to come, she found all of this enchanting. Promising. And yet because she helped with the holiday food baskets, she knew that for many, times were hard. She caught a glimpse of the elderly mother and daughter she'd met at Thanksgiving, talking to neighbors and pointing up at the height of the tree.

"Well, if I didn't know better, I'd say you're actually enjoying the holiday," came Mel's voice.

"Oh!" she said, turning to Mel and giving her a hug. "Thanks largely to you, I'm having a very nice time. Mallory is doing pretty well. We talk about her mom a lot but we're doing other things that are as distracting for me as for her. We're reading together—I can't believe how smart that kid is. We play board games and watch some movies and she loves Lady and the puppies. Now, I'd really like to find out who brought me some of the Christmas treats I found on my porch."

"I think if whoever it was didn't want to be anonymous, you'd have gotten a card," Mel said. "I think Jack let it slip that you were dreading Christmas on account of your mother's passing. If there's ever a time you want to get the word out about something, just tell Jack."

"You're saying he's a big mouth?" Kaylee asked with a laugh.

"He's a bartender," Mel said. "He can't help it."

"He said you never tell," Kaylee pointed out.

"I'm a midwife," she said, grinning. "Requirement of the job." Then she stood on her toes as if to look over heads.

"One thing about raising kids in Virgin River. They're relatively safe."

"Relatively?" she asked hesitantly.

"Well, we do have wildlife and miles of woods and rivers you should try not to fall into, but we haven't had a kidnapping in a long time." Kaylee grabbed Mel's arm so suddenly, Mel laughed. "It was a long time ago, like ten years or so. Paige Middleton was kidnapped by her abusive ex-husband, but he didn't have her long. Preacher went looking for her and found her. Her ex-husband regained consciousness before long."

"We really need to spend more time talking," Kaylee said.

"It was in the newspaper or I wouldn't have mentioned it," Mel said.

"How long do you plan to be a midwife?" she asked. "Because you must have loads of tales to tell."

"Forever," Mel said. "But just spend a little time with Jack. Are you looking for book material?"

"Always." At that moment Howard came down the porch stairs and handed Kaylee a steaming cup of hot chocolate. "Mel, this is my father, Howard. Dad, this is Mel Sheridan, local midwife and Jack's wife. Did you meet Jack when you were in the bar?"

"I might've," he said. "It's a pleasure."

"I had no idea you were having family for the holiday, Kaylee," Mel said. "That's fantastic. Howard, let me show you around a little, introduce you to a few people. Kaylee...?"

"I'll stay here and have my hot chocolate, thanks. It's where I told Mallory I'd stay."

She watched as Howard walked off beside Mel and stopped at the first couple they happened upon—Vanessa and Paul Haggerty. Then the minister and his wife. Then Tom Cavanaugh with three girls, a couple of teenagers and a younger one.

Then she saw Mallory and her best friend, Ali. They were

running around the tree with a couple of other girls and Mallory was laughing. They were holding glittery streamers on sticks that sparkled in the lights of the tree.

Kaylee remembered when she and her mom used to sing that Helen Reddy song, "You and Me Against the World," a mother-daughter song. She wished her mother could see the tree. Or know Mallory. But she also knew that if Mallory's situation had presented itself before Meredith passed away, Kaylee wouldn't have done it, wouldn't have taken her on. She wouldn't have gone to Virgin River to seclude herself and ended up with dozens of friends, a new boyfriend, a bunch of pets and a child.

Because you weren't that person then.

Boy, that sounded very much like Meredith. She felt her eyes getting a little moist.

Landry walked up behind her and slid an arm around her waist. "Where's Howard?" he asked.

"Mel's taken him to meet the town. What a glorious night, isn't it?"

"There must be two hundred people in town tonight," he said. "There's food in the bar, if you want a little something to eat."

"Do you have any idea how much my life has changed since I came up here?"

He grinned at her. "Do you have any idea how much my life has changed since you came? Everything is different. I went from being a solitary artist to having trouble spending time in my studio because I'd rather be with you."

"I think I'm going to have to stay a while longer," she said. "Mallory should go back to her classroom after Christmas break, where she's acclimated and comfortable. I can go down to Newport Beach and pick up a few things or we can all go check it out later. In fact, I don't even know if I'm allowed to take her out of this county. I'm not even an official, certified foster parent. I'm a friend of the family. A neighbor."

"Don't worry," he said. "We have room to grow. We have an abundance of possibilities."

"I wish my mom could see this," she said.

"She can see it, honey," he said, pulling her a little tighter against him.

After all the singing and visiting and snacking, Kaylee and her family headed home for a late spaghetti dinner, which they enjoyed at Landry's house. Because of Mallory, he had found nice medium-size trees to put up in both houses so there would be one in Landry's house where they were having their holiday meals and one in Kaylee's house where Mallory had her room.

By the time they finished eating, it was obvious Mallory was worn out from playing with her friends and there would be no games or movies with Landry and Howard on Christmas Eve. Kaylee took Mallory home while Landry checked on the dogs and made sure Howard was settled in his room.

When Kaylee and Mallory walked up to the house, there were two small packages leaning against the front door. "What's this?" Kaylee said, reaching for one. "One says 'Mallory' and one says 'Kaylee' and both say 'Open on Christmas Eve.' I guess we should do as we're told."

"I guess we should," Mallory agreed.

They went inside and didn't wait for Landry. They opened their boxes immediately and discovered matching pajamas, red with white polka dots. They were expensive, classy, grown-up pajamas and they looked to be exactly the right size.

"Oh my gosh, these are so cool," Mallory said.

Mel, Kaylee thought. She had told Mel about how her mother gave her really nice pajamas every year, the joke being if she was going to work in her pajamas, she ought to have good ones. She couldn't think of anyone else she had told about their tradition.

They wore their pajamas to bed, and woke up on Christmas morning to presents under the tree and Landry working on breakfast in Kaylee's kitchen. Kaylee called Howard and told him to come next door for Christmas morning, and he came bearing gifts he'd kept in his trunk.

Kaylee had tried not to go overboard on gifts for Mallory, but she did buy her an iPad and a couple of very expensive books—a leather-bound copy of Harry Potter and one of *Watership Down*. She got her father a couple of shirts and also some books and for Landry some big picture books of art and dogs.

"I guess books are going to be a way of life from now on," Landry observed.

Kaylee and Mallory stayed in their pajamas for a long time, playing with Mallory's new iPad, reading, lounging, talking. For a while in the late morning Kaylee noticed that Mallory became a little quiet and morose. So they talked about her mother, about missing both their mothers, and it was just the two of them remembering and wishing things could have been just a bit different.

But for Kaylee, this Christmas was very special. The Christmas she had hoped would never come was magical and filled with love, filled with people who had never been in her life before. She was in love with a man she could not have even hoped for, he was so wonderful. She had a little girl who depended on her, a little girl she had quickly grown to love and hoped would be with her forever. And there was a prodigal father who had found a way back into her heart.

Mel called. "Merry Christmas! How's it going?" she asked.

"It's lovely. And thank you for the pajamas."

"Pajamas?" Mel asked.

"Mel, it had to be you! Red matching pajamas for me and Mallory? I told you my mother gave me wonderful pajamas every Christmas! There were two boxes leaning up against the door when we got home last night!"

"Kaylee, I was in town. At the tree. I didn't leave any gifts. I bet it was Landry."

But he said no when she asked him. He swore he wasn't lying. "I'm telling the truth. There was a note, wasn't there?"

"But it was printed," she said.

"I think you should accept the fact that you have a guardian angel. And she might be walking the earth or maybe not. But there is one thing I noticed that you didn't."

"What's that?"

"You didn't fall apart at 11:04."

She hadn't. She had glided right through the time and when she noticed a while later, it made her smile. It was as if Christmas had been given back to her. Times ten.

Epilogue

One year later

KAYLEE WAS THRILLED TO BE BACK. SHE COULDN'T imagine spending Christmas anywhere but Virgin River. They'd spent a couple of weeks in Newport Beach early in the year, long enough to check out the house, the towns, the galleries and the beaches. Then they moved back in the fall so that Mallory could start school there. Kaylee arranged to have a small studio erected behind the house in the backyard, just on the other side of the small pool. It was big enough for Landry to use as his studio when they were there.

Mallory was now eleven and had friends in Newport as well as friends in Virgin River. The majority of their time was spent in Newport Beach where the house was larger and the winters milder. And there was a more convenient airport for the traveling they wanted to do. Landry was updating his Virgin River studio, but leaving everything else the same. They had become one of those very fortunate families with a summer home. Their plan was to live in Newport Beach for the school year and spend summers and Christmas in Virgin River. Luckily Tux, Otis and Lady didn't mind long car rides.

Landry liked Newport and there were many opportunities for him in the shops and galleries around Southern California. And Mallory took to the town and the ocean very quickly. She also took to the idea of being part of the family she'd helped to create.

Kaylee was now officially a certified foster parent. The county had found a couple of distant relatives of Mallory's, her mother's second cousins living in Seattle. They hoped to meet them soon, but Mallory was very happy with Landry and Kaylee and had no interest in finding other guardians.

It was as if the three of them came together at exactly the right time. Landry had been lonely, Kaylee had been bereaved and Mallory had been in need of a family to help her with the rest of her growing up.

Kaylee and Landry balanced their work and family life like synchronized swimmers. There were times Landry had to visit stores and galleries to sell his art just as there were writers' conferences and promotional trips Kaylee was anxious to return to.

In the new year Kaylee and Landry were planning to get married.

But they were back in Virgin River for their first Christmas as an official family. They had seen the raising and decorating of the tree, and Kaylee had spent days working with the volunteers who put together food baskets and bought Christmas gifts for residents in need. There were many social gatherings, and Howard was invited to stay with them for the holidays.

The anonymous Christmas fairies again delivered gifts to Kaylee's porch. Sometimes it was obvious where they came from—winter crops from Jillian, canned delicacies from Kelly, handmade fishing flies from Jack, baked goods from Paige and many others who just appreciated all that Kaylee and Landry did for the town. This time Kaylee reciprocated with her own gifts of signed books and baked goods, scattering them around the mountain village.

And a few days before Christmas a small decorated tree had appeared on Kaylee's porch. Her mother had not appeared, which was very disappointing. But there was an ornament on the tree that looked like a pair of pajamas, the kind with feet in. It was made of red glass, something Landry could have crafted. There was a white streamer, also glass, swirling out from the ornament. And on the streamer it said, You'll Be Fine.

And they were.

★ ★ ★ ★ ★

Turn the page for an exclusive look at Robyn Carr's thoughts on visiting the set of the Netflix production of Virgin River.

VIRGIN RIVER IS ALIVE! REALLY!

When my readers write to me to say my characters have become real to them, that they have become like friends or family, I always smile and think, *You have no idea how much so.* Sometimes they're almost *too* real for me. When I am writing a novel, my characters occupy so much space in my mind. I join them for meals, take them on walks, lie beside them in bed, wake up to them in the morning. Sometimes I feel like covering up in the shower!

They talk to me inside my head; I can imagine the sound of their voices, and there are times I've created writing exercises to help bring them to life. A few times I've interviewed characters to get a better fix on who they are. To a novelist, especially this novelist, the most authentic writing doesn't look like writing at all. It looks more like scribbling or daydreaming or, in the best of times, rocking in a hammock. I took this approach when I started writing Virgin River. Me to Mel: *What are you running away from?* Mel to me: *I lost my husband, and it was a brutal loss.*

From the very beginning of my Virgin River novels, I imagined a televised series. Over the years there has been interest from a variety of production companies, but I always knew it wasn't a story that could be told quickly. It's an ongoing story with the potential for growth and an infinite opportunity for expansion.

The Netflix production of the series is a dream come true. And I was very pleased to be invited to visit the set and watch my characters come to life.

Of course, once the announcement was made, before a single cast member was selected, I began to get letters. "They better get Jack's character right!" And the less threatening version: "I hope you have input in selecting the cast!"

However redundant these thoughts may be, we all have our own image in our heads as to what characters might look like. That's the true beauty of fiction—while our eyes scan the page, our mind is busy turning it into a movie in our minds. Will that vision be the same for everyone? Of course not.

But I knew my characters were in good hands, and I could hardly contain my excitement when visiting the set. Inside a giant warehouse was Jack's Bar and several other structures, including Doc's house and clinic. There were enormous painted backdrops of the great outdoors—the monument-size trees, mountains, rivers. As I walked around the set, I was in awe. It was a town, incredible down to the smallest detail. I wandered in and out of the structures, touching the stacks of papers on Doc's desk, checking out the exam table in one of the exam rooms, looking at the small kitchen where so much action happened in the book.

I mounted the steps to Jack's Bar with some trepidation—so much of the series takes place there—would it look anything like I'd imagined? I stopped just inside the door. It took my breath away. Every detail was precise. I sat on a stool at the bar and about a hundred scenarios ran through my mind. A little later in the day I watched the filming of a scene in which Mel was talking to Jack about her life as an urban nurse practitioner, tossing back a couple of shots, wobbling off the stool and needing a little assistance from Jack! Yes, the place was Jack's, down to the animal trophies on the walls. It was exactly as I'd pictured it when I first wrote about it.

And there were so many people everywhere. A large gathering of people at picnic tables outside of Doc's house turned out to be extras. They'd be called on to walk up and down the street, sit in the bar, maybe be waiting for a doctor's appointment, whatever the need. Also within the crowd there were tradesmen: carpenters, painters, builders, cameramen, grips. A good many of them approached me, introduced themselves and asked me, usually a bit shyly, if the set met my expectations. I had to be honest—it far exceeded my wildest desires. When I said so, their faces would light up with pride. They, too, want the show to meet the expectations of the fans of the books.

Also gathered were production people: the director, sound techs and others. I found a chair with my name on the back and we gathered to watch them shoot a scene, then reshoot from several different angles. I must say, I've always had this image of actors as having a glamorous job, but what I saw was very unglamorous. They worked hard, over and over again, standing, sitting, walking, moving. And the days were long—they kept the set open, working twelve hours a day. There were trailers in the parking lot for the stars to relax between scenes, study their lines, rest, rehearse or catch up on emails or phone calls when they weren't required on set.

And the food! This was my biggest surprise of the day. The unions are strict, and those hardworking folks need regular breaks. Every few hours tables full of catered food were put out. Between breaks, great bowls of fruit appeared.

I sat through a table reading of the ninth episode. Every actor read their lines from the script. They did this every day for several days. It was an opportunity for questions and so they could discuss their lines or delivery with the director.

The scenes that I saw or read were not what I wrote in the original book. The script can't follow the book exactly. It would be confusing, too long and the meaning could be lost in translation. The screen is a completely different format. There's no way to film a character's thoughts or internal dialogue, so adjustments are made to make the spirit of the story fit the new format. There were things I didn't recognize but so many new twists I wished I had thought of. It was true to the spirit of my work and it was excellent!

It was a brand-new adventure with some of my most beloved characters. And those people who see the televised series first will have the same experience when they read the books—fresh adventures with favorite characters.

I was on the set for two days and it was magical. I fell in love with everything I saw, but there were a couple of things that stood out. First of all, the extreme gratitude of the cast and crew, to the last. There were hundreds of people working on this series. We provided jobs—hundreds of them. This wasn't something I had done alone, even if I had created the setting and characters. This was something that evolved out of the millions of readers' love for the series.

And the second thing was nestled in the heart. One of the tradesmen asked if I'd seen the sign in the bar. He took me over to show me what he meant. A closer look revealed a slice of tree trunk with some words burned into it. "Virgin

River—Built By Men Of Honor For The Women They Love." It was perfect.

That is the spirit and essence of Virgin River—the town we all want to call home. I hope you enjoy the books and the Netflix series as much as I do. Please visit my website, robyncarr.com, for more behind-the-scenes information about the show.

*If you enjoy the Virgin River series,
you'll love Sullivan's Crossing!*

*Keep reading to discover this series from #1 New York Times
bestselling author Robyn Carr.*

*Neurosurgeon Maggie Sullivan knows she needs to slow down
before she burns out completely, and the best place she can do that
is the campground owned by her eccentric estranged father in rural
Colorado.*

What We Find
*The first story in the Sullivan's Crossing series.
Available now from MIRA Books.*

Just living is not enough…
One must have sunshine, freedom,
and a little flower.

—Hans Christian Andersen

1

Maggie Sullivan sought refuge in the stairwell between the sixth and seventh floors at the far west end of the hospital, the steps least traveled by interns and residents racing from floor to floor, from emergency to emergency. She sat on the landing between two flights, feet on the stairs, arms crossed on her knees, her face buried in her arms. She didn't understand how her heart could feel as if it was breaking every day. She thought of herself as much stronger.

"Well, now, some things never change," a familiar voice said.

She looked up at her closest friend, Jaycee Kent. They had gone to med school together, though residency had separated them. Jaycee was an OB and Maggie, a neurosurgeon. And... they had hidden in stairwells to cry all those years ago when med-school life was kicking their asses. Most of their fellow students and instructors were men. They refused to let the men see them cry.

Maggie gave a wet, burbly huff of laughter. "How'd you find me?" Maggie asked.

"How do you know you're not in my spot?"

"Because you're happily married and have a beautiful daughter?"

"And my hours suck, I'm sleep-deprived, have as many bad days as good and…" Jaycee sat down beside Maggie. "And at least my hormones are cooperating at the moment. Maggie, you're just taking call for someone, right? Just to stay ahead of the bills?"

"Since the practice shut down," Maggie said. "And since the lawsuit was filed."

"You need a break. You're recovering from a miscarriage and your hormones are wonky. You need to get away, especially away from the emergency room. Take some time off. Lick your wounds. Heal."

"He dumped me," Maggie said.

Jaycee was clearly shocked. *"What?"*

"He broke up with me. He said he couldn't take it anymore. My emotional behavior, my many troubles. He suggested professional help."

Jaycee was quiet. "I'm speechless," she finally said. "What a huge ass."

"Well, I was crying all the time," she said, sniffing some more. "If I wasn't with him, I cried when I talked to him on the phone. I thought I was okay with the idea of no children. I'm almost thirty-seven, I work long hours, I was with a good man who was just off a bad marriage and already had a child…"

"I'll give you everything but the good man," Jaycee said. "He's a doctor, for God's sake. Doesn't he know that all you've been through can take a toll? Remove all the stress and you still had the miscarriage! People tend to treat a miscarriage like a heavy period, but it's a death. You lost your baby. You have to take time to grieve."

"Gospel," Maggie said, rummaging for a tissue and giving her nose a hearty blow. "I really felt it on that level. When I found out I was pregnant, it took me about fifteen minutes to start seeing the baby, loving her. Or him."

"Not to beat a dead horse, but you have some hormone issues playing havoc on your emotions. Listen, shoot out some emails tonight. Tell the ones on the need-to-know list you're taking a week or two off."

"No one knows about the pregnancy but you and Andrew."

"You don't have to explain—everyone knows about your practice, your ex-partners, the lawsuit. Frankly, your colleagues are amazed you're still standing. Get out of town or something. Get some rest."

"You might be right," Maggie said. "These cement stairwells are killing me."

Jaycee put an arm around her. "Just like old times, huh?"

The last seven or eight miles to Sullivan's Crossing was nothing but mud and Maggie's cream-colored Toyota SUV was coated up to the windows. This was not exactly a surprise. It had rained all week in Denver, now that she thought about it. March was typically the most unpredictable and sloppiest month of the year, especially in the mountains. If it wasn't rain it could be snow. But Maggie had had such a lousy year the weather barely crossed her mind.

Last year had produced so many medical, legal and personal complications that her practice had shut down a few months ago. She'd been picking up work from other practices, covering for doctors on call here and there and working ER Level

1 Trauma while she tried to figure out how to untangle the mess her life had become. This, on her best friend and doctor's advice, was a much-needed break. After sending a few emails and making a few phone calls she was driving to her dad's house.

She knew she was probably suffering from depression. Exhaustion and general misery. It would stand to reason. Her schedule could be horrific and the tension had been terrible lately. It was about a year ago that two doctors in her practice had been accused of fraud and malpractice and suspended from seeing patients pending an investigation that would very likely lead to a trial. Even though she had no knowledge of the incidents, there was a scandal and it stank on her. There'd been wild media attention and she was left alone trying to hold a wilting practice together. Then the parents of a boy who died from injuries sustained in a terrible car accident while on her watch filed a wrongful death suit. Against her.

It seemed impossible fate could find one more thing to stack on her already teetering pile of troubles. *Hah. Never challenge fate.* She found out she was pregnant.

It was an accident, of course. She'd been seeing Andrew for a couple of years. She lived in Denver and he in Aurora, since they both had demanding careers, and they saw each other when they could—a night here, a night there. When they could manage a long weekend, it was heaven. She wanted more but Andrew was an ER doctor and also the divorced father of an eight-year-old daughter. But they had constant phone contact. Multiple texts and emails every day. She counted on him; he was her main support.

Maggie wasn't sure she'd ever marry and have a family but she was happy with her surprise. It was the one good thing in a bad year. Andrew, however, was *not* happy. He was still in divorce recovery, though it had been three years. He and his ex still fought about support and custody and visits. Maggie didn't understand why. Andrew didn't seem to know what to do with his daughter when he had her. He immediately suggested terminating the pregnancy. He said they could revisit the issue in a couple of years if it turned out to be that important to her and if their relationship was thriving.

She couldn't imagine terminating. Just because Andrew was hesitant? She was thirty-six! How much time did she have to *revisit the issue*?

Although she hadn't told Andrew, she decided she was going to keep the baby no matter what that meant for their relationship. Then she had a miscarriage.

Grief-stricken and brokenhearted, she sank lower. Exactly two people knew about the pregnancy and miscarriage—Andrew and Jaycee. Maggie cried gut-wrenching tears every night. Sometimes she couldn't even wait to get home from work and started crying the second she pulled the car door closed. And there were those stairwell visits. She cried on the phone to Andrew; cried in his arms as he tried to comfort her, all the while knowing he was *relieved*.

And then he'd said, "You know what, Maggie? I just can't do it anymore. We need a time-out. I can't prop you up, can't bolster you. You have to get some help, get your emotional life back on track or something. You're sucking the life out of me and I'm not equipped to help you."

"Are you kidding me?" she had demanded. "You're dropping me when I'm down? When I'm only three weeks beyond a miscarriage?"

And in typical Andrew fashion he had said, "That's all I got, baby."

It was really and truly the first moment she had realized it was all about him. And that was pretty much the last straw.

She packed a bunch of suitcases. Once she got packing, she

couldn't seem to stop. She drove southwest from Denver to her father's house, south of Leadville and Fairplay, and she hadn't called ahead. She did call her mother, Phoebe, just to say she was going to Sully's and she wasn't sure how long she'd stay. At the moment she had no plan except to escape from that life of persistent strain, anxiety and heartache.

It was early afternoon when she drove up to the country store that had been her great-grandfather's, then her grandfather's, now her father's. Her father, Harry Sullivan, known by one and all as Sully, was a fit and hardy seventy and showed no sign of slowing down and no interest in retiring. She just sat in her car for a while, trying to figure out what she was going to say to him. How could she phrase it so it didn't sound like she'd just lost a baby and had her heart broken?

Beau, her father's four-year-old yellow Lab, came trotting around the store, saw her car, started running in circles barking, then put his front paws up on her door, looking at her imploringly. Frank Masterson, a local who'd been a fixture at the store for as long as Maggie could remember, was sitting on the porch, nursing a cup of coffee with a newspaper on his lap. One glance told her the campground was barely occupied—only a couple of pop-up trailers and tents on campsites down the road toward the lake. She saw a man sitting outside his tent in a canvas camp chair, reading. She had expected the sparse population—it was the middle of the week, middle of the day and the beginning of March, the least busy month of the year.

Frank glanced at her twice but didn't even wave. Beau trotted off, disappointed, when Maggie didn't get out of the car. She still hadn't come up with a good entry line. Five minutes passed before her father walked out of the store, across the porch and down the steps, Beau following. She lowered the window.

"Hi, Maggie," he said, leaning on the car's roof. "Wasn't expecting you."

"It was spur-of-the-moment."

He glanced into her back seat at all the luggage. "How long you planning to stay?"

She shrugged. "Didn't you say I was always welcome? Anytime?"

He smiled at her. "Sometimes I run off at the mouth."

"I need a break from work. From all that crap. From everything."

"Understandable. What can I get you?"

"Is it too much trouble to get two beers and a bed?" she asked, maybe a little sarcastically.

"Coors okay by you?"

"Sure."

"Go on and park by the house. There's beer in the fridge and I haven't sold your bed yet."

"That's gracious of you," she said.

"You want some help to unload your entire wardrobe?" he asked.

"Nope. I don't need much for now. I'll take care of it."

"Then I'll get back to work and we'll meet up later."

"Sounds like a plan," she said.

Maggie dragged only one bag into the house, the one with her toothbrush, pajamas and clean jeans. When she was a little girl and both her parents and her grandfather lived on this property, she had been happy most of the time. The general store, the locals and campers, the mountains, lake and valley, wildlife and sunshine kept her constantly cheerful. But the part of her that had a miserable mother, a father who tended to drink a little too much and bickering parents had been forlorn. Then, when she was six, her mother had had enough of hardship, rural living, driving Maggie a long distance to a school that Phoebe found inadequate. Throw in an unsatisfactory husband and that was all she could take. Phoebe took Maggie away to Chicago. Maggie didn't see Sully for several years and her mother married Walter Lancaster, a prominent neurosurgeon with lots of money.

Maggie had hated it all. Chicago, Walter, the big house, the private school, the blistering cold and concrete landscape. She hated the sound of traffic and emergency vehicles. One thing she could recall in retrospect—it brought her mother to life. Phoebe was almost entirely happy, the only smudge on her brightness being her ornery daughter. They had switched roles.

By the time Maggie was eleven she was visiting her dad regularly—first a few weekends, then whole months and some holidays. She lived for it and Phoebe constantly held it over her. *Behave yourself and get good grades and you'll get to spend the summer at that god-awful camp, eating worms, getting filthy and risking your life among bears.*

"Why didn't you fight for me?" she had continually asked her father.

"Aw, honey, Phoebe was right, I wasn't worth a damn as a father and I just wanted what was best for you. It wasn't always easy, neither," he'd explained.

Sometime in junior high Maggie had made her peace with Walter, but she chose to go to college in Denver, near Sully. Phoebe's desire was that she go to a fancy Ivy League college. Med school and residency were a different story—it was tough getting accepted at all and you went to the best career school and residency program that would have you. She ended up in Los Angeles. Then she did a fellowship with Walter, even though she hated going back to Chicago. But Walter was simply one of the best. After that she joined a practice in Denver, close to her dad and the environment she loved. A year later, with Walter finally retired from his practice and enjoying more golf, Phoebe and Walter moved to Golden, Colorado, closer to Maggie. Walter was also seventy, like Sully. Phoebe was a vibrant, social fifty-nine.

Maggie thought she was possibly closer to Walter than to Phoebe, especially as they were both neurosurgeons. She was grateful. After all, he'd sent her to good private schools even when she did every terrible thing she could to show him how unappreciated his efforts were. She had been a completely ungrateful brat about it. But Walter turned out to be a kind, classy guy. He had helped a great many people who proved to be eternally grateful and Maggie had been impressed by his achievements. Plus, he mentored her in medicine. Loving medicine surprised her as much as anyone. Sully had said, "I think it's a great idea. If I was as smart as you and some old coot like Walter was willing to pick up the tab, I'd do it in a New York minute."

Maggie found she loved science but med school was the hardest thing she'd ever taken on, and most days she wasn't sure she could make it through another week. She could've just quit, done a course correction or flunked out, but no—she got perfect grades along with anxiety attacks. But the second they put a scalpel in her hand, she'd found her calling.

She sat on Sully's couch, drank two beers, then lay down and pulled the throw over her. Beau pushed in through his doggy door and lay down beside the couch. The window was open, letting in the crisp, clean March air, and she dropped off to sleep immediately to the rhythmic sound of Sully raking out a trench behind the house. She started fantasizing about summer at the lake, but before she woke she was dreaming of trying to operate in a crowded emergency room where everyone was yelling, bloody rags littered the floor, people hated each other, threw instruments at one another and patients were dying one after another. She woke up panting, her heart hammering. The sun had set and a kitchen light had been turned on, which meant Sully had been to the house to check on her.

There was a sandwich covered in plastic wrap on a plate. A note sat beside it. It was written by Enid, Frank's wife. Enid worked mornings in the store, baking and preparing packaged meals from salads to sandwiches for campers and tourists. *Welcome Home*, the note said.

Maggie ate the sandwich, drank a third beer and went to bed in the room that was hers at her father's house.

She woke to the sound of Sully moving around and saw that it was not quite 5:00 a.m. so she decided to go back to sleep until she didn't have anxiety dreams anymore. She got up at noon, grazed through the refrigerator's bleak contents and went back to sleep. At about two in the afternoon the door to her room opened noisily and Sully said, "All right. Enough is enough."

Sully's store had been built in 1906 by Maggie's great-grandfather Nathaniel Greely Sullivan. Nathaniel had a son and a daughter, married off the daughter and gave the son, Horace, the store. Horace had one son, Harry, who really had better things to do than run a country store. He wanted to see the world and have adventures so he joined the Army and went to Vietnam, among other places, but by the age of thirty-three, he finally married and brought his pretty young wife, Phoebe, home to Sullivan's Crossing. They immediately had one child, Maggie, and settled in for the long haul. All of the store owners had been called Sully but Maggie was always called Maggie.

The store had once been the only place to get bread, milk, thread or nails within twenty miles, but things had changed mightily by the time Maggie's father had taken it on. It had become a recreational facility—four one-room cabins, dry campsites, a few RV hookups, a dock on the lake, a boat launch, public bathrooms with showers, coin-operated laundry facilities, picnic tables and grills. Sully had installed a few extra electrical outlets on the porch so people in tents could charge their electronics and now Sully himself had satellite TV and Wi-Fi. Sullivan's Crossing sat in a valley south of Leadville at the base of some stunning mountains and just off the Continental Divide Trail. The camping was cheap and well managed, the grounds were clean, the store large and well stocked. They had a post office; Sully was the postmaster. And now it was the closest place to get supplies, beer and ice for locals and tourists alike.

The people who ventured there ranged from hikers to hikers to cross-country skiers, boating enthusiasts, rock climbers, fishermen, nature lovers and weekend campers. Plenty of hikers went out on the trails for a day, a few days, a week or even longer. Hikers who were taking on the CDT or the Colorado Trail often planned on Sully's as a stopping point to resupply, rest and get cleaned up. Those hearties were called the thru-hikers, as the Continental Divide Trail was 3,100 miles long while the Colorado Trail was almost 500, but the two trails converged for about 200 miles just west of Sully's. Thus Sully's was often referred to as *the crossing*.

People who knew the place referred to it as Sully's. Some of their campers were one-timers, never seen again, many were regulars within an easy drive looking for a weekend or holiday escape. They were all interesting to Maggie—men, women, young, old, athletes, wannabe athletes, scout troops, nature clubs, weirdos, the occasional creep—but the ones who intrigued her the most were the long-distance hikers, the thru-hikers. She couldn't imagine the kind of commitment needed to take on the CDT, not to mention the courage and strength.

She loved to hear their stories about everything from wildlife on the trail to how many toenails they'd lost on their journey.

There were tables and chairs on the store's wide front porch and people tended to hang out there whether the store was open or closed. When the weather was warm and fair there were spontaneous gatherings and campfires at the edge of the lake. Long-distance hikers often mailed themselves packages that held dry socks, extra food supplies, a little cash, maybe even a book, first-aid items, a new lighter for their campfires, a fresh shirt or two. Maggie loved to watch them retrieve and open boxes they'd packed themselves—it was like Christmas.

Sully had a great big map of the CDT, Colorado Trail and other trails on the bulletin board in the front of the store; it was surrounded by pictures either left or sent back to him. He'd put out a journal book where hikers could leave news or messages. The journals, when filled, were kept by Sully, and had become very well-known. People could spend hours reading through them.

Sully's was an escape, a refuge, a gathering place or recreational outpost. Maggie and Andrew liked to come for the occasional weekend to ski—the cross-country trails were safe and well marked. Occupancy was lower during the winter months so they'd take a cabin, and Sully would never comment on the fact that they were sharing not just a room but a bed.

Before the pregnancy and miscarriage, their routine had been rejuvenating—they'd knock themselves out for a week or even a few weeks in their separate cities, then get together for a weekend or a few days, eat wonderful food, screw their brains out, get a little exercise in the outdoors, have long and deep conversations, meet up with friends, then go back to their separate worlds. Andrew was shy of marriage, having failed at one and being left a single father. Maggie, too, had had a brief, unsuccessful marriage, but she wasn't afraid of trying again and had always thought Andrew would eventually get over it. She accepted the fact that she might not have children, coupled with a man who, right up front, declared he didn't want more.

"But then there was one on the way and does he step up?" she muttered to herself as she walked into the store through the back door. "He complains that I'm too sad for him to deal with. The *bastard*."

"Who's the bastard, darling?" Enid asked from the kitchen. She stuck her head out just as Maggie was climbing onto a stool at the counter, and smiled. "It's so good to see you. It's been a while."

"I know, I'm sorry about that. It's been harrowing in Denver. I'm sure Dad told you about all that mess with my practice."

"He did. Those awful doctors, tricking people into thinking they needed surgery on their backs and everything! Is one of them the bastard?"

"Without a doubt," she answered, though they hadn't been on her mind at all.

"And that lawsuit against you," Enid reminded her, *tsk*ing.

"That'll probably go away," Maggie said hopefully, though there was absolutely no indication it would. At least it was civil. The DA had found no cause to indict her. *But really, how much is one girl supposed to take?* The event leading to the lawsuit was one of the most horrific nights she'd ever been through in the ER—five teenage boys in a catastrophic car wreck, all critical. She'd spent a lot of time in the stairwell after that one. "I'm not worried," she lied. Then she had to concentrate to keep from shuddering.

"Good for you. I have soup. I made some for your dad and Frank. Mushroom. With cheese toast. There's plenty if you're interested."

"Yes, please," she said.

"I'll get it." Enid went around the corner to dish it up.

The store didn't have a big kitchen, just a little turning around room. It was in the southwest corner of the store; there was a bar and four stools right beside the cash register. On the northwest corner there was a small bar where they served adult beverages, and again, a bar and four stools. No one had ever wanted to attempt a restaurant, but it was a good idea to provide food and drink—campers and hikers tended to run out of supplies. Sully sold beer, wine, soft drinks and bottled water in the cooler section of the store, but he didn't sell bottled liquor. For that matter, he wasn't a grocery store but a general store. Along with foodstuffs there were T-shirts, socks and a few other recreational supplies—rope, clamps, batteries, hats, sunscreen, first-aid supplies. For the mother lode you had to go to Timberlake, Leadville or maybe Colorado Springs.

In addition to tables and chairs on the porch, there were a few comfortable chairs just inside the front door where the potbellied stove sat. Maggie remembered when she was a little girl, men sat on beer barrels around the stove. There was a giant ice machine on the back porch. The ice was free.

Enid stuck her head out of the little kitchen. She bleached her hair blond but had always, for as long as Maggie could remember, had black roots. She was plump and nurturing while her husband, Frank, was one of those grizzled, skinny old ranchers. "Is that nice Dr. Mathews coming down on the weekend?" Enid asked.

"I broke up with him. Don't ever call him nice again," Maggie said. "He's a turd."

"Oh, honey! You broke up?"

"He said I was depressing," she said with a pout. "He can kiss my ass."

"Well, I should say so! I never liked him very much, did I mention that?"

"No, you didn't. You said you loved him and thought we'd make handsome children together." She winced as she said it.

"Obviously I wasn't thinking," Enid said, withdrawing back into the kitchen. In a moment she brought out a bowl of soup and a thick slice of cheese toast. Her soup was cream of mushroom and it was made with real cream.

Maggie dipped her spoon into the soup, blew on it, tasted. It was heaven. "Why aren't you my mother?" she asked.

"I just didn't have the chance, that's all. But we'll pretend."

Maggie and Enid had that little exchange all the time, exactly like that. Maggie had always wanted one of those soft, nurturing, homespun types for a mother instead of Phoebe, who was thin, chic, active in society, snobby and prissy. Phoebe was cool while Enid was warm and cuddly. Phoebe could read the hell out of a menu while Enid could cure anything with her chicken soup, her grandmother's recipe. Phoebe rarely cooked and when she did it didn't go well. But lest Maggie completely throw her mother under the bus, she reminded herself that Phoebe had a quick wit, and though she was sarcastic and ironic, she could make Maggie laugh. She was devoted to Maggie and craved her loyalty, especially that Maggie liked her more than she liked Sully. She gave Maggie everything she had to give. It wasn't Phoebe's fault they were not the things Maggie wanted. For example, Phoebe sent Maggie to an extremely good college-prep boarding school that had worked out on many levels, except that Maggie would have traded it all to live with her father. Foolishly, perhaps, but still... And while Phoebe would not visit Sully's campground under pain of death, she had thrown Maggie a fifty-thousand-dollar wedding that Maggie hadn't wanted. And Walter had given her and Sergei a trip to Europe for their honeymoon.

Maggie had appreciated the trip to Europe quite a lot. But she should never have married Sergei. She'd been very busy and distracted and he was handsome, sexy—especially that accent! They'd looked so good together. She took him at face value and failed to look deeper into the man. He was superficial and not trustworthy. Fortunately, or would that be unfortunately, it had been blessedly short. Nine months.

"This is so good," Maggie said. "Your soup always puts me right."

"How long are you staying, honey?"

"I'm not sure. Till I get a better idea. Couple of weeks, maybe?"

Enid shook her head. "You shouldn't come in March. You should know better than to come in March."

"He's going to work me like a pack of mules, isn't he?"

"No question about it. Only person who isn't afraid to come around in March is Frank. Sully won't put Frank to work."

Frank Masterson was one of Sully's cronies. He was about the same age while Enid was just fifty-five. Frank said he had had the foresight to marry a younger woman, thereby assuring himself a good caretaker for his old age. Frank owned a nearby cattle ranch that these days was just about taken over by his two sons, which freed up Frank to hang out around Sully's. Sometimes Sully would ask, "Why don't you just come to work with Enid in the morning and save the gas since all you do is drink my coffee for free and butt into everyone's business?"

When the weather was cold he'd sit inside, near the stove. When the weather was decent he favored the porch. He wandered around, chatted it up with campers or folks who stopped by, occasionally lifted a heavy box for Enid, read the paper a lot. He was a fixture.

Enid had a sweet, heart-shaped face to go with her plump

body. It attested to her love of baking. Besides making and wrapping sandwiches to keep in the cooler along with a few other lunchable items, she baked every morning—sweet rolls, buns, cookies, brownies, that sort of thing. Frank ate a lot of that and apparently never gained an ounce.

Maggie could hear Sully scraping out the gutters around the store. Seventy and up on a ladder, still working like a farmhand, cleaning the winter detritus away. That was the problem with March—a lot to clean up for the spring and summer. She escaped out to the porch to visit with Frank before Sully saw her sitting around and put her to work.

"What are you doing here?" Frank asked.

"I'm on vacation," she said.

"Hmm. Damn fool time of year to take a vacation. Ain't nothing to do now. Dr. Mathews comin'?"

"No. We're not seeing each other anymore."

"Hmm. That why you're here during mud season? Lickin' your wounds?"

"Not at all. I'm happy about it."

"Yup. You look happy, all right."

I might be better off cleaning gutters, she thought. So she turned the conversation to politics because she knew Frank had some very strong opinions and she could listen rather than answer questions. She spotted that guy again, the camper, sitting in his canvas camp chair outside his pop-up tent/trailer under a pull-out awning. His legs were stretched out and he was reading again. She noticed he had long legs.

She was just about to ask Frank how long that guy had been camping there when she noticed someone heading up the trail toward the camp. He had a big backpack and walking stick and something strange on his head. Maggie squinted. A bombardier's leather helmet with earflaps? "Frank, look at that," she said, leaning forward to stare.

The man was old, but old wasn't exactly rare. There were a lot of senior citizens out on the trails, hiking, biking, skiing. In fact, if they were fit at retirement, they had the time and means. As the man got closer, age was only part of the issue.

"I best find Sully," Frank said, getting up and going into the store.

As the man drew near it was apparent he wore rolled-up dress slacks, black socks and black shoes that looked like they'd be shiny church or office wear once the mud was cleaned off. And on his head, a weird WWII aviator's hat. He wore a ski jacket that looked to be drenched and he was flushed and limping.

Sully appeared on the porch, Beau wagging at his side, Frank following. "What the hell?"

"Yeah, that's just wrong," Maggie said.

"Ya think?" Sully asked. He went down the steps to approach the man, Maggie close on his heels, Frank bringing up the rear and Enid on the porch waiting to see what was up.

"Well, there, buddy," Sully said, his hands in his pockets. "Where you headed?"

"Is this Camp Lejeune?"

Everyone exchanged glances. "Uh, that would be in North Carolina, son," Sully said, though the man was clearly older than Sully. "You're a little off track. Come up on the porch and have a cup of coffee, take off that pack and wet jacket. And that silly hat, for God's sake. We need to make a phone call for you. What are you doing out here, soaking wet in your Sunday shoes?"

"Maybe I should wait a while, see if they come," the man said, though he let himself be escorted to the porch.

"Who?" Maggie asked.

"My parents and older brother," he said. "I'm to meet them here."

"Bet they have 'em some real funny hats, too," Frank muttered.

"Seems like you got a little confused," Sully said. "What's your name, young man?"

"That's a problem, isn't it? I'll have to think on that for a while."

Maggie noticed the camper had wandered over, curious. Up close he was distracting. He was tall and handsome, though there was a small bump on the bridge of his nose. But his hips were narrow, his shoulders wide and his jeans were torn and frayed exactly right. They met glances. She tore her eyes away.

"Do you know how you got all wet? Did you walk through last night's rain? Sleep in the rain?" Sully asked.

"I fell in a creek," he said. He smiled though he also shivered.

"On account o' those shoes," Frank pointed out. "He slipped cause he ain't got no tread."

"Well, there you go," Maggie said. "Professor Frank has it all figured out. Let's get that wet jacket off and get a blanket. Sully, you better call Stan the Man."

"Will do."

"Anyone need a hand here?" Maggie heard the camper ask.

"Can you grab the phone, Cal?" Sully asked. Sully put the man in what had been Maggie's chair and started peeling off his jacket and outer clothes. He leaned the backpack against the porch rail and within just seconds Enid was there with a blanket, cup of coffee and one of her bran muffins. Cal brought the cordless phone to the porch. The gentleman immediately began to devour that muffin as Maggie looked him over.

"Least he'll be reg'lar," Frank said, reclaiming his chair.

Maggie crouched in front of the man and while speaking very softly, she asked if she could remove the hat. Before quite getting permission she pulled it gently off his head to reveal wispy white hair surrounding a bald dome. She gently ran her fingers around his scalp in search of a bump or contusion. Then she pulled him to his feet and ran her hands around his torso and waist. "You must've rolled around in the dirt, sir," she said. "I bet you're ready for a shower." He didn't respond. "Sir? Anything hurt?" she asked him. He just shook his head. "Can you smile for me? Big, wide smile?" she asked, checking for the kind of paralysis caused by a stroke.

"Where'd you escape from, young man?" Sully asked him. "Where's your home?"

"Wakefield, Illinois," he said. "You know it?"

"Can't say I do," Sully said. "But I bet it's beautiful. More beautiful than Lejeune, for sure."

"Can I have cream?" he asked, holding out his cup.

Enid took it. "Of course you can, sweetheart," she said. "I'll bring it right back."

In a moment the gentleman sat with his coffee with cream, shivering under a blanket while Sully called Stan Bronoski. There were a number of people Sully could have reached out to—a local ranger, state police aka highway patrol, even fire and rescue. But Stan was the son of a local rancher and was the police chief in Timberlake, just twenty miles south and near the interchange. It was a small department with a clever deputy who worked the internet like a pro, Officer Paul Castor.

Beau gave the old man a good sniffing, then moved down the stairs to Cal who automatically began petting him.

Sully handed the phone to Maggie. "Stan wants to talk to you."

"He sounds like someone who wandered off," Stan said to Maggie. "But I don't have any missing persons from nearby. I'll get Castor looking into it. I'm on my way. Does he have any ID on him?"

"We haven't really checked yet," Maggie said into the phone. "Why don't I do that while you drive. Here's Sully."

Maggie handed the phone back to her dad and said, "Pass the time with Stan while I chat with this gentleman."

Maggie asked the man to stand again and deftly slid a thin wallet out of his back pocket. She urged him to sit, and opened it up. "Well, now," she said. "Mr. Gunderson? Roy Gunderson?"

"Hmm?" he said, his eyes lighting up a bit.

Sully repeated the name into the phone to Stan.

"And so, Roy, did you hurt anything when you fell?" Maggie asked.

He shook his head and sipped his coffee. "I fell?" he finally asked.

Maggie looked at Sully, lifting a questioning brow. "A Mr. Gunderson from Park City, Utah," Sully said. "Wandered off from his home a few days ago. On foot."

"He must've gotten a ride or something," Cal said.

"His driver's license, which was supposed to be renewed ten years ago, says his address is in Illinois."

"Stan says he'll probably have more information by the time he gets here, but this must be him. Dementia, he says."

"You can say that again," Maggie observed. "I can't imagine what the last few days have been like for him. He must have been terrified."

"He look terrified to you?" Frank asked. "He might as well be on a cruise ship."

"Tell Stan we'll take care of him till he gets here."

Maggie went about the business of caring for Mr. Gunderson, getting water and a little soup into him while the camper, Cal, chatted with Sully and Frank, apparently well-known to them. When this situation was resolved she meant to find out more about him, like how long he'd been here.

She took off Roy's shoes and socks and looked at his feet—no injuries or frostbite but some serious swelling and bruised toenails. She wondered where he had been and how he'd gotten the backpack. He certainly hadn't brought it from home or packed it himself. That would be too complicated for a man in his condition. It was a miracle he could carry it!

Two hours later, the sun lowering in the sky, an ambulance had arrived for Roy Gunderson. He didn't appear to be seriously injured or ill but he was definitely unstable and Stan wasn't inclined to transport him alone. He could bolt, try to get out of a moving car or interfere with the driver, although Stan had a divider cage in his police car.

What Maggie and Sully had learned, no thanks to Roy himself, was that he'd been cared for at home by his wife, wandered off without his GPS bracelet, walked around a while before coming upon a rather old Chevy sedan with the keys in the ignition, so he must have helped himself. The car was reported stolen from near his house but had no tracking device installed. And since Mr. Gunderson hadn't driven in years, no one put him with the borrowed motor vehicle for a couple of days. The car was found abandoned near Salt Lake City with Roy's jacket in it. From there the old man had probably hitched a ride. His condition was too good to have walked for days. Roy was likely left near a rest stop or campgrounds where he helped himself to a backpack. Where he'd been, what he'd done, how he'd survived was unknown.

The EMTs were just about to load Mr. Gunderson into the back of the ambulance when Sully sat down on the porch steps with a loud huff.

"Dad?" Maggie asked.

Sully was grabbing the front of his chest. Over his heart. He was pale as snow, sweaty, his eyes glassy, his breathing shallow and ragged.

"Dad!" Maggie shouted.

If you tell the truth you don't have to remember anything.

—MARK TWAIN

2

It's different when it's your father, when your father is Sully, the most beloved general-store owner in a hundred square miles. Maggie felt a rising panic that she hoped didn't show. First, she gave him an aspirin. Then she rattled off medication orders to the EMT, though she wasn't the physician in charge and it would have to be approved via radio. Poor Mr. Gunderson ended up in the back of Stan's squad car and Sully was put on the gurney. The emergency tech immediately started an EKG, slapping electrodes onto his chest, getting an oxygen mask over his nose and mouth.

Maggie was in the ambulance immediately, reading the EKG as it was feeding out. Beau was barking and jumping outside the ambulance door, trying to get inside.

"Beau!" Maggie yelled. "No, Beau! Stay!"

She heard a whistle, then a disappointed whine, then the door to the ambulance closed and they pulled away.

"Maggie," Sully said, pulling the mask away. "See he didn't follow. I don't leave him very much."

Maggie peeked out the back window. "It's okay, Dad. He's in front of the porch with that guy. That camper. Enid will see he's taken care of."

The driver was on the radio saying they were en route with a possible coronary.

"The lost guy with dementia?" the dispatcher asked.

"Negative, we got Sully from the store. Chest pains, diaphoretic, BP 190 over 120, pulse rapid and thready. His daughter is with us. Dr. Maggie Sullivan. She wants us to draw an epi and administer nitro. She stuck an aspirin in his mouth."

"Is he conscious?"

"I'm conscious," Sully whispered. "Maggie. I ain't quite ready."

"Easy, Dad, easy. I'm right here for you," Maggie said. "Let's start some Ringer's, TKO."

"Not you," Sully said. "You're shaking!"

"You want me to do it, Sully?" the young EMT asked.

"Better you than her. Look at her." Then he moaned.

"We need morphine," Maggie said. "Get an order for the morphine and ask for an airlift to Denver. We have to transport to Denver stat. Gimme that IV setup."

She got the IV started immediately, so fast the EMT said, "Wow!"

A few years ago Walter, her stepfather, had suffered a small stroke. *Stroke*. That was her territory and she handled him with calm and ease. He was treated immediately, the recovery was swift, his disability minor and addressed in physical therapy in a matter of weeks. A textbook case.

This felt entirely different.

"Gimme your cell phone," she said to the EMT. She didn't have hers, of course, because it was back at Sully's in her purse. The young man handed it over without question and she called Municipal Hospital. "This is Dr. Maggie Sullivan. I'm in an ambulance with my father, en route to you. I don't have my cell. Can you connect me with Dr. Rob Hollis? It's an emergency. Thank you."

It took only a moment. "What have you got, Maggie?" her friend Rob asked.

"My dad—seventy-year-old male," she said, running through his symptoms. "The EMT is running an EKG and we can send it." She looked at the EMT. "We can send it, right?"

"Right."

"If we get a medical airlift from Timberlake, we'll be there in no time. Will you meet me?"

"Absolutely," he said. "Try to stay calm."

"I'm good," she said.

"She's a wreck," Sully muttered. "Airlift. Gonna cost a goddamn fortune."

"I gave him nitro, oxygen and morphine. He seems to be comfortable. EKG coming to the ER for you."

It was not like this with Walter. With Walter, whom she'd become close to once she'd passed through adolescence, she was able to be a physician—objective, cool, confident. With Sully, she was a daughter clinging to her medical training with an internal fear that if anything terrible happened to him she would be forever lost.

Sully was not experiencing terrible pain once the morphine kicked in; his breathing was slightly labored and his blood pressure remained high. Maggie watched over him through the transfer into a medical transport helicopter and stayed with him while he was taken into the emergency room where Dr. Hollis waited.

"Jesus, Maggie," Rob said, his stethoscope going immediately to Sully's chest. "Nothing like making an entrance."

"Who are you?" Sully asked.

"Rob Hollis, cardiac surgeon. And you must be Sully." He picked up a section of the EKG tape, glancing at it almost casually. "We're going to run a few tests, draw some blood, bring down that blood pressure if possible and then, very probably, depending on the test results, go to the OR and perform a bypass surgery. Do you know what that is?"

"Sure I do," Sully said, his voice tired and soft. "I'm the last one on my block to get one."

"Maggie, this is going to take a while even though we'll push it through with stat orders. Maybe you should go to the doctor's lounge and rest."

"She should go grab a beer and find a poker game but she don't need no rest," Sully said. "She's plenty rested."

"I'll stay with my dad," she said. "I'll keep out of your way."

"You're going to be bored," Rob said.

Not as long as he's breathing, she thought. "I'll manage."

Maggie knew almost everyone in the hospital, in the ER and the OR. Because of her stature as a surgeon, she was given many updates on the tests, the results, the surgery. She even thought to ask one of her friends, an operating room charge nurse, for the loan of her car once Sully was out of recovery, out of danger, and resting comfortably in the coronary care unit. Here she was in Denver with no vehicle, no purse, credit cards, phone, nothing, but there was a spare key to her house under the flowerpot on the back patio and she could write a counter check at her bank for cash. There might even be a duplicate or extra credit or debit card she didn't keep in her purse. In her closet there would be something to wear. In fact, there were drawers full of scrubs, if it came to that.

She wasn't bored and she'd had plenty of sleep before Sully's medical emergency, but by the time she stood at his bedside in the CCU at five in the morning she was so exhausted she could hardly stand up. She had the wiggles from too much caffeine, looked like bloody hell and hadn't had a shower since leaving Denver for Sullivan's Crossing. It reminded her of some of those days in residency when she stayed at the hospital for over forty-eight hours with only a catnap here and there. This time it was all stress.

She went home in her borrowed car to freshen up. She located an old wallet and purse, found a credit card she didn't often use in her file cabinet and was back at the hospital by eight. By nine they were rousing Sully.

"Maggie, you gotta get me out of here," he rasped. "They won't leave me alone."

"There's nothing you can do but be your charming self," she said.

"They got some breathing thing they force on me every hour," he complained. "And I'm starving to death. And it feels like they opened my chest with a Black & Decker saw."

"I'll ask for more pain meds," she offered. She lifted a hand toward the nurse and got a nod in return.

"Maggie, you gotta go run the store..."

"The store is fine. I called Enid an hour ago, gave her a progress report and checked on them. Frank stayed with her yesterday till closing, they took Beau home with them and they should be opening up about now. She's going to call Tom Canaday and see if he has any extra time to help out. It's all taken care of."

He just groaned and closed his eyes. "'Bout time Frank worked off some of that coffee he's been freeloading. What about you?" he asked.

"What about me? I'm here with you."

He opened his eyes. They were not his usual warm or mischievous brown eyes. They were angry. "I'm not good with hospitals. I've never been in one before."

She thought for a moment because surely he was wrong. "Huh," she finally said. "Never? That's something, Sully. Seventy years old and never spent a night in a hospital."

"Turns out I knew what I was doing. Look what happens. They have a tube shoved up my—"

"Catheter," she said.

"Get it out! *Now!*"

The nurse arrived with a syringe, putting it in the IV. "You should feel a lot better in just a few minutes, Mr. Sullivan."

"How long do I have to stay here?"

"In the care unit? Just a day or two."

"Then I can go home?"

"That's a good question for the doctor, but it's usually anywhere from three to eight days."

"I'll do two," he said without missing a beat. "That's all I got."

"There's recovery time involved after heart surgery, Dad," Maggie said.

"And what are you going to do?"

"I'm going to stay with you. Take care of you."

He was quiet for a moment. "God help me," he whispered.

We're going to need a lot more drugs, Maggie thought.

A great deal of maneuvering was required for Maggie to get her affairs in order, so to speak.

According to Enid, Tom Canaday, their handyman and helper, was going to adjust his schedule to spend more time at Sully's. Tom had a lot of jobs—he drove a tow truck, worked on car repairs in a service station, drove a plow in winter and did roadwork in summer, which kept him on the county payroll. He did a variety of handyman and maintenance jobs around the area. He'd do just about anything if the money was right because he was a single father with four kids aged twelve to nineteen. Sometimes he'd bring one or two along to help him or just to hang out with him. And now, when Tom couldn't work, he could send his oldest son, Jackson, the nineteen-year-old.

Maggie asked Enid if she could come to Denver to pick her up, drive her back to Sully's where she would get her own car and some incidentals like her cell phone, purse, extra clothes, makeup and the like. Also, she would get some clothing and a shaving kit for Sully, who was not going back home soon, a subject she was not looking forward to discussing with him.

Enid said she'd be at the hospital in the morning. "Can I see him when I get there?" she asked.

"You don't want to see him, Enid. He's a huge pain in the ass. He's been complaining and trying to get out of here from the minute he arrived and the fact that he can hardly get out of bed hasn't deterred him one bit."

"Well, I could've told you it would be like that."

Maggie was waiting outside the hospital's front entrance for Enid when who should pull up in a banged-up old red pickup truck but Frank. Maggie sighed. *Just what I need—two hours held captive by Frank.*

All the way back to Sullivan's Crossing, Frank droned on and on about the evils of government in every conspiracy theory ever imagined, including his belief that commercial jetliners were spraying the atmosphere with enhanced jet stream in an effort to lower the temperature of the earth to combat global warming. "Of which there ain't no damn such thing anyhow."

By the time they got back to the crossing, she was exhausted all over again. "I can't believe you did that to me," she said to Enid.

"You find him a little talkative, Maggie?" she asked with a teasing smile. "He got there, didn't he? We're a little short-handed around here, you know."

Maggie hurried to gather up what she needed and asked Enid to make her a sandwich.

"Already done, cupcake. Turkey and swiss on whole grain. And I packed up a box of cookies and muffins for Sully."

"I'm afraid his cookie and muffin days are over for now. Listen, Enid, we can put a sign on the door. Close up for a while. You and Frank just can't handle the whole place on your own."

"We're getting by all right, honey. People understand about stuff like this. Tom's been here with his boy. That camper with the pop-up trailer has even been pitching in. Nice fella, Cal."

"Oh, Enid, he'll probably steal the silver! If we had any."

"Nah, he's a good enough fella. He's got that spot and asked for a weekly rate. I offered him the house for his shower but he said he's doing just fine."

"He's probably homeless," Maggie said. "You know we don't really know these people."

"Tom offered to try to spend some nights around here, but we don't hardly have anybody in the park anyhow. And besides, we got Cal here if there's trouble, which there ain't likely to be. Cal's got a cell phone."

"He'll probably break into the store and clean us out the first night and—"

"Maggie, the first night's come and gone and he's still here, helping out. You've been in the city too long. That isn't gonna happen, honey. And for sure not in March! No one's passing through in this muck and mess."

But there had been times when the police or sheriff or

ranger had to be called, when a few campers had a little too much fun, too much to drink, got aggressive. Sully had a baseball bat he took with him if he went out to see what was going on late at night. There was a domestic once when Maggie was young—some man knocking around his woman and Sully just couldn't resist. He decked him, knocked him out. Maggie had been stunned, not just that her dad would do that but that he was that strong. Plus, even though she'd always been told, *we never hit, no matter what*, she had adored him for it.

It was true the crossing was mostly peaceful. But they were isolated, especially from November to March, and from time to time had a little trouble. They didn't have any paid security like some of the bigger or state-operated campgrounds. Just Sully. Maggie could count on one hand the number of nights Sully had spent away from the campground. Her graduations, her wedding.

"Was it awful?" Enid asked of Sully's heart attack.

"I was terrified," Maggie whispered back.

Maggie went back to Denver, to a hospital she knew well, and commenced what would become three of the longest weeks of her life. Sully was healing nicely and making great progress...and he was incorrigible. He sulked, he didn't follow explicit instructions, he got very constipated and it riled him beyond measure. He began speaking abusively to the nursing staff. He went from stonily silent to loud and abrasive; he wouldn't eat his food and he was moved to a private room because Maggie couldn't bear the effect he had on his roommate.

"What is the *matter* with you?" she ground out.

"Besides the fact that my chest was ripped open and I haven't had a good shit in ten days? Not a goddamn thing!"

"You haven't been here ten days, but I'm going to get you fixed right away. And you're going to be sorry you complained to me." She put two residents on the job; she told them to use any means available and legal, just make it happen. She said she didn't want to know how they did it but they were to see to it he had a bowel movement by morning.

When she came in to see Sully the next day, he was smiling. And he was passably pleasant most of the day.

After seven days in the hospital she took him home to her house where she was cloistered with him, fed him low-sodium and low-fat foods, took him to rehab every other day and listened to him bitch for another thirteen days.

Finally, she took him back to Sullivan's Crossing.

And Sully was reborn. His temperament immediately smoothed over. His facial features relaxed. He greeted Enid, Frank and Tom, and spent about fifteen straight minutes greeting Beau. Then Sully ate a salad with turkey slices and complimented Maggie's thoughtfulness for the lunch.

"I think you dropped twenty pounds," Enid said.

"Twelve. And I could spare it. Now, Enid, it looks like I'm going to be keeping Frank company for a while. Maggie says I have to go slow. We should get Tom's boy to help out with things like stocking shelves; get Tom to finish cleaning the gutters and clearing that trench around the house to the stream so we don't get flooded, if we aren't already."

"You aren't," a voice said. "I finished clearing that trench and I checked the basement at your house."

Everyone turned to see the man standing in the doorway of the store. Cal. Maggie looked at him closely for the first time. He was somewhere just under forty, with dark brown hair and light brown eyes that twinkled.

"Cal," Sully said. "You're still here? Good to see you! You been helping out?"

Cal stuck out a hand. "Sorry about the heart trouble, Sully.

Glad to see you're doing so well. To tell the truth, you look better than ever."

"What the devil you doing here so long?" Sully asked, shaking his hand.

"Well, I could say I was here to help out, but that wouldn't be true. I'm waiting for better weather to check out the CDT. Since I was here, I tried to lend Enid a hand."

"He did a great job, Sully," Enid said. "He's been bringing in the heavy boxes from the storeroom, helped stock shelves, swept up, hauled trash, the kind of stuff that's on your schedule."

"That's awful neighborly," Sully said. "We'll cut you a check."

The man chuckled and ducked his head with a hint of shyness that Maggie was immediately taken with.

"No need, Sully. I didn't mind helping out. It gave me something to do."

"If you're camping, you must have had other things on your mind to take up time."

"To tell the truth, I messed up my planning. I thought I'd pick up the CDT out of Leadville but where it's not icy, it's flooding. A few chores weren't anything. Enid took care of me. I appreciate the hospitality."

"Are you planning to leave your vehicle in Leadville?" Sully asked.

"That was the plan."

"Well, you can leave it here if it suits you and pick up the trail just over that hill," Sully said, pointing. "Whenever you're ready and no charge. No charge on the campsite, either."

"You don't have to do that, but it's appreciated. In fact, this being your first day home, I'll stick around a few days in case you need a hand. I don't have urgent plans."

"Are you homeless?" Maggie asked.

Everyone stared at her.

"I mean, you don't need money and you're in no hurry and you're happy to help and... It's unusual. Not that people aren't friendly, but..."

He flashed her a beautiful smile. His front teeth were just slightly imperfect and it gave him a sexy, impish look. "No problem. In fact, I am homeless. I'm on the road, probably till fall. But I have the truck, the camper, I'm always on the look-out for places to charge up the laptop and phone and I think Enid gave me special treatment—some of the meals I got here were way better than what's for sale in the cooler. I have what I need for now. And yes, I can pay my way."

"Independently wealthy?" Maggie asked. And for someone who didn't mean to be rude, she realized she certainly sounded it. "Trust-fund baby?"

"Maggie!" Sully reprimanded. "She might be a little cranky, Cal, on account of I turned out not to be the best patient on record."

"No problem at all. I'm the suspicious type myself. No, not a trust-fund baby, Dr. Sullivan. Just a little savings and a lot of patience." He shifted his gaze to Sully. "Right now I have time for a game of checkers. Any takers?"

"Don't do it, Sully," Frank said. "He's brutal."

"That makes it irresistible, now, don't it?"

That's when Maggie wandered off to the house.

Sully's house was over a hundred years old. It had been built when Maggie's great-grandfather was a young man, before he and his wife had their first child. The improvements and changes since it was originally built were haphazard at best. When old refrigerators died, new ones appeared and they never matched the original kitchen color or design. The washer and dryer started in the basement but eventually made it up to the back porch; the porch was finally closed in so a person wouldn't freeze doing laundry in winter. Furniture was replaced as it wore out but never was a whole room remodeled. It was long overdue.

But the design was surprisingly modern for a house built in 1906 and Sully himself had reroofed it. There was a living room, dining room and a kitchen with nook on the main floor. There had been three bedrooms and a bath but Sully had installed a master bath attached to the largest bedroom. He had burrowed into the third bedroom for the space, which left a smaller than usual room, so it became his office. Over time he'd finished off the attic into a cozy loft bedroom but Maggie had no idea why. He didn't marry again. It wasn't like there were offspring wrestling for space. He'd recently remodeled the basement into what he called a rumpus room. "For the grandchildren I guess I'll never get," he said. "No pressure."

"It's not really too late," Maggie said. "If I ever find the time." *And the right man...*

"There wasn't that much to do in winter so I worked on the house a little bit," was all he said.

She loved the house, though it was in serious need of a face-lift.

She spent the afternoon settling their belongings into their rooms. Sully didn't make an appearance. It crossed her mind to check on him, to make sure he wasn't doing too much, but she trusted Enid to keep an eye on him.

She came back across the yard to the store a little after four and found Sully sitting by the stove with only Beau for company.

"Tired?" she asked him.

"I never been the nap kind of man but I'm starting to see the merits," he said.

"Did you send Enid and Frank home?"

"Nothing going on around here, no need for them to stay. We can close up early. After we have a little nip." He lifted his bushy salt-and-pepper brows in her direction. "Your friend the doctor, he said that's all right."

"Did he, now? You wouldn't lie about that, would you?"

"I would if need be, but he did indeed say that." Sully got up, a bit slower than he used to, and walked through the store to the little bar. He went behind while she grabbed a stool. "What's your pleasure?" he asked.

"Is there a cold white wine back there with the cork out?" she asked.

"No, but it would be my pleasure to uncork this really nice La Crema and let you steal it. You can take it back to the house with you."

"That sounds like a plan."

"Now, I'd like you to do something for me, Maggie."

"What's that, Dad?"

"I'd like you to go out to the porch where that nice Cal Jones just sat down, and invite him to join us. Right after you apologize for being such an ass."

"Dad..."

"You think I'm kidding around? Really, I didn't raise you like that and maybe Phoebe did but I doubt it. She's snooty but not nasty. I've never seen the like."

She took a breath. "After your behavior in the hospital..."

"After you get your chest sawed open, we'll compare notes. For now, the man was decent enough to help Enid and we're grateful. Aren't we, Maggie?"

She sighed. "You know what this is like? This is like getting in trouble at school and being marched back to the classroom to humbly take your medicine. How do you know he's not a serial killer?"

"I'm not," said an amused voice.

"Don't you just have the worst habit of sneaking up on people!" she said. "This old man is a heart patient!"

"That's no way to worm back into my good graces, calling me old," Sully said. "Besides, I saw him coming. Say what I told you, Maggie."

"I might've been a little impatient today," she said. "And perhaps I didn't show my gratitude very well..."

"She was an ass," Sully said. "Not like her, neither. You want a little pop, son?"

"You're on," he said, sitting on one of the stools. "How about a Chivas, neat, water back."

While Sully pulled the cork out of the wine, he talked. "So, Maggie here is very tough but tenderhearted and usually very good with her manners. Much better than I am. But I think putting up with me for three weeks since this operation just plain ruined her." He pushed a glass of wine toward Maggie. "She isn't going to do that again. Unless you give her trouble. Don't give her trouble, son. She's very strong."

Maggie the bold and strong, she thought.

"I don't have any trouble in me, Sully," Cal said with a chuckle. "I'm just checking out Colorado."

"And what are you doing here?" she asked. When both men looked at her, she held up a hand. "Hey, no offense, but people usually have a reason for finding themselves at Sullivan's Crossing."

"No offense taken," he said. "I've been doing some hiking here and there. Hiking and camping. There's a lot of stuff online about hiking the Divide, but you don't want to hit the Rockies before May, and that might even be too soon..."

"Not this year," Sully said. "It's an early thaw. We damn near washed into the lake one year with an early thaw. The snowpack flows to the west, but we're not without our wash.

I gotta figure out how to get that garden in without lifting a finger."

Maggie laughed. "Once again, he talks about me like I'm not even here. Of course I'll help with the garden. So, you think you might hike the whole CDT?"

Cal shook his head. "I don't think so, just a little piece of it, but I'd like to get up there and see what I see. I'll hike and camp for a few weeks, then I'll decide what's next. Montana, maybe. Or Idaho. Canada. But not in winter."

Over the years, Maggie had learned that you don't ask a hiker why they take on something like the Appalachian Trail or the CDT. They're driven. They want to be stronger than the trail, to break it or maybe just survive it. "The CDT is the longest one," Maggie pointed out. "It can get lonely out there."

"I know. I like the solitude. I also like the people I run into. People who want to do that are... I don't know how to explain it. It's like they have things to understand about themselves and every single one of them has different things to figure out."

"And what do you have to figure out, Mr. Jones?" she asked.

"I don't know. Nothing too deep. How about what to do next? Where to settle?"

That sounded like true freedom to Maggie—choosing something new. She'd eventually have to go back to work in Denver. Right now she was using Sully's rehabilitation as an excuse. She was needed here.

"If you like solitude, then that must be why you chose this campground in March," Sully said, sipping from his glass and letting go a giant *ahhhh* as he appreciated it. Maggie and Cal laughed. "Doc says this is all right but you can bet your sweet ass that bitch of a nurse didn't bring me no nightcap!"

"Dad!"

"You expect me to apologize for saying that? That was a simple, true statement!" He shook his head. "That one nurse, the one at night with the black, black hair and silver roots, she was mean as a snake. If I die and go to hell, I'll meet her there."

Cal looked at Maggie and with a wry smile said, "Long convalescence?"

"Three weeks of my life I'll never get back," Maggie said.

No man can, for any considerable time,
wear one face to himself, and another to the multitude,
without finally getting bewildered as to which
is the true one.

—Nathaniel Hawthorne

3

Once Sully had gone to bed, Maggie got on her computer. She might not be a trained investigator, but she was damn sure an experienced researcher. She started by collecting the possible variants on the name Cal. Calvin, Calhoun, Caleb, Callahan, Calloway, even Pascal. Then she tried just plain Cal Jones. She found several obituaries but not a single reference that could be their camper, so if he was a serial killer he was still an unknown one. She wasted two hours on that.

She heard her phone chime with a text. She was surprised to see it was from Andrew.

I heard about Sully. Is he doing well? Are you?

We're fine, she texted back.
There was no response and she went back to tinkering on

her laptop. About ten minutes later her phone rang and she saw the call was from Andrew. She sent it to voice mail. There was a ping—message received.

There were so many times over the past three weeks she had wished to hear Andrew's confident and reassuring voice. To feel his arms closing around her. She had a few close women friends. There was Jaycee, her closest friend. Jaycee had called or texted every day to see how they were getting along. There were a few of the women she worked with, but Andrew had been the only man in her life for a long time. Since Sergei. And Sergei had been a total mistake. An artist of Ukrainian descent who, she eventually realized, wanted to marry an American doctor or someone of equal income potential. He'd had the mistaken impression she came from money because of the show Phoebe and Walter could put on. Walter could affect an image of aristocracy.

"I am so lousy at men," she muttered to herself.

But Andrew shouldn't have been a mistake. Her eyes had been wide-open—they were both professionals with young practices and bruised hearts. She'd been thirty-four, he almost forty. His marriage had been longer but far more expensive than hers, and his ex had been so mean. Sergei hadn't been mean, not at all. In fact he'd been charming. Sweet. And after nine months of marriage expected a house, a car and 50 percent of her income for the next twenty years.

It turned out she'd had good instincts about lawyers. Thank God.

She didn't listen to Andrew's message, but she saved it. There would probably be a time soon when she'd crave that soothing voice. She wondered if he even realized that after all the storms she'd weathered lately one of her darkest hours had been the sight of Sully gripping his chest, panting, washing pale. She knew true terror in that moment.

It was amusing to Maggie that her mother thought Sully was such a loser, a simple, laid-back general-store owner, a country boy, an underachiever. Maggie didn't see him that way at all. Sully was her rock. In fact, he was a rock for a lot of people. He had a strong moral compass, for one thing. He worked hard but he wasn't a slave to his work, he saw the merits to a balanced life. He was possessed of a country wisdom attained through many years of watching people and learning about human nature. And he was true. He was the most loyal individual on earth. Sully thought Maggie was smart to strive to be as successful as Walter. But Maggie wished she could be more like Sully.

She settled back on the couch and decided to listen to Andrew's message.

"Maggie, listen, babe, I'm sorry about your crisis with Sully. Is he there with you in Denver? When I get a day I can come up and check on you both..."

"I don't want to be checked on," she said to the phone.

"It's been pretty crazy here or I might've heard sooner. I just heard about the bypass a couple of days ago but I was told he was doing great and you were with him so I didn't jump on the phone."

"Yeah, why would you do that?"

"And what's this I hear that you took a vacation? Of indefinite duration? I hope that doesn't have anything to do with our disagreement. I know you're probably upset with me, I know that. Honey, I just want what's best for you and I could tell I wasn't helping anything. Maybe I made the wrong call but I thought it was probably best if you looked further than me to get support right now. I don't know anyone who could cope with all you've been through any better than you have, but I just felt so helpless, and that wasn't good for you..."

"I sucked the life out of you, remember?"

"Call me, please. Or email me or something. Let me know what I can do, when we can talk. You know how much I care about you and Sully."

"Actually, I'm a little murky on that…"

"Maggie?" Sully said from the hall. "Who the devil are you talking to?"

She jumped in surprise. He was wearing his pajamas, his white hair mussed and spiking. "Um…the television?"

"The TV isn't on," he said.

"Okay, I was talking back to a message from Andrew. You don't dump someone and then leave a kind and caring message. Too little, too late."

"Hmm," he said, thinking on that for a moment.

"I guess I need a fresh start," she informed him. "I'd like to go back to eighth grade and redo everything."

"I think this heart attack business has taken a toll on you," he said. "I'm sorry about that."

"It wasn't exactly your fault," she said. "Aside from your genetics, you've been in good health. Your father and grandfather probably had health issues they didn't even know about. At least yours is resolved."

"I understand all that, but there's one thing you're going to have to make peace with one way or another. I'm seventy. I'm going to die before you do."

"*That* takes a toll," she informed him. "Remember you said you weren't quite ready? You remember saying that? In the ambulance?"

"If God takes me home in March it's only because he means to punish everyone I hold dear, from the folks who help run this little place to all the folks who pass through. I wasn't done with the cleanup. That's all I meant by that. Now, will you take one of them anxiety pills that are so popular and get some sleep? Unless you want to bitch at Andrew's message some more, of course."

"I thought coming back here would help me get perspective," she said.

"We been in Denver, Maggie. We haven't been back two full days. Even God needed seven to get it together. Jesus." He ran a hand over his head and wandered back to his bedroom.

"I've always had kind of high expectations of myself," she yelled at his back.

"No shit," he returned.

Maggie woke up at first light and walked into the kitchen. There were no signs of life and Sully's bedroom door stood open. He'd made his bed and was gone. This was typical of life here—he rarely put on a pot of coffee at the house, only in the worst of winter when venturing to the store was a useless chore. In spring, summer and fall he dressed and trudged over to the store where he'd start the big pot for Enid.

Before she even got up the steps to the back porch, she spied Sully. He was down at Cal Jones's campsite sitting on a small camp stool, holding a mug of coffee on his knee, petting Beau with the other hand. Cal, on the other hand, was crouched before a small grill, sitting on the heel of his boot, stirring something in a frying pan. She caught the unmistakable aroma of bacon.

When Beau saw her he got up, started wagging his tail and ran to her as though he hadn't seen her in weeks. "Good morning, gentlemen. Something smells good."

Cal cracked two eggs on top of his bacon and covered the pan. "I'd be happy to make you breakfast," he said.

"That's very nice of you. I'll get some in the store in a minute. Dad, I was hoping you'd sleep in."

"And here I was hoping you would," Sully said. "I can't stay in bed, Maggie. I get all creaky and it takes too long to work out the kinks. Besides, this is the best time of day."

"It is a beautiful morning," she agreed. She wanted to discuss the coffee—just one cup, please. And activity today—nothing strenuous. Diet, they could talk about diet, and it wouldn't include bacon... But Cal distracted her by popping open a camp stool for her to join them. "Thanks," she said.

She watched as Cal put two pieces of bread he'd toasted on the grill onto a plate. Then he lifted his bacon and eggs out of the pan. He sat across the grill from Sully, plate on his knees, and worked away at his breakfast.

"That bacon smells every bit as good as I recall," Sully said.

"If you stay away from the wrong foods you'll live longer," Maggie reminded him.

"I probably won't. But it'll damn sure seem longer." Cal laughed.

"What's Cal short for?" Maggie asked.

He swallowed and looked at her. "You've been googling me."

"I have not!" she said.

"Is that what you were doing on the computer half the night?" Sully asked.

She scowled at him. "I'm just curious. Calvin? Caleb?"

"Why? Does one of those guys have a record?" Cal asked.

"How would I know?" she returned, but she colored a little. She'd always been a terrible liar.

He laughed at her. "I just go by Cal," he said.

"You won't tell me?"

"I think this is more fun."

A car pulled into the grounds followed by Frank's beat-up red truck. "There's Enid and Frank. I take it you started the coffee?" Maggie asked.

"I did. And ate a bowl of that instant mush," Sully said.

"What've you got to do today, Sully?" Cal asked. "What can you use help with?"

"Just the regular stuff. I can probably handle it with Maggie's help. You know—shelf stocking, cleaning up, inventory. Hardly any campers yet so we're not too far behind, but they're coming. We have spring break coming up. I'm gonna have Tom and two of his kids to help this weekend and we'll get that garden in. Once it's in, I can handle it, plus the doctor said I should be back in the swing of things in a couple of weeks."

"No. He didn't," Maggie pointed out. "He said you'd probably be moving slow for six weeks and in a few months you'd be in good shape. But no lifting anything over ten pounds for at least six weeks, preferably ten."

"Thank God you were listening, Maggie," he said sarcastically. "Otherwise I might've just killed myself planting a carrot."

Maggie got up, turned and started walking to the store. "I don't appreciate the attitude," she said.

"I'm about ready to get out a big cigar and see how strong *your* heart is!"

"Do that and you'll see how strong my right arm is!"

"This is going to be one giant pain in the ass, that's what."

"Sully, can't you appreciate that I'm just being responsible? If you live right you have many good years ahead," she said, a pleading quality to her voice.

"Let's try to relax, Maggie. The doctor said I'd be fine and to keep an eye on too much bruising from the blood thinner. He didn't tell me to stay in bed until I die of boredom." Sully stood from his camp chair to follow Maggie. "He did tell me not to have sex or take my Viagra for a while," Sully said to Cal.

Maggie whirled and gave him a dirty look as Cal smirked.

"Bummer," Sully said.

★ ★ ★

Cal puttered around his campsite, cleaning up and stowing things. Then he ambled over to the store to check things out before Sully got himself in any more trouble with Maggie. Sully was full of mischief and reminded Cal a lot of his grandfather. His grandfather had died at the age of seventy-five and it had seemed so premature at the time. He, like Sully, had been so physically strong, mentally sharp.

Maggie was a very interesting character. He didn't know all the details but he'd peg her for either a firstborn or only child. She was strong like her father, that was undeniable. Or maybe she was strong-willed like a doctor? Cal had had plenty of experience with doctors and he knew they could be arrogant, stubborn and nurse a great need to be right about everything. They were also often brilliant, compassionate, sensitive and yet not sentimental. Maggie seemed to embody those qualities.

And she wasn't hard to look at, either. She had good teeth, he thought, then laughed at himself. Like he was judging a horse? He was just one of those people who noticed eyes and mouths first. It was somehow natural to him and also something he consciously thought about—you can tell a lot about a person from their mouth and eyes.

Maggie's eyes were brown like his but darker. Chocolate. She had thick lashes, fine, thin, arching brows and a sparkle in her eyes. They reflected humor, anger, curiosity and embarrassment. He'd caught her; it was written all over her face—she'd been trying to research him. Probably because he was hanging around the campground so long, even during inclement weather. And not just hanging around the grounds but also the store—she was naturally protective of her father and his property.

He said good morning to Frank, who sat by Sully near the stove. Sully had another cup of coffee and Cal guessed he must have gotten rid of Maggie somehow to score another cup. Who knew how many he'd had before walking with his steaming mug over to Cal's campsite? Cal wasn't sure whether Sully was hard to manage or he just enjoyed watching Maggie's attempts. He was extremely curious about their family history. Where was Maggie's mother?

"What would you like me to get out of that storeroom for you, Sully?"

"Aw, I don't want to work you, Cal…"

"I don't feel put-upon at all. I don't have anything on the calendar. Another week and your campground will get busy, the weather will get warmer and I'm going to take you up on your offer to park and see what these trails have to offer. So—want to tell me?"

"I'll go with you and show you," Sully said.

"As long as you don't get in trouble with the warden."

Cal went about the business of bringing out boxes of supplies and restocking the shelves. He rotated the goods so the newest went in the back and the oldest would sell first. He checked the dates on the food products if necessary and he used a dampened rag to wipe the shelving clean.

It brought back memories of his student days. Stocking supermarket shelves didn't pay particularly well but it was something he could do at night. He went to classes and study groups during the day and early evening, worked at night. And sleep? When he could. He learned to work quickly, study every second he could spare, power nap, eat on the run. He recorded facts, stats, case studies and lectures into his pocket recorder, listened and repeated as he showered, drove, shelved. The days were long, the nights short, the labor intense.

Yet it was a happy time. He was achieving all his goals, was deeply bonded with his friends and fellow students, his life felt challenging but very stable. And he met Lynne.

Lynne Aimee Baxter was the smartest, kindest, strongest, funniest person he'd ever known. They weren't headed in the same direction, not really. They both wanted to work in the legal system. He wanted to make a good living, put down roots, build a house that could hold him till he died and with space to accommodate a growing family. Lynne wanted to help people. He might end up in criminal law...maybe tax law...same thing, they would joke. She might end up a public defender or, better still, a storefront operation for the under-privileged in need of legal counsel. What was so comical— he came from nothing while she was a trust-fund baby.

Maybe that explained it. He longed for security; she wanted to shed the excesses of her life.

"You're better at this than I am," Sully said behind him.

He turned around with a grin. "I've done this before."

"I'll say it again—I just don't pay you enough. Listen, Maggie's gone over to town to pick up my seeds and starters and maybe to get away from me. Want to join me for a hot dog?"

Cal smiled. "You eat a hot dog, you're going to pay. That's for sure."

"You thinking I'll get caught?" Sully asked.

"Someone is bound to talk," Cal said. "But I was thinking more along the lines of indigestion. You've been on a pretty bland diet, haven't you? I'd work up to a hot dog if I were you. And then there's the high sodium, fat, et cetera."

"That mean you don't want one?"

"Oh, *I* want one," Cal said. "You should have something a little more easy on the stomach. If you ever want to have sex again in your life."

"Hell, I gave up on that a long time ago. Don't tell Maggie. I'd like to think of her having nightmares about it."

When he was done with the shelf stocking and his hot dog, Cal went to the area Sully had mentioned was his garden. It was easily identifiable. It was behind the house, kind of hidden from the campgrounds. Cal wondered if that was sometimes an issue—a thriving garden being tempting to campers. Did they occasionally help themselves to the tomatoes?

It wasn't too big, maybe sixteen by sixteen feet. He could see the rows from last year. He went to the shed that stood back from the property, tucked in the trees. There was a lot of equipment, from snowblower to plow attachment, lawn-grooming equipment, riding mower, wheelbarrow and gardening supplies.

Snowblower. He kept reminding himself to head south. Maybe southwest. It was just all that smog and sand and those hot rocks they called mountains…

He'd gone to school in Michigan, the state that invented winter. He was from everywhere, usually moderate climates, while Lynne was from New York. Westchester, to be exact.

He chose the wheelbarrow, spade, shovel and rake, and started clearing away the winter debris. He hadn't asked what Sully meant to do with the stuff so he made two piles—one of fallen leaves that could constitute fertilizer and the other rocks, winter trash and weeds. You wouldn't want to use weeds in mulch; that would just invite them back.

He'd been at it a couple of hours when he heard her approach. He knew she'd get around to it. He leaned on his spade and waited.

"You let my father eat a hot dog? Does that sound heart healthy to you?"

He just shook his head. "You know he's a liar and he's having fun with your close medical scrutiny. What do you think?"

"He got me, didn't he?"

"He ate a sandwich—lean turkey, tomato, lettuce on wheat bread. He asked for doughy white bread and lost out to Enid, who obviously knows him better than you do. He wanted chips—he got slaw—made with vinegar, not mayo. Really, Maggie?" He laughed and shook his head.

"He's antagonizing me, is that what you're saying?"

"Over and over. But you can stop pressing the panic button. He's doing great."

"Have you seen his incision?" she asked.

"Oh, about ten times. I offered to sell tickets for him. He's running out of people to show. But no worries. He tells me the camp is going to attract people like crazy any second now. Spring break, then weekends, then summer. I just hope he doesn't scare the children."

She thought about that for a moment. "It's impolite to act like you know more about my closest relative than I do."

"And yet, that's usually the case. You're too bound up by baggage, expectation and things you need for yourself. Like a father who lives much longer." He pulled a rag out of his back pocket to wipe off his brow. "Stop letting him bait you. He's very conscious of the doctor's orders. He's taking it one step at a time."

"Did he pay you to say this? Or are you Dr. Phil on vacation?"

Cal laughed. "You two have quite a dynamic going. You could be a married couple. Married about forty years, I'd say."

"Remind you of your parents?" she asked, raising one brow. She crossed her arms over her chest.

"My parents are unnaturally tight," he said. "They're kind of amazing, I guess. Deeply supportive of each other, almost to the exclusion of everything around them and everyone else. Protective. They're in their sixties, as in love as the day they met, and total whack jobs. But sweet. They're very sweet."

Her arms dropped to her sides. "What makes them whack jobs?"

"Well, they always described themselves as hippies. New age

disciples. Free thinkers. Intelligent and experimental and artistic. They're from that dropout generation. And Deadheads."

"As in, the Grateful Dead?"

"Exactly. Just a little more complex."

She dropped down to the ground like a child fascinated by a bedtime story filled with adventure and excitement. She circled her knees with her arms. He'd seen this before. It was kind of fun, as a matter of fact.

"Where are they now?" she asked.

"Living on my grandfather's farm in Iowa. My grandfather passed away quite a while ago and my grandmother, just a few years ago."

"Are they still whack jobs?" she asked.

"Oh yeah," he said, working his spade again. "Or maybe it's more kind to say they're eccentric. My mother doesn't hear voices or anything." Then he smiled. "But my dad is another story. My father fancies himself a new age thinker. He's incredibly smart. And he regularly gets…um…*messages*."

"Oh, this is fascinating," she said. "What kind of messages?"

"Come on, nosy. How about you? Are you the oldest in the family?"

"The only. My parents divorced when I was six. My mother lives in Golden with my stepfather. What kind of messages?"

"Well, let's see… There have been so many. One of the most memorable was when my father believed space aliens were living among us and systematically killing us off by putting chemicals in our food. That was a very bad couple of years for meals."

"Wow."

"It definitely hits the wow factor. They—*we*—were gypsies with no Romany heritage and my parents glommed on to a lot of bizarre beliefs that came and went."

"And this has to do with Jerry Garcia how?"

"He appealed to their freedom factor—no rules, no being bound by traditional ideas or values, crusaders of antisocial thinking, protesting the status quo. They were also very fond of Timothy Leary and Aldous Huxley. My father favors dystopian literature like *Brave New World*. My mother, on the other hand, is a very sweet lady who adores him, agrees with everything he says, likes to paint and weave and is really a brilliant but misguided soul. She usually homeschooled us since we were wanderers." He took a breath and dug around a little bit. "My father is undiagnosed schizophrenic. Mild. Functional. And my mother is his enabler and codependent."

"It sounds so interesting," she said, kind of agog. "And you're an only child, too?"

He shook his head. "The oldest of four. Two boys, two girls."

"Where's the rest of the family?" she asked.

"Here and there," he told her. "My youngest sister was on the farm with my parents last I checked. There's a sister back East living a very conventional life with a nice, normal husband and two very proper children. My brother is in the military. Army. He's an infantry major. That's taken years off my mother's life, I'm sure."

She laughed and it was a bright, musical sound. "You are no ordinary camper! What are you doing here?"

He leaned on the spade. "What are *you* doing here?" he asked.

"Looking after Sully," she said.

"Oh, but that's not all," he said. "Neurosurgeons don't just take weeks off when duty calls."

"True. Not weeks off anyway. I was already here for a vacation. My practice in Denver shut down because two of my former partners are not only being sued but being investigated by the attorney general for fraud and malpractice. I am not being indicted. I had no knowledge of their situation. But I can't float a practice alone."

"And that's not all, either."

"My father had a heart attack," she said indignantly.

"I know, but there's something else. Something that made you run home, run to your father, who is a remarkable man, by the way. There's at least one more thing…"

"What are you talking about?" she demanded.

"That little shadow behind your eyes. Something personal hurt you."

"I don't know what you mean."

"A man," he said. "I bet there was a man. You had a falling out or fight or something. Or he cheated. Or you did."

"There was no cheating! We just parted company!"

"Now we're getting somewhere," he said, grinning at her.

"That's just plain rude, prying like that. I didn't do that to you. I was only curious and I asked, but if you'd said it was none of my business, I wouldn't have pushed. And I wouldn't have given you some bullshit about something behind your eyes."

"I think I'm getting a name," he said, rolling his eyes upward as if seeking the answer in the heavens. "Arthur? Adam? Andrew, that's it."

She got to her feet, a disgusted smirk marring her pretty face. "Oh, that was good, Calhoun," she said.

"Frank told me," he said. "You weren't thinking of keeping a secret around here, were you?" He laughed, very amused with himself. "And it's not Calhoun."

She brushed off the butt of her jeans. "You're going to pay for that. I don't know how yet, but trust me…"

"Someone has to teach you how to have a little fun, Maggie," he said.

"Well, it's not going to be you, Carlisle."

He just shook his head and laughed. Then he worked on tilling the garden plot.

Escape to Virgin River and read the books that everyone is talking about!

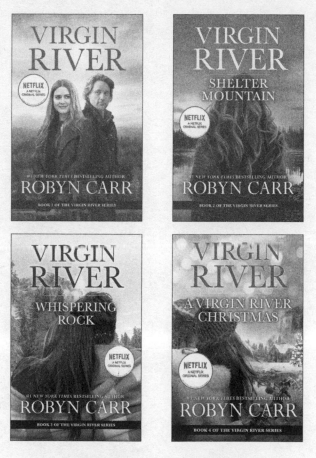